SHIP OF FLAMES

Despite a wipe-out air attack, the Japanese forces did nothing to protect themselves by sea.

Suddenly, a fleet of American torpedoes shot through the Phillipine Sea waters, dead straight for the Japanese carrier, the Taiho. The Taiho, detecting the wakes of the torpedoes, managed to steer clear of five of them. The sixth only shuddered the carrier when it hit the ship's bow—according to the Japanese sailors' reports.

But the U.S. torpedo had ruptured two of the vessel's gasoline tanks. Air vents soon blew the deadly vapors throughout the entire ship, making the Taiho a gigantic supercharged gas cylinder.

Then the explosion came, heaving the flight deck upward, twisting it like paper.

500 Japanese men trapped below deck met their watery graves. The ship ignited instantly, blowing sky-high like a miniature Mount Fuji . . .

DEPTH FORCE
by Irving Greenfield

Built in secrecy, launched in silence, and manned by a phantom crew *The Shark* is America's unique submarine whose mission is to stop the Russians from dominating the seas. There's no room for anything other than victory or death, and the only way to stay alive is to dive deep and strike hard.

PACIFIC
BREAKTHROUGH

BY LAWRENCE CORTESI

ZEBRA BOOKS
KENSINGTON PUBLISHING CORP.

ZEBRA BOOKS

are published by

KENSINGTON PUBLISHING CORP.
475 Park Avenue South
New York, N.Y. 10016

SECOND PRINTING   APRIL 1987

Printed in the United States of America

BATTLE of the PHILIPPINE SEA

THE GREAT MARIANAS TURKEY SHOOT
19-20 JUNE 1944

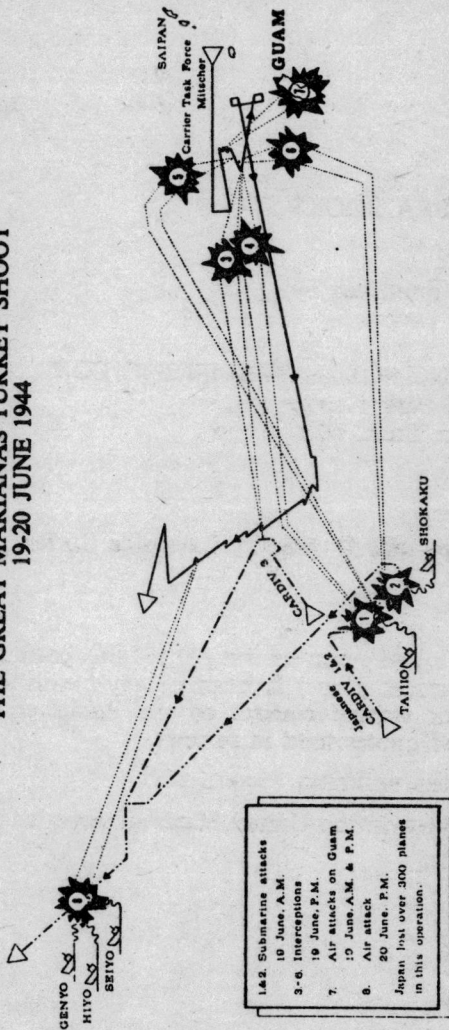

SAIPAN

Carrier Task Force
Mitscher

GUAM

SHOKAKU

CARDIV 2

CARDIV 1

Japanese Fleet

TAIHO

GENYO
HIYO
SEIYO

1 & 2. Submarine attacks
19 June, A.M.

3 - 6. Interceptions
19 June, P.M.

7. Air attacks on Guam
19 June, A.M. & P.M.

8. Air attack
20 June, P.M.

Japan lost over 300 planes
in this operation.

This map gives a quick, visual view of the carrier battle of June 19-20, from first sub attacks on the Japanese fleet, to the Japanese air attacks on TF 58, the American air attacks on Guam, and the late afternoon attacks by U.S. planes.

Chapter One

In April of 1944, a unique bomber landed in China to join the new U.S. 20th Air Force. The plane, the B-29 Superfortress, had an estimated 4,000-mile range and a potential bomb-load capacity of 10,000 pounds. The half-dozen Superforts had landed on a field near Kumming, a huge runway completed by 700,000 Chinese laborers. With this giant new bomber, the United States hoped to begin the first systematic bombing of Japan proper. However, the plan failed from the start. The China air base lay 2,000 miles away from Japan and the route from Kumming followed a path saturated with Japanese fighter planes and antiaircraft guns. The United States had no fighter plane that could escort a B-29 all the way to Japan.

"We just can't use the Superfort out of China," U.S. Army Air Force chief Hap Arnold told the J.C.S. in Washington. "We'll need a base a lot closer to Japan, and along a route where Japanese fighter planes and antiaircraft guns won't plague the Superfort.''

Gen. George Marshall, the U.S. Army commander in chief, looked at a huge map on the table. He put a finger on an island chain far across the Pacific. "Here, in the Mariana Islands. If we take these islands, we can have B-29's less than fifteen hundred miles from Tokyo. The whole route is over water so we'd meet very few Japanese interceptors and no antiaircraft guns.'' Then, General Marshall turned to Adm. Chester Nimitz, commander of the U.S. Pacific fleet. "Can we take these islands?''

"If you want the Mariana Islands, we'll take them,'' Nimitz said.

Thus did the J.C.S. in Washington, DC initiate the beginning of Operation Forager, a plan to capture the islands of Saipan, Tinian, and Guam in the Mariana Island chain. The operation would require the largest journey for an invasion fleet in the history of amphibious warfare. And worse, at this very moment, the Japanese were assembling the biggest carrier and surface fleets of the war for a showdown with the U.S. Navy.

In mid-June, when the Americans launched Operation Forager, they would find a double problem. Not only would the Americans need to invade and secure Saipan, but they would need to fight the biggest carrier battle of World War II. When the battle ended, one of the fleets would no longer be an effective fighting force.

The Mariana Islands chain included more than a dozen islands, of which the Japanese had fortified four: Guam, Rota, Saipan, and Tinian. The southern tip of the island chain lay but 250 miles north of the Caroline Islands chain of which Truk was a major Japanese base. The north end of the Mariana Islands lay only 1,000 miles from the southernmost point in Japan itself on the island of Honshu. To the west, 900 miles away across the Philippine Sea, lay the Philippine Islands, still under firm Japanese control. The nearest American base lay in the Marshall Islands, 1,000 miles east of the Mariana Islands.

While Admiral Nimitz believed his navy was strong enough to capture the Mariana Islands, many staff officers of the J.C.S. expressed doubt. The nearest base at Kwajalein did not have the facilities to launch the kind of amphibious operation the Americans needed to capture the Mariana Islands. Most of the invading forces would need to sortie in Hawaii, some 2,500 miles from the Mariana Islands.

"We had some army air bases in the Marshalls," Gen. Hap Arnold said, "but, except for long-range B-24's, we didn't have anything else that could hit the Mariana Islands chain. Sure, we'd take Hollandia in New Guinea, but even an air base here would be too far from the Mariana Islands. The navy could not depend on army air units for help. I would have preferred to invade the Caroline chain first because then our medium bombers and P-47

9

fighters could reach the Mariana Islands."

But, Adm. Chester Nimitz, fully confident, believed his U.S. Pacific fleets were powerful enough to support an amphibious landing in Saipan, even though most of the invading forces must come from Hawaii.

"The Japanese are pretty well finished in the Pacific," Nimitz said. "We've got more than enough carrier units and surface ships to take care of anything the Japanese send against us."

Nimitz set June 15, 1944 as the date for the Saipan invasion. As soon as invading marines secured the island, and especially Aslito Airdrome, engineers would immediately expand the field into a base for long-range B-29 Superfortresses.

Nimitz planned to use the U.S. Fifth Fleet under the command of Adm. Raymond Spruance to carry out Operation Forager. The fleet included TF 58, a combat armada that included 11 carriers, six battleships, 21 cruisers, and 64 destroyers, along with 950 navy bombers and fighters. The fleet also included TF 51, the amphibious fleet under Adm. Richard Turner and that included cruisers, destroyers, and hundreds of transports, LST's, and other ships. TF 51 would carry 50,000 combat troops, 50,000 support troops, and countless tons of supplies and ammunition for the Saipan invasion. Finally, TF 17, the U.S. submarine fleet, would supply submarines for Operation Forager.

TF 58, the U.S. fast carrier fleet, was under

the command of Adm. Marc Mitscher. He expressed the same confidence as Admiral Nimitz. "We had no reason to expect the Japanese to mount very much against a powerful carrier-surface fleet like TF 58," Mitscher said. "I saw no problems in succeeding with Operation Forager, even though the TF 51 invasion fleet would sortie hundreds of miles away to reach the Mariana Islands invasion site."

On May 15th, Admiral Mitscher began the preliminaries for the invasion. He sent out carrier planes to attack Japanese air bases in the Caroline Islands, south of the Mariana Islands; to the Bonin Island group north of the Mariana Islands; and against the Mariana Islands themselves. The sustained air strikes reduced the number of Japanese planes and badly damaged Japanese air fields on these island bases.

"We hoped to have these Japanese air bases pretty well knocked out so they couldn't interfere with the Saipan invasion," Mitscher said. "Our reconn reports indicated we were indeed knocking out their bases and aircraft faster than the Japanese could repair the bases or bring in more planes."

By early June of 1944, B-24's from Kwajalein also struck the Mariana Islands, hitting all four major islands: Guam, Rota, Saipan, and Tinian. Further, hordes of reconn planes took hundreds of photos of the Japanese defenses on Saipan. And finally, U.S. Navy frogmen continually entered the lagoons and bays around Saipan to check depths, mine fields, and obstacles to amphibious landings.

Despite the U.S. Navy efforts against the Caroline, Mariana, and Bonin Islands, the Japanese had not suspected an invasion of the Mariana Islands. Adm. Soemu Toyoda, the new commander of the Japanese combined fleet, believed the Americans would move into Japan's inner Pacific empire through the southwest Pacific, especially after the landings on Hollandia in northwest New Guinea and on the island of Biak on May 27, 1944. Toyoda thus planned for a showdown in the southwest or western pacific.

While the Americans planned Operation Forager to seize the Mariana Islands, the Japanese formulated their own plans. Admiral Toyoda had devised the A-Go plan, a strategy to lure the American carrier fleet into the western Pacific waters for a decisive carrier battle. Toyoda maintained dozens of air bases in the East Indies and the Philippines: Borneo, the Celebes, Java, Mindanao. His land-based navy aircraft at these bases could help his own carrier fleet to destroy the Americans.

The Japanese also possessed two large naval anchorages in the western Pacific, one at Lungga Roads off Singapore in southeast Asia and the other at Tawi Tawi on the northeast coast of Borneo and southeast of Mindanao in the Philippines.

When the Americans invaded Biak to wrest a

good anchorage and the four airbases there, Toyoda saw his opportunity to lure the American carrier fleet into the western waters. He initiated the Kon plan for the relief of Biak. He sent out the 2nd Amphibious Fleet under Adm. Naomasa Sakonju for a counterinvasion of Biak with 2,500 troops. They would land on Biak in mid-June with air support from the 23rd Air Flotilla that had air bases throughout the East Indies. Toyoda also ordered the Batjan battleship-cruiser force to support the 2nd Amphibious Fleet.

"The units sailing to Biak will not only relieve our garrison there," Toyoda told Sakonju, "but would force the Americans to send their carrier fleets to the Biak area. We can then carry out our A-Go plan and destroy the Americans."

Admiral Sakonju agreed.

Admiral Toyoda also called on Adm. Yoshioka Ito, commander of the 23rd Air Flotilla to intensify his air strikes on Biak. "You will muster every available aircraft to strike the American invaders and force them to send their carriers to the Biak area."

"Yes, Admiral," the 23rd Air Flotilla commander answered.

Admiral Yoshioka Ito immediately launched massive air strikes against the American invaders at Biak. Ito brought 50 new fighter planes and 50 new bombers down from the Philippines on May 28th. On May 31st, an additional 28 bombers and 48 fighters flew into

Sorong on the northwest tip of New Guinea. Finally, 20 bombers and 20 fighters landed at the Japanese base of Batjan on the island of Halmehara just west of northwest New Guinea.

By June 3rd, 1944, the 2nd Amphibious Fleet and its supporting Batjan battleship-cruiser fleet left Tawi Tawi and started southeastward toward Biak. Meanwhile, the 2nd Air Flotilla began its aerial attacks on Biak on the same June 3rd. Thirty-two Zeke and 19 Judy dive bombers attacked Biak, damaging several U.S. LST's and LCT's. Less than an hour later, 41 more Japanese planes attacked Biak, damaging two American destroyers before a few American fighter planes from Hollandia drove them off.

In the face of the heavy air attacks, both U.S. Gen. Walter Krueger of the U.S. 41st Infantry Division and Adm. Daniel Barbey of the U.S. TF 77 fleet considered the Biak situation quite serious. When these American commanders learned further that a Japanese amphibious fleet and a battleship fleet were heading toward Biak, they pleaded for help.

"I don't think we can hang on if we don't get more naval support," General Krueger told S.W.P.A. headquarters.

The S.W.P.A. staff agreed and General MacArthur asked that the huge TF 58 carrier fleet be sent at once to Biak waters to save the American invasion. Had Toyoda known how MacArthur had pleaded for TF 58, Toyoda would have danced with delight. His plan had worked. The U.S. carrier fleet would come into western waters where Toyoda could destroy the armada.

While Admiral Sakonju sailed toward Biak with his 2nd Amphibious Fleet, Admiral Toyoda called into conference several of his admirals to finalize the A-Go plan. Among those in attendance were Adm. Jisaburo Ozawa, commander of the 1st Mobile Fleet that included nine aircraft carriers; Adm. Matome Ugaki, who commanded the battleship-cruiser Batjan fleet; Adm. Kakuji Kakuta of the 1st Air Fleet; and Adm. Takeo Takagi of the 1st Submarine Fleet.

"Gentlemen," Toyoda told his assembled officers, "we have approached the moment for a decisive battle against the enemy's Pacific carrier fleet. Now that Admiral Sakonju sails toward Biak, we can be certain the Americans will bring their mobile carrier fleet into western waters. In such a battle area, we will enjoy a favorable position to do battle, since both our land-based aircraft and naval anchorages will be in close proximity to the battle areas."

"But can we be certain the Americans will send any of their big, fast carriers into western waters from the central Pacific?" Admiral Ozawa asked.

"The American carriers must come to Biak to relieve their invading army who have already suffered severe air strikes from the Twenty-third Air Flotilla," Toyoda said. "I cannot believe they will abandon their army and navy units at Biak. I would ask you, Admiral Takagi, to use the submarine fleet to the utmost. Is it possible to establish an NA scouting line along the length of the Philippine Sea?"

"We have enough RO and I boats in the 1st Submarine Fleet to do so," Admiral Takagi answered. "We will ascertain the position of the enemy carrier fleet long before it comes into position to do battle with our own mobile carrier fleet."

"Excellent," Admiral Toyoda said. He turned to Admiral Ozawa. "You will sortie the First Mobile Fleet from Tawi Tawi and prepare for this decisive battle." He then turned to Admiral Ugaki. "I would ask that you sortie your own Batjan surface fleet to protect the 1st Mobile Carrier Fleet in this A-Go operation as soon as you have escorted the Second Amphibious Fleet to Biak."

"Yes, Honorable Toyoda," Ugaki answered.

Unfortunately for Admiral Toyoda, the U.S. Navy would not accommodate him. The Americans had already planned Operation Forager and both the TF 51 amphibious fleet and the TF 58 carrier fleet were already headed for Saipan. When General MacArthur asked for carriers to relieve Biak, he got a sharp "no" from the J.C.S. in Washington. MacArthur should accelerate his airfield construction at Hollandia, he was told, so he could then move his 5th Air Force bombers and fighters there to support the Biak invasion forces.

The Saipan landings, scheduled for June

15th, would prompt the Japanese to alter their own plans. The Japanese would need to come out of their sanctuary in the western Pacific instead of luring the Americans into western waters. Toyoda would need to send his own 1st Mobile Fleet and Batjan Fleet eastward to relieve Saipan, instead of the Americans sending their fleets westward to relieve Biak.

Nonetheless, both the 1st Mobile Fleet and the Batjan Fleet were powerful naval forces and hardly the "pretty well finished navy" that Adm. Chester Nimitz believed.

Adm. Jisaburo Ozawa's 1st Mobile Fleet included nine carriers with a total of 225 Zero fighter planes, 136 Judy and Val dive bombers, and 101 Jill torpedo bombers: 462 combat aircraft. In the land bases of the Mariana, the Caroline, and the Bonin Islands, Adm. Kakuji Kakuta counted more than 450 land-based planes in his 1st Air Fleet. Further, the 23rd Air Flotilla in the East Indies could transfer some of the more than 300 planes to the 1st Air Fleet if the Japanese needed to fight the decisive A-Go battle to the east.

Adm. Matome Ugaki's Batjan fleet included five battleships, including the powerful *Yamato* and *Musashi* with their eighteen-inch guns. The surface fleet also included 11 heavy cruisers, two light cruisers, and 28 destroyers.

Finally, Adm. Takeo Takagi's 1st Submarine Fleet numbered about forty RO and I boats, of which 27 had already taken station in the Philippine Sea.

Not since the beginning of World War II had the Japanese amassed such a powerful fleet in the Pacific. Toyoda was probably as ready as he would ever be to carry out his A-Go plan. The commander in chief of the Japanese combined fleet felt certain he could defeat the Americans wherever he met them.

No sooner had Toyoda finalized his A-Go plan when the U.S. TF fleet began pounding the Japanese airfields in the Caroline, the Mariana, and the Bonin Islands. By the second week of June, after the sustained air attacks, the Japanese finally suspected that the Americans planned to invade the Mariana Islands. Admiral Toyoda was stunned. The Americans would have to mount their amphibious force from hundreds of miles away and he could not believe the Americans would attempt such a giant step in the Pacific.

Still, Toyoda now canceled the Kon operation to relieve Biak. He recalled the 2nd Amphibious Fleet to Tawi Tawi and he decided to send both the 1st Mobile Fleet and the Batjan fleet eastward, across the Philippine Sea, to stop any invasion of the Mariana Islands. He expected the land-based planes of the 1st Air Fleet to support strongly the 1st Mobile Fleet. Thus, even to the east, beyond the sanctuary of the inner Japanese empire, Toyoda believed he possessed enough ships and aircraft to win a carrier battle against the Americans.

But, as Nimitz had underestimated the strength of the Japanese Navy in the Pacific,

Toyoda had underestimated the strength of the U.S. TF 58. Marc Mitscher's carrier fleet represented the greatest combat fleet ever assembled in World War II. So huge was Mitscher's fleet that he had organized the fleet into four carrier units and one battleship unit. With its 15 light and fast carriers, 956 combat planes, and six battleships, TF 58 had plenty of muscle.

While Admiral Toyoda ordered the 1st Mobile Fleet and Batjan fleet eastward, the garrison on Saipan prepared for the expected American invasion. Gen. Yoshitsugu Saito counted 32,000 men in his 31st Army on Saipan, another 10,000 troops on Tinian, and about 15,000 men on Guam. Because of active submarine patrols by U.S. TF 17 submarines during the latter part of May and early June, the Japanese had lost nearly a dozen transports and freighters that had been bringing reinforcements to the Mariana Islands.

Still, General Saito, the overall commander in the Mariana Islands, believed he possessed enough men, materiel, and defenses to hold the island against any American invaders. Saito had done a creditable job in preparing defenses on Saipan. At various points along the coastal areas, the Japanese had emplaced six eight-inch guns and nine 140-mm guns. They had also emplaced more than a dozen 120-mm artillery pieces. Further, Saito had already completed the construction of concrete block houses and about a dozen concrete pillboxes. However, because the American plan to invade the Mariana Islands had not been suspected until early June, the Japanese had not yet completed trench-system defenses on the beaches.

Adm. Chuichi Nagumo, the famed commander of the Battle of Midway and of the Pearl Harbor attack itself, had lost favor with Imperial Headquarters in Tokyo. He had been reduced to commander of the small 1st Naval Defense Force in the Mariana Islands. Under his command were a few submarines, an array of patrol boats, a few dozen barges, and other small craft. He also commanded 5,000 naval combat troops. The duties of the 1st Naval Defense Force required a defense of the sea approaches to Saipan, the laying of mines, and the construction of obstacles to deter an invasion fleet. However, thus far, Nagumo's 1st Naval Defense Force had laid very few mines and built few obstacles around Saipan to deter any invasion.

Also, from a headquarters on Saipan, Adm. Takeo Takagi directed his 1st Submarine Fleet that included about 40 RO and I boats.

Adm. Kakuji Kakuta, however, maintained his 1st Fleet headquarters on Guam. Despite heavy American air strikes, Kakuta had managed to bring in another 200 planes to Aslito Field on Saipan and Orote Field on Guam. He had also brought in new planes to Rota. Thus, Kakuta still counted nearly 300 planes to support the 1st Mobile Fleet.

But, the forces under the Americans were

still quite superior. The TF 51 amphibious fleet under Adm. Richmond Turner included two full transport groups that carried the entire 4th Marine Division along with all the division's supplies, equipment, and ammunition. Several LST groups carried the full 2nd Marine and full 27th Army divisions, also with all their supplies and equipment. Two dozen baby flattop carriers, a dozen cruisers, and countless destroyers screened the huge TF 51 invasion force. Besides the combat troops, TF 51 also carried thousands of support troops. In fact, the Saipan invasion fleet was 30 miles long and ten miles wide. Only the invasion fleet at Normandy would surpass in number the ships and men of the Operation Forager force.

Adm. Marc Mitscher of TF 58, meanwhile, had learned about the A-Go Japanese plan from captured documents on Hollandia in northwest New Guinea. He would have welcomed a decisive battle with the 1st Mobile Fleet, but not in the waters of the East Indies. Mitscher hoped the coming invasion of Saipan would force the Japanese fleet to sail eastward and perhaps Mitscher's fast carrier fleet could engage the 1st Mobile Fleet in the more neutral waters of the Philippine Sea, somewhere between the Mariana and the Philippine Islands. He could not guess that such a battle would come to pass.

In any event, for Operation Forager, Adm. Marc Mitscher sortied his TF 58 carrier fleet from Majuro in the Marshall Islands on June

6, 1944. By June 9th, the American carrier planes began once more to pound the Mariana Islands airfields, now on almost a daily basis. Over a four-day period, American Navy planes knocked out a dozen airfields and destroyed over 200 Japanese planes on the ground and in the air. By June 14th, the day before the Saipan invasion, the Americans had reduced Admiral Kakuta's 1st Air Fleet to less than a hundred operable planes. Kakuta would be in no position to offer much air resistance against the American invasion of Saipan.

By June 14th, the Americans had approached Saipan with the big battleships of TF 58. All day, the heavy surface ships pounded Saipan and by afternoon the Japanese braced themselves for an obvious invasion. Adm. Soemu Toyoda, now certain the Americans would land on Saipan, ordered both Ozawa and Ugaki to increase speed toward the Mariana Islands with the 1st Mobile and Batjan fleets. Toyoda wanted these fleets not only to relieve the Japanese garrison on Saipan, but also to engage the enemy carrier fleet.

Toyoda also called Adm. Kakuji Kakuta at the 1st Air Fleet headquarters on Guam. "Prepare aircraft for attacks on the American fleet and for support of the garrison on Saipan," Toyoda told Kakuta.

Incredibly, Kakuta did not tell Toyoda that he had lost most of his 1st Air Fleet aircraft to American carrier-plane attacks. He merely promised Toyoda that he would carry out air strikes against both the U.S. carrier fleet and the American landing forces. So, Toyoda and Ozawa expected land-based air support from the 1st Mobile Fleet in any coming battle with the Americans.

On Saipan itself, General Saito reiterated his confidence to throw back any American invading forces. "No matter how many ships or men the Americans bring to Saipan," Saito told Toyoda, "they will fail to take this island. We have constructed permanent defense positions in strategic areas and our troops on Saipan will destroy the invaders on the beaches."

Adm. Chuichi Nagumo also expressed confidence. "Be assured, Admiral Toyoda, we are ready for the invaders. We have done whatever is necessary to deter the enemy," he told the commander of the Japanese combined fleet. "I am certain we can delay the Americans until the Honorable Ozawa and the Honorable Ugaki arrive with their 1st Mobile and Batjan fleets to destroy the American invaders."

In the early hours of June 15, 1944, the first transports of Adm. Richmond Turner's TF 51 invasion force approached Marpi Point at the extreme north end of Saipan. As the first band of daylight rose above the eastern horizon, Japanese sentinels spotted the greatest array of ships ever seen in the Pacific. The Japanese were utterly astounded. One of the sentinels hurried to the 41st Army headquarters to report the huge invasion fleet. But, neither

General Saito nor Admiral Nagumo showed undue fear.

"The Americans have outwitted themselves this time," General Saito scoffed. "Saipan is not an inconsequential atoll like Tarawa or Eniwetok. I have every confidence in the ability of our ground troops to hold off the Yankee invaders until the mobile and surface fleets arrive here from Tawi Tawi. Then, we shall destroy the Americans—all their troops, all their transport ships, and all their aircraft carriers."

"Are all troops at battle stations?" Admiral Nagumo asked.

"Every man," Saito answered.

The beginning of a great land battle, the struggle for Saipan, was now only hours away. But, unknown to the thousands of marines and army troops of U.S. TF 51, and unknown to the thousands of Japanese ground troops on Saipan, a more awesome sea battle would dominate Operation Forager.

Before the week ended, on the vast surface of the Philippine Sea between the Mariana Island group and the Philippine Islands, the biggest Japanese carrier fleet of World War II would clash with the biggest American carrier fleet of World War II. If the Japanese lost, their western Pacific empire would crumble and collapse. If the Americans lost, their steady two-year advance across the central Pacific, their steady reduction of the Japanese, would come to a devastating end. And further, there would be no B-29 base in the Mariana Islands to send Superfort bombers against the Japanese homeland.

BATTLE OF THE PHILIPPINE SEA,

MOVEMENTS OF JAPANESE FLEET,
JAPANESE AND AMERICAN AIR SEARCHES
13–17 June 1944

The route of the Japanese 1st Mobile Fleet (Ozawa's main body and the Batjan Force under Vice Admiral Masatome Ugagi).

Chapter Two

At 0445 hours, June 15, 1944, combat troops from both the 2nd and 4th Marine divisions sat down to breakfast on the transport ships, even as Japanese sentinels on Saipan watched the huge American invasion fleet approach the island. Daylight on this June day had broken with a golden sunrise under a clear sky. In every direction they looked, the Japanese troops on Saipan and Tinian saw nothing but ships from U.S. TF 51 offshore. Adm. Richmond Turner, aboard the TF 51 flagship, U.S.S. *Rocky Mount*, stood on the bridge with his staff to scan the island of Saipan through binoculars. American battleships and cruisers had completed their early bombardment of the island and now, U.S. destroyers skimmed into the shallows offshore to support the marines with close-up fire.

"What's ashore?" Turner asked his chief aide.

The aide shook his head. "We don't know how many of the enemy defenses we've cleared on the island with naval gunfire and air bombardment, but I think we've knocked out most of them."

"Obstacles?" Turner asked.

"Frogmen have cleared obstacles, and minesweepers have eliminated the few mines they found."

Then, a flight of 20 droning Avengers overhead drew Admiral Turner's attention. He watched the navy bombers zoom across the emerging daylight, the low sun erupting bright, scintillating sparkles on the wings of the aircraft. Moments later, Turner heard whistling bombs explode along the island's shoreline. Like the American destroyers, these aircraft would also support the U.S. invaders all day to soften Japanese defenses or to knock out artillery and machine-gun positions that might pin down American combat troops.

At 0500 hours, supporting U.S. battleships and cruisers, Fire Group 2, sent new salvos of heavy shells into the island of Saipan, erupting palls of black smoke that covered the island from one end to the other. Each new staccato of explosions from eight-inch and sixteen-inch guns shook the very sea off the coast of Saipan, shuddering the wallowing transport ships and numbing the battle-geared marines who waited on decks to climb into LSI landing barges.

When the heavy naval bombardment ended

at 0542 hours, a new roar of Avengers echoed across the sky. Once more, U.S. Navy bombers zoomed over the beaches to release countless SAP bombs and five-inch rockets, erupting more palls of smoke.

At 0552 hours, Admiral Turner turned to his aide. "O.K., away landing force."

"Aye, sir."

Chaplains aboard the transports had held their last prayer meetings and noncoms had made final checks, making certain their squads of marine infantry had proper supplies, ammo, medical kits, and gas masks. The marines themselves had written final letters home, for all knew that some of them would not come out of Saipan alive.

Then came the cries over ship loudspeakers: "Lower away!"

Now, the sober-faced marines spilled over the sides of transports, crawled down the nets, and plopped into rocking LCI boats, one squad to a boat. Bluejackets at the wheels or on the machine guns of the LCI's watched the marines settle themselves in crowded boats. They hoped that Japanese shore guns did not blow away either themselves or their passengers.

Meanwhile, big LST's also plowed toward the island. From the inside of the LCI's or from the decks of LST's, the battle-geared marines and sailor crews squinted at the shoreline ahead: narrow sandy beaches rising into low dunes. Beyond the dunes lay scrub brush, an occasional palm tree, or a flame tree sparkling brilliant vermillion flowers. The Americans could also see quaint, Japanese-style houses, covered with rose-colored pagoda roofs, and surrounded by low escarpments with quaint green railings. Finally, the invaders squinted at Mount Topatchau that dominated the island of Saipan.

The marines were awed by the landscape, the kind one saw in the travel folders on exotic Pacific isles. The shoreline appeared far different from the dense green foliage of the Solomons or Cape Gloucester. Saipan had none of the thick, humid, insect-infested jungles that these combat marines had known for nearly two years.

Besides the main invasion units heading for Marapi Point, Admiral Turner had also sent a diversionary force to Mutcho Point, but General Saito was not fooled. He knew the enemy would not land on this rocky shoreline of Mutcho Point. So, he only kept a single battalion of troops here, while he concentrated most of his forces inside blockhouses along the Marapi and Charon-Kanoa area, on the southwest coast of Saipan.

And, as Saito expected, the landings did indeed come on the beaches in these areas. The LST's hit the beaches and opened their big front maws like huge amphibians that had awakened with wide yawns on this bright, sunny morning: temperature 82 degrees. Out of the open maws poured troop-laden amphtracs that rolled off the lips of the LST ramps and chugged toward shore. Nearby, the LCI's also hit the beaches and dropped their ramps before marines poured ashore.

As soon as the LCI's and LST's hit shore, Japanese shore guns opened up, spewing heavy fire at the LCI's, LST's, and amphtracs. Japanese gunners scored an array of hits, even hitting one of the warships offshore.

And, as marines hit the Saipan beaches under heavy fire, Tokyo Rose interrupted her usual hot jazz music over the radio to warn the sailors aboard the ships off Saipan: "We know about Operation Forager, and you can be sure the invasion will fail. Each member of the American expeditionary force is doomed on the beaches or to a watery grave."

But, despite losses, the marines made progress after they hit Beach Red and Beach Yellow at 0844 hours on June 15, 1944. They pressed over the dunes and within eight minutes the Americans had fought their way toward the Charon-Kanoa airstrip. A second wave of marines hit the beaches at 0857 hours, while the first amphtracs were moving back and forth to LST's to bring in supplies. Within two hours, the amphtracs would unload tons of supplies on shore, including 75-mm and 105-mm artillery pieces. A few of them even became emergency first-aid stations.

By dark on this first day, the Americans had secured a stretch of beach four miles long and one and a half miles wide. They also captured Angingan Point. LCM's had also come ashore to unload Sherman tanks, despite the continued Japanese gunfire, sometimes heavy and sometimes sporadic. Of 36 tanks brought to the beaches, the Americans lost only one of them.

Even though U.S. carrier planes had knocked out practically all opposition from the 1st Air Fleet, and even though ships and planes had dumped tons of explosives on the beaches, the capture of Saipan still became a tough, dangerous job. The Saipan defenders had not been hurt badly because Japanese troops had sheltered themselves into deep caves and concrete bunkers, safe havens from the heavy aerial and naval bombardments.

By D plus one, the U.S. Marines had suffered 800 dead and more than 3,000 wounded. Medics had evacuated American casualties to certain LST's designated as hospital ships.

During the first night on Saipan, between 2200 hours, June 15th, and 0300 hours, June 16th, the Japanese launched three Banzai charges. Marines stiffened everytime they heard the Japanese buglers from somewhere in the distant darkness. And they stiffened even more when they heard the dreaded cries: "Banzai! Banzai!"

The Americans on the beaches called for star shells that whooshed off the decks of destroyers and blossomed into descending lights over the hordes of Japanese troops pouring toward the beaches in their Banzai charges. The marines ogled in awe, but they stood their ground and answered each Japanese charge with almost point-blank machine-gun, mortar, and artillery fire that left hordes of the enemy dead in the terrain beyond the secured beachheads. Still, the marines knew that the capture of Saipan would be another of those slow, casualty-ridden chores of rooting Japanese troops out of pillboxes, blockhouses, and caves with flame throwers, satchel charges, and hand grenades.

On the same morning of June 16th, Gen. Yoshitsugu Saito, Adm. Chuichi Nagumo, and Adm. Takeo Takagi peered from a pillbox to study the U.S. Marines who had firmly entrenched themselves in beachhead positions. General Saito now knew he would not annihilate the American Marines on the beaches.

"What are your thoughts, Honorable Saito?" Admiral Takagi asked.

"It is evident we cannot drive the Americans from the beaches," Saito answered. "Still, if we can hold the enemy on his little won ground, the powerful mobile and surface fleet of the combined fleet can annihilate the Yankee dogs when these fleets arrive from Tawi Tawi." He turned to Nagumo. "Have you heard further word on Ozawa's progress?"

"They are on the way," Nagumo said, "and they can be expected to be here within two or three days. Ozawa's fleet holds countless aircraft and the Batjan fleet under Admiral Ugaki has huge eighteen-inch guns on two of his battleships. These huge warships can destroy the beaches from beyond the range of any

American battleship."

General Saito nodded. "I have requested more aircraft and I was promised that new Aichi bombers are expected to reach the Bonin airfields sometime today. Then, the 1st Air Fleet can again offer air support to our troops on Saipan."

General Saito peered again at the beaches from the sheltered blockhouse and he then turned to the Japanese naval officers once more. "We must simply hold the enemy until help arrives. I would urge you, Honorable Nagumo, to deploy your combat sailors to help in this defense."

"They are ready to fight," Nagumo said. "Just tell me where you want them."

"I would like them in the areas beyond Agingan Point, for we can be certain the enemy's first objective will be the capture of Aslito Airdrome."

"I will do so," Admiral Nagumo answered.

Two days before the landings on Saipan, the 1st Mobile carrier fleet had left its anchorage at Tawi Tawi off Borneo to steam toward Saipan. Adm. Jisaburo Ozawa had sortied his entire nine carriers with supporting cruisers and destroyers. The carrier force had steamed northeastward, clearing the Guimaras Strait between the islands of Panay and Negros in the Philippines at about 0900 hours, June 15th. The Japanese heavy battleship fleet, the Batjan force under Adm. Matome Ugaki, had left the

Halmaheras about the same time. Ugaki's surface fleet included four big battleships, *Haruna, Kongo,* and the two huge eighteen-inch gun vessels, *Yamato* and *Musashi.* The force also included eight heavy cruisers and eight destroyers. Adm. Matome Ugaki kept his flag on battleship *Yamato.* By the same 0900 hours, June 15th, the Batjan force had come far into the Philippine Sea, east of the Philippine island of Mindanao.

When Adm. Soemu Toyoda received word of the Saipan landings, he had sent word to increase speed of the Ozawa and Ugaki fleets. He now sent the two fleet commanders another urgent message: "The Americans are making progress on Saipan and the 1st Mobile Fleet must activate the A-Go plan against the enemy in the Mariana Islands. The fleet must annihilate the American invaders."

Aboard 1st Mobile Fleet flagship, carrier *Taiho,* Admiral Ozawa read the message soberly. The next morning, June 16th, he himself exhorted the commanders and sailors of his command with his own message:

"I humbly relay the message which has been received from the Emperor through the navy commander in chief. The enemy has invaded the Mariana Islands and we must annihilate them. This operation has immense bearing on the fate of the empire. It is hoped that all sailors and airmen of this command will exert their utmost to achieve as magnificent results as the Battle of Tsushima."

The Tsushima battle referred to the great naval battle in the early 1900's between the Japanese and Russian navies. The Japanese had decisively destroyed the Russian fleet, erasing any further Russian threats to Japan.

When Ozawa sent the message throughout the ships of his fleet, he took a short respite for some tea and cakes. By 1030 hours, Admiral Ozawa stood on the bridge of carrier *Taiho* with Adm. Matake Yoshimura, his chief of staff, and other members of the 1st Mobile Fleet staff. He peered through binoculars at the Philippine Islands now fading behind him as his large carrier fleet moved deeper into the Philippine Sea.

"How long before we reach Saipan?" Ozawa asked.

"Perhaps three or four days at our present eighteen knots," Admiral Yoshimura said, "unless you wish to increase speed."

"No, the sea is too rough," Ozawa said. "We would not want any of our aircraft to break their lines and perhaps fall overboard. We will maintain present speed and course."

"Yes, Honorable Ozawa."

"What of Admiral Ugaki's Batjan fleet?"

"He is well into the Philippine Sea," Yoshimura said, "and we should rendezvous with him tomorrow for the sail to the Mariana Islands."

Admiral Ozawa peered through his binoculars again and then looked once more at his chief aide. "And what of the submarine line?"

"Admiral Takagi has more than two dozen submarines patrolling the waters west of the Mariana Islands," Yoshimura said. "Should the enemy fleet come westward, the RO and I boats will detect them and report their location to us immediately."

"Can we expect help from the First Air Fleet?"

"Despite the American invasion of Saipan, Admiral Kakuta assures us that he has ample aircraft on the Mariana Islands to aid our own carrier planes in an attack on the American fleet."

"Excellent," Ozawa nodded.

Admiral Kakuta did not tell the 1st Mobile Fleet staff of his heavy losses, but fortunately, Kakuta now found the distasteful chore unnecessary; the 1st Air Fleet commander had once again obtained new planes, more than 200 of them, in the Bonin and Mariana Island groups to bolster the 1st Air Fleet. So, he expected to help Ozawa considerably in a showdown with the American carrier fleet.

Adm. Jisaburo Ozawa, meanwhile, was satisfied that all would go well. At age 57, Ozawa was one of the ablest admirals in the Japanese Navy. He had been at war since 1938 and he had directed ships and fleets in several naval battles. Ozawa had commanded the naval octopus that had strangled Malaysia and Indonesia early in 1942. In late 1942, after the setbacks at Guadalcanal, Admiral Ozawa had relieved Admiral Nagumo as commander of the famed 3rd Carrier Fleet.

Since the end of 1942, Ozawa had personally organized the huge 1st Mobile Carrier Fleet in the hope of someday engaging the American fleet in a decisive battle. Ozawa, a man with a scientific brain and a seaman's instinct, was a strategist. He had learned that no surface ship fleet, no matter how powerful, could do much without air support. He had also learned that no carrier fleet without screens against enemy surface ships and enemy submarines could survive too well. So, Ozawa had been a strong advocate of the combined carrier-surface fleet, the technique of using surface ships in conjunction with heavy aircraft carriers. Now, Ozawa expected to meet the powerful Batjan fleet that would sail with the 1st Mobile Fleet toward Saipan. These two fleets, along with planes from the 1st Air Fleet, would assure victory for the Japanese over the Americans.

But, even before the end of June 16th, the first full day for the marines on Saipan, events went awry for Admiral Ozawa.

During early June, American Desron 94, a fleet of sub hunters in the Philippine Sea, had found the Japanese submarines on the NA line. With their highly advanced sonar systems, the U.S. destroyers sent one after another of the Japanese subs to the bottom of the Philippine Sea. Of 24 Japanese subs, only RO-41, RO-43, RO-47, RO-112, RO-113, and RO-115 had escaped destruction from the U.S. Desron 94. In particular, the destroyer U.S.S. *England* under the command of Lt. Cmdr. Bill Pendleton had scored six kills within 24 hours.

By late in the day of June 16th, the 1st Submarine Fleet NA had been shattered. Ozawa would get no reports from Admiral Takagi's submarines.

Then, at 1835 hours, June 16th, the U.S. submarine *Flying Fish* spotted the 1st Mobile Fleet at 13.3° north latitude, 130° east longitude, northeast of Samar Island. The nine carriers, in three divisions, were sailing eastward on a course of 120°. An hour later, the U.S.S. *Seahorse* sighted the Batjan battleship-cruiser fleet under Admiral Ugaki sailing north by northeast up the Philippine Sea. The Batjan force was then 200 miles east of Mindanao. The two American sub commanders immediately radioed coded reports to Admiral Lockwood of TF 17. In turn, Lockwood sent a message to Adm. Marc Mitscher aboard flag carrier U.S.S. *Lexington*. Mitscher read the message soberly and then turned to his chief of staff, Capt. Arleigh Burke.

"Well?" Mitscher asked.

"They're no doubt heading for Saipan," Burke said.

"Then we've got a fight on our hands," Mitscher said. "How many carriers have they got?"

"The sub report says the Japanese carrier fleet is in three divisions, so they must have at least six, maybe more. The *Seahorse* report says that surface fleet has four or five battleships."

39

"At their reported position, they're still a couple of days from Saipan," Mitscher said, referring to a map in his flag room. "I suggest we make more air strikes on their island air bases to make certain they don't get help from land-based aircraft."

"Yes, sir," Burke said.

On the same afternoon of June 16th, therefore, carrier planes from TF 58 renewed their attacks on the Japanese bases in the Mariana and Bonin Islands groups. Air Group 28 from carrier U.S.S. *Monterey* made a heavy strike on Guam. Twenty Avengers, led by Lt. Ron "Rip" Gift set the stage for subsequent American bomb runs over Guam, when Gift and his Avenger crews came in low and knocked out more than a dozen grounded planes. The U.S. planes also chopped up Orote Field. Thus, the Japanese could not take off to intercept the American aerial intruders. However, a burst of anti-aircraft fire struck Gift's Avenger as he made his glide bomb run. The plane wobbled and smoked, but Lt. Jim Edwards, Gift's wingman, guided the AG-28 bomber leader safely back to carrier *Monterey*.

Meanwhile, Lt. Tom Dries and Lt. Bob Bennett led other AG-28 Avengers over Guam, knocking out more installations, destroying more planes, and punching more holes in the runway.

Other American aircraft struck Rota and Tinian. In fact, all afternoon, until dusk, U.S. carrier planes blasted Japanese airfields in the

Mariana Islands and destroyed dozens of grounded planes. Other TF 58 air groups attacked Japanese airfields on the Bonin Islands group to knock out more Japanese planes on the ground and in the air. The U.S. carrier-plane airmen also wrecked Bonin airfields.

By the end of the day, Kakuta was stunned by the heavy losses. Twice he had brought in replacement aircraft and once more American airmen had devastated his air units. He now counted only 50 planes in his 1st Air Fleet still capable of combat. Thus, the 1st Air Fleet would offer next to nothing to help Admiral Ozawa in the planned decisive A-Go sea battle with the American TF 58 carrier fleet.

However, nobody sent reports to Admiral Ozawa. Admiral Takagi did not tell the 1st Mobile Fleet commander of his submarine losses and Admiral Kakuta did not tell Ozawa of his aircraft losses. Perhaps both men lacked the courage to do so. Thus, Ozawa sailed on, unaware that no sightings would come from the Japanese submarines and no help would come from land-based planes.

Despite the air and submarine losses, however, Ozawa still had an advantage. Because his aircraft lacked armor and self-sealing gas tanks, he could launch planes for both search and attack missions from a 500-mile range, while the Americans could not launch combat formations beyond a 300- to 325-mile range. Further, since Ozawa sailed eastward, his carriers could launch directly into the eastward trade winds, while the Americans would need to launch from the east, forcing aircraft to circle back before flying to the westward. And, in any naval engagement, the side that found the other first would use to best advantage the element of surprise.

By the morning of June 17th, the American submarines had lost sight of the Japanese fleets, with no idea of their present locations in the Philippine Sea. Admiral Mitscher notified Adm. Raymond Spruance, commander of the U.S. Fifth Fleet, "All we know is they're coming eastward and we can expect a fight."

"We'll have to take care of that," Spruance said.

The Fifth Fleet commander ordered a postponement of the Guam invasion. The 27th U.S. Army Infantry Division would instead join the marines in seizing Saipan. Spruance also agreed to detach some of Turner's support cruisers and battleships from TF 51 to join TF 58 for a search-and-attack against the Japanese fleets. Then, Spruance ordered all transports, freighters, LST's, and other non-combat vessels out of Saipan waters to retire eastward as soon as the vessels unloaded.

"I suggest you keep your battleships about twenty-five miles off Saipan to intercept the enemy carrier fleet that is obviously coming on to relieve the enemy garrison on Saipan," Spruance told Mitscher. "Meanwhile, set sail to the westward to find and engage that enemy fleet. We'll keep the baby flattops off Saipan to give the marines air support as needed."

"Aye, sir," Mitscher answered Spruance.

The marines on Saipan had felt a measure of safety with the huge TF 58 fleet offshore. Both the aircraft and naval guns of this fleet had supplied plenty of fire, enabling the U.S. Marines to advance inland and to repel Banzai charges. But, at 0400 hours, June 18, 1944, another American submarine again sighted the Japanese carrier fleet. The enemy force was now within 600 miles of Saipan at 14° north latitude by 134° east longitude. The enemy fleet still sailed at an east, northeast course. The sighting prompted Admiral Mitscher to weigh anchor in a hurry and sail westward.

At dawn, June 18th, the U.S. Marine troops on Saipan prepared to eat breakfast before they continued their push inland. Some of them stared out to sea from their beachhead positions and noticed a strange absence: the faint outline of big carriers and battleships was no longer on the horizon.

"Holy Christ!" one of the marines hissed. "The fleet's gone!"

"What the hell do you mean gone?"

"Take a look."

Fellow marines stared out to sea in astonishment. The big, powerful TF 58 was nowhere in sight. Many of these green combat troops suddenly felt abandoned by the pull-out of TF 58. They cursed Spruance, Mitscher, and anyone else in authority.

In reality, however, the fate of these marines

did not lie with the enemy troops on Saipan, but with the powerful combined Japanese 1st Mobile and Batjan fleets to the westward. If TF 58 failed, the American troops on Saipan would truly face annihilation. Their survival would depend on an upcoming sea fight that would be the biggest carrier-fleet battle of World War II.

Chapter Three

By sunup of June 18th, TF 58 had sailed
more than two hours to the westward. But,
neither submarine *Flying Fish* nor submarine
Seahorse, nor anyone else had reported any
further information on the whereabouts of the
Japanese fleets. Adm. Marc Mitscher only
knew the enemy was somewhere to the
westward in the Philippine Sea. The TF 58
commander estimated that the Japanese armada was probably some 600 miles from
Saipan, far beyond the range of American
naval planes.

At 0830 hours, June 18th, Mitscher met in
his flag room aboard carrier *Lexington* with his
chief of staff, Capt. Arleigh Burke, TF 58
deputy commander, Adm. James Whitehead,
and TF 58 air commander, Capt. William Gus
Widhelm.

"Gentlemen," Mitscher told the assembled
staff, "our last report from the submarine

Seahorse came at zero three forty-five hours this morning. She reported at least fifteen combat vessels, of which at least half were carriers. There's no doubt the Japanese mobile fleet is coming on to relieve Saipan."

"We've got no further reports?" Admiral Whitehead asked Captain Burke.

"None," Burke answered. "From the information we have, we can only assume that surface fleet coming into the Philippine Sea from the south intends to join the enemy carrier fleet to the north."

Admiral Whitehead squeezed his face. "Is it possible the Japanese intend to keep this other fleet to the south as a decoy and then make an end run from the north with their main carrier fleet?"

Capt. Arleigh Burke shook his head.

"We'll have Admiral Harill's TF 58.4 group stay to the north of us to guard against that possibility," Mitscher said. "If the Japanese try a flanking move, we'll know about it in a hurry."

Admiral Whitehead nodded.

"How about the air groups?" Admiral Mitscher now looked at the TF 58 aircraft commander.

"Every air unit is on alert," Capt. Gus Widhelm answered. "The maintenance crews have bombed up and fueled every bomber and fighter. Our carriers can launch within a half-hour. Radar-equipped destroyers are screening in a one-hundred-eighty-degree arc far to the

46

front of us. If the Japanese launch planes, we'll know about it before they come within one hundred miles."

"That should give us plenty of time to respond," Admiral Whitehead said.

"Yes, sir," Captain Widhelm answered.

"If we assume that the enemy fleet is about six hundred miles from Saipan and still closing, we should be within search range this afternoon," Mitscher said, "and we'll launch search planes after noon mess. If our aircraft search in a one-hundred-eighty-degree arc, we should find that enemy fleet again. By evening, Admiral Lee should be able to conduct a night surface-ship engagement with his battleship-cruiser fleet and do a lot of damage, especially with his radar-controlled fire. Then, we'll launch aircraft at first light to hit that Japanese fleet with heavy air strikes."

"We don't know the complement of that Japanese surface fleet that's covering their carrier fleet," Whitehead said.

"I don't think the Japanese can have more than three or four battleships and maybe a dozen cruisers," Admiral Mitscher said. "Lee's got a half-dozen battlewagons with radar-controlled guns, and he's got about twenty heavy cruisers. He'll be more than a match for a Japanese surface fleet."

"Still," Admiral Whitehead scowled, "we don't know if those enemy ships are on a straight eastward course or veering off to the northeast or southeast."

"I can promise, sir," Captain Widhelm said to Whitehead, "our search planes will know the whereabouts of that fleet by fifteen hundred hours, sixteen hundred at the latest. That should give Admiral Lee time to set course for a night surface engagement."

"I suggest you contact TF Seventeen headquarters to intensify submarine searches in the Philippine Sea," Mitscher said. "Maybe they can relocate that enemy fleet by morning."

Admiral James Whitehead nodded.

Mitscher now looked at his aide, Captain Burke. "Arleigh, contact Lee and tell him to prepare for a night surface-ship engagement." When Burke nodded, Mitscher turned to Widhelm. "Gus, please notify your air groups to expect takeoff for air strikes at about zero five hundred hours in the morning. Be sure all carriers are turned into the wind by zero four forty-five hundred hours for launch."

"Yes, sir."

Admiral Mitscher straightened from his map table. "O.K., gentlemen, that's it. We can't do anything more until our search planes or TF Seventeen submarines find that enemy fleet again. We'll maintain our west-by-southwest course at one hundred sixty degrees and twenty knots. We'll keep Lee's battle line twenty-five miles ahead of us."

For the bulk of the morning, June 18th, the powerful American TF 58 fleet sailed westward. Seven battleships, with 20 cruisers and some 30 destroyers, steamed in the van, with destroyers making 20-mile sweeps ahead of the larger surface ships. To the rear steamed the U.S. carrier groups: TF 58.4 to port, the main TF 58.3 in the center, and TF 58.2 to starboard. Admiral Harill's TF 58.4 carriers sailed to the north in a flanking position to detect and engage any Japanese fleet element that attempted to make an end run.

On the deck of the *Lexington*, Cmdr. Ralph Weymouth and Lt. Alex Vraciu stared up at the bridge. Neither of these air group pilots knew the gist of the flag room discussions this morning, but they expected action soon. They might get a scramble call at any hour to attack the huge enemy fleet reported last night by the submarines. Both men had been in combat for well over a year. Weymouth, a Dauntless dive-bomber pilot, had attacked and damaged enemy cruisers and destroyers on several occasions and, along with other Dauntless pilots, he had sunk a Japanese submarine. However, Weymouth had never seen a Japanese carrier, for the enemy had not committed any of its carriers into battle during the American Navy's sweep westward across the Pacific. So, Weymouth felt a mixture of excitement and uncertainty. The prospect of attacking an enemy carrier would be exhilarating, but the enemy carriers might also send up swarms of interceptors.

Lt. Alex Vraciu, a squat man with a moon face, had been one of the most successful naval fighter pilots in the Pacific war. He had fought across the central Pacific as a Lady Lex pilot for more than a year. Vraciu had already downed six enemy planes to rank among TF 58's top six aces. He had downed two planes over Makin, another Zero over Tarawa, and three Japanese bombers during the Marshall Islands campaign.

Now, the AG 16 VB bomber pilot and the AG 16 VF pilot stared out to sea, relatively calm. Overhead, not a single cloud lay in the blue sky. But, even with the slight breeze whispering across the Philippine Sea, the hot sun drew perspiration from the two men.

"What do you think, Ralph?" Alex Vraciu asked. "Will we find that Nip carrier fleet again?"

"I don't know," Weymouth shrugged. "The communications room hasn't had another word on the whereabouts of that fleet in the past six hours."

"Maybe those Nips will find us first and get in the first punch."

Weymouth grinned. "If they do, you'll be the one flying off; you and the other fighter jocks."

Vraciu grinned. "We could handle that."

The two men continued their stroll along *Lexington's* huge deck, staring at the heavy complement of Dauntless dive bombers and Hellcat fighter planes on the fantail. Ordnance crews had loaded and armed both the SBD's and the F-6's. As soon as somebody found the Japanese fleet again, these planes would be off.

Only a mile off *Lexington's* starboard sailed the other big carrier of TF 58.3, U.S.S. *Enterprise*. In the officer's rec room of Big E, Cmdr. Bill "Killer" Kane, the commander of Big E's Air Group 10, and Lt. Bob Shackford of AG 16's VF squadron, sat at the table sipping coffee. The two naval pilots had been waiting anxiously for new word on the position of the enemy fleet.

Killer Kane had been a fighter pilot for two years. But, despite more than 300 hours of combat in the sweep across the Pacific, he had only shot down one Japanese plane. And, three days ago, the Japanese had retaliated. Kane had been coordinating air strikes during the Saipan landings, when two bursts of shrapnel fire from Japanese antiaircraft guns had blown out his engine. Kane had luckily made a water landing and a friendly destroyer had fished him out of the water. Kane had suffered a deep gash in his head, but he had conned the Big E doctors to fit him with a special helmet so he could get into action if or when they scrambled after the Japanese carrier fleet.

Lt. Bob Shackford had already shot down four enemy planes during the central Pacific campaign and he was eager to score a few more kills. When they said the Japanese might have 1,000 aircraft to resist the Mariana Islands invasion, Shackford had reacted with joy rather than fear. With so many enemy planes flying in and around the Mariana Islands, how could he fail to get a few more kills?

"What do you think, Will?" Shackford asked Kane.

Kane shrugged. "Nobody knows where the hell that Japanese carrier fleet is, right now. They haven't had a word since last night. We can't go after that Nip task force until search planes or subs find them again, maybe this afternoon."

"Would they send us out that late in the day?"

Kane shook his head. "They'd have to recover at dark, and they can't do that. Very few of our pilots have had training in night landings. No, if they spot that enemy fleet this afternoon, they'll try to get in a few licks tonight with our big battleships. Then they'll send us out in the morning."

"Yeah," Shackford nodded, "that makes sense." Then he grinned at Commander Kane. "But you won't go; not with your head wound."

"Like hell I won't," Kane said. "Why do you think I had the docs improvise this special helmet for me?"

"They will let you go?" Shackford asked.

"I'm going to see the doc again," Commander Kane said. "I want to make sure he lets me fly. They're not keeping me out of this."

Lt. Bob Shackford stared out of the starboard porthole at the calm sea, blue sky, and the carrier U.S.S. *Princeton* in the distance, the third big carrier of the four-carrier TF 58.3 group. The search planes would fly from

Princeton as soon as the flag people aboard *Lexington* thought the American fleet had come close enough to the enemy fleet to find the Japanese with search planes. Lieutenant Shackford felt an excited tremor race through his tall, hefty frame. A thousand planes! That was a lot of target, with plenty of chances to score. He could not wait to scramble. The AG 10 fighter pilot waited hopefully for someone to rush excitedly into the rec room and report a new sighting of the Japanese carrier fleet.

The Japanese had none of the uncertainties of the Americans. On the morning of June 18th, Admiral Jisaburo Ozawa had a good idea of the TF 58's location in the Philippine Sea. Scout planes from Guam and Rota in the Mariana Islands chain had been out all night and into this morning. The aircraft had reported the departure westward of the massive American TF 58 carrier fleet just before dawn. The planes from Guam had subsequently reported the American fleet sailing on a 160-degree bearing, west-southwest, at about 20 knots. However, nothing had been reported after 0700 hours, for the American fleet had by then sailed out of range from the Guam and Rota 1st Air Fleet bases. Still, the 0700 hour report had given Ozawa a good idea of TF 58's location west of Saipan. At 0800 hours, Ozawa called a staff meeting in the flag office of carrier *Taiho*.

At the conference with Ozawa were Adm.

Matake Yoshimura, Ozawa's chief of staff; Capt. Toshikazu Ohmae, 1st Mobile Fleet communications officer; and Capt. Mitsuo Fuchida, air commander of the fleet's 1st Mobile Air Division.

"We know the American carrier fleet left Saipan waters two hours before dawn," Ozawa said, "and our last search-plane report at zero seven hundred hours placed the enemy fleet about one hundred miles west of the Mariana Islands. We can assume the enemy is now about one hundred twenty-five miles from Saipan and therefore some five hundred fifty miles from our own position. This range gives us an advantage and we should make the best use of this advantage."

"What do you propose, Admiral?" Yoshimura asked.

"We should launch search aircraft at once," Ozawa said. "Within two or three hours, such aircraft should locate the enemy carrier force." He turned to Captain Fuchida. "You do have aircraft that can make reconnaisance flights that far, do you not?"

Fuchida nodded. "We can search to at least six hundred miles."

"Good," Ozawa said. "Once we have located the enemy fleet, we will keep them under constant observation and launch our air strikes in the morning." He paused. "Captain, it is my understanding that American naval aircraft are only effective within a two hundred fifty-mile range, perhaps three hundred miles at the most. Is that not so?''

Captain Fuchida nodded again. "Yes, Admiral. Their aircraft are quite heavily armored, so they have much more inferior range than do our own aircraft.''

"When we locate the enemy fleet," Ozawa gestured, "we will then remain outside the striking range of the enemy's carrier aircraft, while we ourselves attack their carriers.''

"Yes, Admiral," Fuchida said.

"And," Ozawa continued, "even if some of our attacking aircraft become low on fuel because of a long flight, or if they suffer damage from enemy interceptors or anti-aircraft, they can fly on to Guam or Rota to rearm and refuel to attack the enemy again.'' He leaned closer to his air chief. "Our aircraft *can* fly on to Rota or Guam, can they not?''

"The latest word from the 1st Air Fleet headquarters in Guam indicates the airfields are open," Captain Fuchida said.

Admiral Ozawa now looked at his communications officer, Toshikazu Ohmae. "Captain, you will notify all ship commanders to maintain present speed of twenty-two knots and present course of zero two zero, north-northwest. You will also contact Admiral Ugaki and ask that destroyers of the Batjan force assume a van position of fifteen to twenty-five miles ahead of our carrier divisions. His battleships and cruisers are to hold next to us to protect the carriers.''

"Yes, Admiral," Captain Ohmae said.

"How soon will the Batjan force rendezvous with us?"

"By noon, Honorable Ozawa," Captain Ohmae said.

"Once we locate the enemy fleet again," Ozawa said, "we will maintain a four-hundred-mile range between ourselves and the enemy. We can thus strike the enemy with our combat aircraft, but deny the enemy the opportunity to strike us with his own combat aircraft."

"An excellent suggestion, Honorable Ozawa," Admiral Yoshimura said.

"You will notify all carrier commanders to prepare aircraft for an attack on the American carriers at first light tomorrow," Ozawa continued. "I fully expect that our search aircraft will know the enemy's position by sometime this afternoon." He then turned to Captain Fuchida again. "You will launch search planes at once."

"Yes, Admiral."

Within the hour, at about 0900 hours, seven special radar-equipped Jill 12 search planes zoomed down *Taiho*'s deck and rose into the east. The Jills, lightly armored and armed only with machine guns, also carried auxiliary fuel tanks. The two-man bombers could thus fly up to 1,644 nautical miles and search far beyond a 600 mile range over the eastern expanse of the Philippine Sea. Fuchida sent the seven reconn planes on a wide sweep so they could snoop as far as 18° north latitude to 12° south latitude.

For the remainder of the morning on this

cloudless June day, the sailors and airmen of 1st Mobile Fleet waited tensely aboard their carriers. Decks had been jammed with Zero fighters, dive bombers, and torpedo bombers. Combat crews were ready. At the noonday meal of fish and rice, the air crews and sailors of the Japanese fleet talked of nothing but the upcoming naval carrier battle against the Americans—a battle no Japanese sailor or airman expected to avoid. They awaited only the order to take off. Ironically, most of the Japanese pilots and bomber crews who waited excitedly to attack the American fleet had never engaged American naval fighter pilots in combat. They did not understand the devastating superiority of either Corsair or Hellcat fighter planes, nor the experience and ability of American fighter pilots.

The hundreds of sailors in Ozawa's fleet had just finished their noonday meal and returned to their work routines when the first report came into the communications room of flag carrier *Taiho*. A hot contact: one of the search planes had spotted the American fleet some 420 miles east of 1st Mobile Fleet.

"Enemy carrier force with unknown number of carriers and other surface ships is sailing westward on a one-hundred-sixty-degree course at twenty knots," the search pilot said. "The force is at fourteen degrees, fifteen minutes north latitude, one hundred forty-two degrees, fifteen minutes east longitude. From what we observe, the enemy force includes at least several carriers and two battleships.''

Capt. Toshikazu Ohmae received the report with elation and he immediately reported the position of the American fleet to Admiral Ozawa. The 1st Mobile Fleet commander checked his charts: 420 miles. Excellent. Ozawa now instituted his 400-mile range strategy. The 1st Mobile Fleet commander turned to his chief of staff, Adm. Matake Yoshimura.

''We will reverse course and sail westward on this same one-hundred-sixty-degree course at slightly under twenty knots until the enemy fleet is four hundred miles to the east of us.''

Before Admiral Yoshimura answered, an aide brought a new message into the flag room of *Taiho*. Another of the Japanese search planes had also found the American carrier fleet. The second message reported an unknown number of carriers and other surface ships at a location of 14° 02' north latitude, and 140° 55' east longitude. This second report left Ozawa somewhat startled, for this second sighting of the U.S. fleet was at a location far to the southeast of the first report. Actually, the first search plane had sighted the north flank of TF 58 and the second search plane had spotted the south flank of the American carrier fleet—a 40-mile spread! Such was the size of the huge American task force, a size that Ozawa could not even comprehend.

Within the next five minutes other reports flowed into the flag room of 1st Mobile Fleet, reports that confirmed the location of the enemy fleet. The vast American task force was definitely in the 40° latitude, 140° longitude area, on a 160° course at 20 knots speed.

With these multiple reports, Ozawa ordered battle disposition. He changed his 60° course northeast by east to a full 200° south-southwest. In the new disposition, the Japanese fleet commander could maintain a 400-mile range from the U.S. carrier fleet.

By mid-afternoon of June 18th, the 1st Mobile Fleet, including all three carrier divisions and the Batjan surface force, had altered course and sailed westward at the same 20 knots as the American fleet. Thus, the Japanese fleet deftly maintained its 400-mile range.

At 1500 hours, Captain Ohmae received still another search-plane report. The American carrier fleet had shifted slightly to a 220° course westward and now lay 380 miles east of the Japanese 1st Mobile Fleet and 160 miles east of Saipan.

"Excellent," Ozawa nodded. "We will maintain course until first light. Then, we will turn into the wind for aircraft launch to attack the enemy. Cardiv Three will launch to attack the enemy's south flank and Cardivs One and Two will launch to attack the enemy's north flank."

"Yes, Admiral," Captain Ohmae said.

"You will instruct all groups for attacks at first light."

"Yes, Honorable Ozawa," Captain Ohmae said again.

Communications among the various Japanese vessels were often quite slow because of the erratic chain of command in dispensing messages from the top commander to subordinates. While the division commanders had learned of the sightings of the American fleet, these same commanders had not yet received Ozawa's orders to wait until morning, June 19th, to strike the American fleet.

Adm. Sueo Obayashi, the Japanese commander of Cardiv 3, ordered air strikes as soon as he knew the exact position of the American fleet. Obayashi had remembered the near-fatal naval engagement two years ago during the Battle of Santa Cruz Island in the Guadalcanal campaign. The Japanese carrier fleet had delayed its attack on the American fleet with almost disastrous results. While the Japanese dallied, the Americans had struck. Not only had the U.S. air attacks caused serious damage to the Japanese fleet, but the attacks had also forced the Japanese to break off the Santa Cruz Island naval battle.

Obayashi believed that the side that struck first established an advantage. From his flag room of Cardiv 3 on carrier *Chitose*, he called his 653rd Air Group commander, Masayuki Yamaguchi. "Commander, are your aircraft ready for immediate strikes against the American fleet?"

"Our dive bombers and torpedo bombers have remained on alert all day, Honorable Obayashi," Yamaguchi said.

"It is now sixteen hundred hours," Obayashi said. "If you launch an attack now, you will not be able to return to our carriers because of darkness. Can your aircraft fly on to Guam to land?"

Yes, Admiral," Yamaguchi said. "Our pilots should have little problem in making a land base at night. Some of our pilots have enjoyed training in night carrier landings and they can direct the others."

"If you launch now, can you attack the enemy before dark?"

"We have three hours of daylight remaining," the 653rd Air Group commander said. "We will reach the enemy before dark."

"Then launch an air attack at once."

"Yes, Admiral."

By 1607 hours, the Japanese 653rd Air Group began launching planes. Yamaguchi intended to send out 67 aircraft: 20 Jill torpedo bombers, 25 Judy dive bombers, and an escort of 22 Zero fighter planes. About twenty planes from carrier *Chiyoda* had taken off when Admiral Obayashi received the order from flagship *Taiho:* no attacks on the American fleet would commence before dawn the next day.

"But we are already launching planes," Obayashi said.

"You will recall them," Ozawa answered.

"But Honorable Ozawa," Obayashi protested, "surely we should strike the enemy when he does not expect an attack. A surprise assault can cause considerable damage to the enemy fleet. Commander Yamaguchi and his airmen are determined and eager. Their morale is high. We should not miss this opportunity. The aircraft can fly on and land at Guam.''

"I appreciate your enthusiasm, Sueo, but you must recall your aircraft,'' Ozawa insisted. "We have had no word from Guam for twenty-four hours. We know the Americans have carried out considerable air attacks on Guam, and perhaps they have badly damaged Orote Field. Should your aircraft reach Guam and find no place to land, you would lose your entire complement of attacking planes. They would no longer have sufficient fuel to return to our carriers, and they would certainly have extreme difficulty in trying to land on carrier decks in the dark, even if they did have fuel.''

"But our crews are willing to accept these dangers,'' Obayashi persisted. "If they can sink some of these enemy carriers, they are willing to lose their lives if necessary.''

"I'm sorry, Sueo, you will recall your aircraft.''

"Yes, Honorable Ozawa,'' Obayashi answered, disappointed.

Most of the Cardiv 3 staff officers were shocked and disappointed with the recall order. They could not believe that the 1st Mobile Fleet commander would disapprove of a quick late-afternoon strike.

But, Adm. Jisaburo Ozawa had planned a definite strategy and he would not waver from this strategy. He would launch a series of massive air assaults, beginning at dawn tomorrow, and he wanted every pilot and air crew to enjoy a good night's sleep. Further, he wanted every combat-ready plane available for the strike.

Ozawa ordered Cardiv 3 to continue its southwesterly course after it had recalled its planes. Cardiv 3 would then sail behind the other carrier divisions. Meanwhile, the Japanese fleet continued west-southwest at 20 knots on the 220° course.

Enroute, Ozawa sent out more reconnaisance planes to keep the American fleet in sight at all times. So long as Ozawa maintained his 400-mile range between his own fleet and the American fleet, he would hold the important advantage of launching massive air strikes against his enemy while the Americans could not launch counterstrikes from beyond this 400-mile range.

Then, at 2100 hours, June 18th, Captain Ohmae received a surprising report from a Japanese reconnaisance plane. "The American fleet has reversed course to 135° southeast and is retiring to Saipan waters."

Both Admiral Yoshimura and Admiral Ozawa were shocked by the report. The American fleet retiring? Had the Americans decided to avoid battle with the 1st Mobile Fleet?

Chapter Four

While Japanese long-range reconnaisance planes had successfully tracked the American TF 58 fleet all day on June 18th, the Americans had failed to locate the Japanese fleet. Admiral Mitscher had also sent out search planes all day; but since the maximum range of these American planes was 360 miles, the U.S. search had fallen too short. Ironically, one group of search planes had come within 60 miles of the enemy fleet without finding the Japanese carriers. Further, despite the determined efforts by a dozen submarines of TF 17, no S-boat had again located the Japanese carrier fleet and its supporting surface fleet.

By dark, June 18th, with still no sign of the Japanese fleet, Adm. Raymond Spruance, commander of the U.S. 5th Fleet, decided to withdraw. He consulted with both Admiral Mitscher of TF 58 and with Adm. Willis Lee of the covering TF 58.7 battle-line support fleet of battleships and cruisers.

"We simply cannot overlook the possibility that the Japanese intend to make an end run," Spruance told his commanders. "That's an old Japanese game—make a flanking attack. The Nips tried it at Midway, they tried it in the Coral Sea, and they tried it during the Guadalcanal campaign. If we get too far away from the Saipan area, we would leave the invasion site too open to heavy Japanese carrier-surface ship attacks, while the main body of our own combat fleet got suckered far to the westward. I believe we'd best remain within support distance of Saipan until information on the enemy fleet allows us to take other measures."

"What are you suggesting?" Mitscher asked.

"I think we should play this close to the chest," Spruance said. "I don't think we should wander too far west of Saipan."

"But I thought we had decided on our strategy," Mitscher protested. "As soon as we located the enemy fleet, Lee would make a night engagement and we'd launch air strikes in the morning."

"We haven't found the enemy fleet, and I don't think we will," Spruance said. "As for Lee, he's no longer convinced that a night engagement is a good idea."

Mitscher frowned and looked at Adm. Willis Lee, who merely shook his head. "But you didn't object when I made the suggestion this morning," Mitscher said.

"I've had second thoughts since then," Admiral Lee said. "Marc, even if one of our search planes or submarines finds the Japanese fleet, I don't think it's a good idea to have a night engagement. It's true, all of our battleships are equipped with Mark VIII radar and our battleship guns can straddle a fast-moving target at thirty-five thousand yards. And even though the Japanese have eighteen-inch guns on some of their battleships, we can probably overcome these heavier guns with our radar-controlled guns."

"Then why hesitate?" Mitscher asked.

"We haven't had enough training for a major surface-ship battle at night," Lee said. "Besides, we'd have difficulty in communications at night. We've got to face a hard fact, Marc: the Japanese are superior to us in night-battle tactics, especially with their long-range torpedoes. Anyway, the hour is late. Even if we did locate that enemy fleet now, it would be too late to close for a night engagement. I think we should simply maintain our battleline to protect the carriers and keep the entire force close to Saipan."

"Lee and I agree," Spruance told Mitscher. "We'd best suspend this westerly course and reverse back to Saipan waters. Our radar is good. Should the Japanese launch an air strike, we'll know about it an hour before they reach us. And, if they try a flanking movement, we'll be in a position to protect the Saipan invasion site from an end run."

"But they could make a night air strike,"

Mitscher said.

"No," Spruance answered. "Your search planes have been out to a distance of three hundred sixty miles and found nothing. I doubt if the Japanese carrier fleet is within four hundred miles of us."

Mitscher stared from the *Lexington* flagroom window at the other carriers around Lady Lex. They were still moving on their south-southwest course, still on their 220° direction and still at 20 knots. Mitscher frowned, for not only he, but the men under the TF 58 commander, from his chief of staff to his deck hands, were anxious to find the Japanese fleet and attack their carriers. He turned to Spruance and Lee again.

"I'd like to maintain our course until dark, at least. If we haven't got a sighting by then, we'll reverse course."

Adm. Raymond Spruance did not believe another hour or two would make much difference, especially since the enemy fleet was probably 300 to 400 miles to the west of them. "O.K., Marc, nineteen hundred hours. If we don't know the enemy's location by then, we reverse course and sail back to Saipan."

American aircraft continued searching to the westward until 1730 hours before carrier commanders recalled these aircraft to recover them before dark. Ironically, at the same hour the U.S. search planes began landing on their carriers, Obayashi's earlier launch from Cardiv 3 might have just been reaching the American fleet. The Americans would not have expected a Japanese air attack at dusk, and the Japanese might well have struck with total surprise and caused considerable damage.

Since noon, the American fleet had only made 115 miles to the westward; carriers had continually turned to the eastward into the wind to launch and recover planes.

Then, at 0850 hours, TF 17 submarine headquarters in Hawaii received a garbled message from the U.S. submarine *Stingray*. The message presumably reported the location of the Japanese fleet: 12° 20' north latitude, and 139° east longitude. This would have placed the Japanese fleet less than 360 miles to the west of the American TF 58 task force.

A half-hour later, the U.S. submarine *Finback* sighted what the sub commander believed were searchlights from Japanese carriers, searchlights that were shooting beams up over the horizon. The lights were perhaps 70 miles away from *Finback*, then at a position of 14° 19' north latitude, by 137° 05' east longitude. If the sightings by *Finback* were correct, elements of the Japanese fleet were even closer to the Americans, perhaps no more than 330 miles away.

The submarine reports rattled Adm. Raymond Spruance, commander of the U.S. 5th Fleet. He knew the Japanese were itching for a fight and he feared the Japanese were closing fast to intitiate a night surface-ship action, including possible night air attacks. Spruance knew the Japanese had trained night fighter pilots and he knew the Japanese sailors were adept in night surface-ship battles. So, Spruance ordered an immediate reverse course.

"In view of the reports from our submarines," Spruance told Mitscher, "you'll have to get back to Saipan waters sooner than you planned."

"Yes, sir," Mitscher answered, disappointed.

So, by 1900 hours, the massive American battle fleet, some fifteen carriers with supporting battleships, cruisers, and destroyers, reversed course and headed back to Saipan on an 80° course east by northeast.

By the time the last 1st Mobile Fleet search planes spotted the American fleet at 2000 hours, the Japanese airmen were astonished to see the Americans heading back toward Saipan.

As the U.S. fleet steamed eastward, the Americans received a report from HF/DF stations. By mid 1944, the U.S. had developed a unique high frequency direction-finder system, HF/DF. The Americans had established HF/DF stations in the Hawaiian, the Aleutian, and Marshall Islands, and elsewhere in the Pacific. The HF/DF meters measured the direction of incoming enemy radio transmissions. Then, two or more stations with two or more bearings, calculated the position of the radio transmissions, thus giving the location of the enemy sea forces.

After dark on the evening of June 18th, Admiral Ozawa had broken radio silence in order to safely recover search planes. Ozawa knew that the American task force was at least 400 miles to the east of him and in fact had reversed course back to Saipan. So, he feared no American nighttime attacks and thus he saw no objection to using his fleet radios to help in the recovery of search planes.

At 2135 hours, the first HF/DF report came into Admiral Spruance's radio section aboard the 5th Fleet's flagship, cruiser *Indianapolis*. The HF/DF headquarters in Hawaii reported the Japanese radio transmissions at a position of 13° north latitude and 136° east longitude. During the next half-hour, two more HF/DF reports arrived at the 5th Fleet communications room, indicating the Japanese fleet lay some 400 miles from the American fleet and was steering east by northeast at a leisurely 20 knots.

When Admiral Mitscher received the HF/DF report, he concluded that TF 58 was sailing back to Saipan too swiftly and opening too much range from the Japanese. By morning, he would be too far away to launch planes and attack the enemy fleet. Mitscher could not launch beyond a 300-mile range and he preferred a 200-mile range if possible. He immediately called Admiral Spruance and sought permission to reverse course and close on the Japanese fleet so he could launch air strikes at dawn.

But Spruance objected. "I don't believe a course change advisable. I think the reports from our submarines are more accurate than those direction-finder reports. Don't forget, Marc, we still can't rule out an end run by one of the enemy carrier groups. I'd like to close on the enemy as much as you, but our principal mission is to protect the amphibious operation at Saipan. We can't put the operation in jeopardy."

"But the DF reports put the Japanese at a very advantageous range. They'll be able to launch an air strike on us, but we can't strike back."

"We can't rule out a sham," Admiral Spruance said. "The DF report may come from Japanese deceptions. They know we have high-frequency DF equipment and they may have deliberately put one of their ships far from the actual location of their main body to fool us. No, Marc, the more I study these reports, the more I'm convinced the enemy intends to make a flanking movement and we've got to be ready for this possibility."

So, overruled, Adm. Marc Mitscher continued his eastward sail to Saipan.

Admiral Ozawa, of course, had planned no flanking movement nor any deceptive ruses. He knew the exact location of the American fleet and he maintained his huge 1st Mobile Fleet at the 400-mile range—on the heels of the Americans. Ozawa had every intention of launching planes at first light on June 19th to strike the first blow.

At 0150 hours, submarine U.S.S. *Stingray* again sent a report of a searchlight sighting to the TF 17 submarine headquarters in Hawaii. Again, the position of the searchlight was to the northeast of the HF/DF fix. The new submarine report only strengthened Spruance's decision to keep TF 58 on the retirement course.

Then, at 0115 hours, June 19th, one of Mitscher's PBY Catalina flying boats, a night search plane with a 680-mile range, got radar blips on the Japanese fleet. The PBY radar screen showed 40 enemy fighting ships, disposed in at least two groups, and sailing at a position only 75 miles northeast of the HF/DF fix. The high-frequency equipment had made no mistake. The Japanese fleet was indeed shadowing the American fleet eastward at a 400-mile range, not closing to 300 miles as the submarine reports had suggested to Admiral Spruance.

The lights on the horizon seen by the American submarine were actually from destroyers, far in the van of the main Japanese fleet. The destroyers were simply homing Japanese search planes back to their carriers.

For some reason, the PBY radio report of the radar sighting never reached Admiral Spruance aboard the flagship *Indianapolis;* nor did the radio report reach Marc Mitscher aboard the *Lexington,* nor any other American ship commander. In fact, not until the PBY returned and landed at the American-held island of Garapon, and the pilot filed a personal report, seven hours later, did anybody know about the Catalina flying-boat radar sighting. The radio equipment aboard the PBY had been in good order and the Americans could not understand why the PBY radio report had not reached the U.S. 5th Fleet. Certainly, the flying-boat report had verified the HF/DF fix; and, had Spruance received the Catalina report, he may well have authorized a reverse course for TF 58 to close on the Japanese fleet. The Americans could only conclude that atmospheric conditions west of Saipan had made radio communications impossible.

After the war, Adm. Raymond Spruance acknowledged his disappointment at the delayed radio report from the PBY. "If we had had the report, we would have steamed westward again to close on the Japanese for an air strike."

The Japanese, fortunately for them, had suffered no such radio problems. At 0100 hours, June 19th, Japanese search planes from Guam had again snooped the huge TF 58 fleet. The aircraft not only reported the task force position, 14° 30' north latitude and 143° east longitude, but the planes had even dropped flares over the American carrier fleet to brighten the scene for a better look at the American fleet's complement of ships.

An hour later, the U.S. carrier U.S.S. *Yorktown* launched fifteen torpedo bombers equipped with radar to search to the west-southwest section of the Philippine Sea for 325 miles. The Avengers flew a 255° to 240° arc, with each plane taking a five degree search area. But, once again, the American search planes failed to find the enemy fleet, even on their radar screens. Again, curiously enough, the night-searching Avengers had come within 40 to 50 miles of Adm. Masatome Ugaki's Batjan force that was screening ahead of the Japanese carriers, without locating the Japanese ships.

So, the American TF 58 continued its eastward course, back to Saipan, during the night of June 18–19.

If the Americans were in a state of uncertainty because of the contradictory sighting reports, Admiral Ozawa continually knew the exact location of the American fleet. Except for catnaps during the day and early evening of June 18th, neither Ozawa nor any of his staff had slept much. By 0200 hours, Adm. Jisaburo Ozawa, Adm. Matake Yoshimura, Capt. Toshikazu Ohmae, and other 1st Mobile Fleet officers again met in the flag room of *Taiho*. Capt. Mitsuo Fuchida was missing because he had transferred to the carrier *Shokaku* to brief pilots and crews for air strikes in the morning.

"Gentlemen," Ozawa said, "we have done well. We know the whereabouts of the enemy fleet and we are maintaining our four-hundred-mile range. We are also maintaining Batjan force surface ships twenty-five to fifty miles to the van. They will give us ample warning and ample antiaircraft protection against any retaliating air attacks by the enemy." He looked at Captain Ohmae. "Are all air groups ready?"

"Yes, Honorable Ozawa," Captain Ohmae said.

"We are still sending search aircraft out from Guam," Admiral Yoshimura now spoke. "The aircraft will continue their reconnaisance throughout the night, and they will report immediately on the position of the American carriers at all times. When we launch our first strike in the morning, the formation leader will know exactly where he must go."

Admiral Ozawa nodded.

By 0400 hours, the Japanese 1st Mobile Fleet had assumed the proper launch position from which to strike the American carriers. Ozawa had steadied his course at 50° east-northeast, and his speed at 20 knots. Eighty miles ahead of the other carrier groups sailed Adm. Sueo Obayashi's three light carriers of Cardiv 3: *Chitose, Zuiho,* and *Chiyoda.* The carriers were deployed almost abreast, separated by seven miles, with each carrier surrounded by screening surface ships: battleships *Yamato, Musashi, Haruno,* and *Kongo*, along with four heavy cruisers, light cruiser *Noshiro*, and eight destroyers. Ozawa had deployed Cardiv 3 to avoid a bunched target of ships in the event of American aircraft attacks. Also, the disposition would give Cardiv 3 plenty of fire power.

Cardiv 3 included in its complement of aircraft 26 Jill torpedo bombers, 45 Zero fighter bombers that would dive-bomb with thousand-pound bombs, and 34 Zero fighters to act as escort. Cardiv 3's 653rd Air Group would leave at dawn to carry out the first strike against the Americans.

In the Cardiv 3 flag room on carrier *Chitose*, Adm. Sueo Obayashi and Comdr. Masayuki Yamaguchi stood at a chart table, looking at a huge map. The air commander watched Obayashi tap his finger on the map.

"Here is where you will likely find the enemy fleet, perhaps one hundred fifty miles from Saipan."

Commander Yamaguchi nodded. "We should reach the enemy carrier force within two hours after we leave the carriers."

"If any of our pilots or crews suffer harsh injuries, or if any of their aircraft suffer severe damage, they should fly on to Guam. General Yoshimura has told the 1st Air Fleet headquarters to expect stragglers and damaged aircraft during the day tomorrow, after air attacks on the American carriers. The 1st Air Fleet staff has assured us that they will be prepared to recover any errant aircraft that cannot return to our carriers."

"That is good news, Admiral," Commander Yamaguchi said.

"How many aircraft do you expect to launch?" Admiral Obabyashi asked.

"Between sixty and seventy," Yamaguchi answered. "I myself will lead the torpedo bombers, Lt. Zunkichi Uda will lead the Mitsubishi fighter bombers, and Lt. Shoichi Sugita will lead the Mitsubishi fighter escorts. If we strike with surprise, we should cause considerable damage to the enemy fleet without suffering severe losses to ourselves.''

"And the airmen are ready, Commander?'' Obayashi asked.

"Yes, Admiral,'' the 653rd Air Group commander answered. "They are already awake and will soon eat the morning meal. All pilots and crews will then hold briefings with me in the ready room. We will launch at 0600 hours, as directed by the 1st Mobile Fleet staff.''

"Fine,'' Admiral Obayashi said.

The Cardiv 3 commander looked through his flag-room window at the darkness beyond. He could see the silhouettes of screening cruisers beyond the faint outline of carrier *Chiyoda*. Then, Obayashi ambled to the port window of the flag room and stared down at the mass of aircraft on the fantail of the deck: Zeros and Jills. All was prepared; all had gone well.

Still, Adm. Sueo Obayashi felt an uncertainty. Most of his pilots and crews had enjoyed only minimal training and the Cardiv 3 commander was not sure his airmen would fare well against the more experienced and better trained Americans. Only a few days ago, a Jill had made a poor landing on the deck of a carrier, crashed into a group of aircraft, and destroyed eleven planes. The accident reflected the limited training and experience of 1st Mobile Air Division flyers.

Obayashi also recalled those days gone by when Japanese pilots were the best. He remembered the Battle of Santo Cruz Island during the Guadalcanal campaign in the fall of 1942. His pilots were good then, for they had received good training and long experience in the China war. He could also recall that when a flight of nine Val dive bombers came into a manuevering enemy surface ship, the Val formation made nine hits. But, most of these experienced pilots were gone, lost through attrition in battle after battle during the past two years.

Most recently, during the short training sessions at Tawi Tawi, these new pilots possessed none of the skill of the old pilots. On torpedo training runs against the sunken target ship *Settsu*, the crews assigned to the A-Go operation had done poorly. In their practice attacks, a nine-plane formation had been lucky to score one hit and many times no hits at all. How could these new pilots score when they tried to hit zigzagging, swiftly manuevering U.S. ships, with the added menace of heavy antiaircraft fire?

Still, Obayashi saw hope. His airmen were anxious and determined, willing to suffer whatever necessary, even death, to cripple the enemy fleet. Further, 1st Mobile Fleet was counting on the element of surprise.

Admiral Obayashi looked at his air-group leader. "Commander, you will instruct your air crews and pilots to make a maximum effort. It is vital that we destroy the enemy carrier fleet to relieve our beleaguered garrison on Saipan.''

''I will speak to them when I brief them,'' Commander Yamaguchi said.

Aboard the *Taiho*, Adm. Jisaburo Ozawa stared from the bridge at the swarms of aircraft on the fantail deck of the flag carrier. At 0400 hours he was still awake. He had drunk strong tea all during the night hours and at 0400 he still issued orders to ready his 1st Mobile Fleet aircraft for dawn air strikes. Ozawa stood immobile on the bridge, his face dry from the nighttime breezes whipping across the Philippine Sea. Behind him stood his communications officer, Capt. Toshikazu Ohmae.

''Can I bring you more tea, Admiral?''

But the 1st Mobile Fleet commander never altered his staid face, nor his rigid stance. He stared out to sea, at the calm waters of the Philippine Sea, peering at the silhouettes of his other carriers and the outlines of supporting surface ships. He then looked at the star-filled June night before he once more stared at the swarms of planes on the fantail of the *Taiho*'s long, narrow deck.

''More tea?'' Ohmae asked again.

''Are the air groups ready, Captain?'' Ozawa asked.

''Yes, Admiral,'' Captain Ohmae answered. ''We shall conduct four massive air strikes against the American carrier fleet, with each air group leaving at intervals of one hour. Admiral Obayashi's air group will make the first strike.

They will leave their carriers somewhat later than first planned, at 0700 hours instead of zero six hundred hours. An hour later, the air formation from Cardiv One will leave *Taiho*'s deck. At 0900 the six hundred fifty second Air Group will leave the decks of Cardiv Two for the third strikes. And, at ten hundred hours, Captain Fuchida himself will lead the last strike from our own Cardiv One.''

Ozawa did not answer and Captain Ohmae continued. ''Admiral Ugaki's Batjan force remains in proper battle formation. He is keeping a screen of destroyers and several cruisers twenty-five to thirty miles ahead of our carriers. They will afford extensive antiaircraft protection against any air strikes by the enemy. These screen destroyers and light cruisers will also keep us informed of the approach of any enemy aircraft or submarines. Meanwhile, the Batjan force battleships and heavy cruisers will screen our carriers.''

''Then our disposition is completed as ordered?'' Ozawa asked.

''Yes, Admiral,'' Ohmae said. ''Admiral Joshima's Cardiv Two lies seven miles to port. They are on proper course and speed. Admiral Obayashi's Cardiv Three sails seventy miles to the forward and his carriers are also on proper speed and course.''

''I will have the tea, Captain,'' Ozawa said.

''Yes, Admiral.''

At 0430 hours, after the 1st Mobile Fleet had

made a slight change in course, Ozawa ordered out a new wave of reconnaisance planes to search from 400 to 500 miles to the east. They must report immediately any change on the confirmed location of the American TF 58. At 0445 hours, Adm. Masatome Ugaki of the Batjan force sent off six Jake seaplanes, catapulting the planes from the decks of his battleships and cruisers.

The Jakes moved in a crescent-shaped wedge covering 50 degrees to report any sightings of the American fleet. At 0515 hours, Ozawa ordered sixteen more reconnaisance planes to search the same crescent to the east of the Japanese fleet. The 16 aircraft included nine Kates from Cardiv 3's carrier *Chitose* and seven Judys from carrier *Shokaku* of Cardiv 1. The search planes would fly as far as 600 miles if necessary.

Admiral Ozawa had acted wisely. He wanted no mistakes on the location of the American fleet by the time he launched his first attack. He did not want a formation of 75 to 100 aircraft flying eastward for two hours only to miss the enemy fleet.

At 0520 hours, a report reached the flag room of the *Taiho*. Captain Ohmae read the message with a grin. "Admiral," he told Ozawa, "a reconnaisance plane from Guam has again sighted the enemy fleet. The American carrier force is now at a position of fourteen degrees forty minutes north and one hundred forty-three degrees forty minutes east.

I will direct our carrier search planes to this location. If the Guam sighting is accurate, our combat air crews will know exactly where to find the enemy when the first air strike is launched at zero seven hundred hours."

"Very good," Admiral Ozawa nodded.

BATTLE OF THE PHILIPPINE SEA, IV

"THE GREAT MARIANAS TURKEY SHOOT"
0300–1500 June 19, 1944

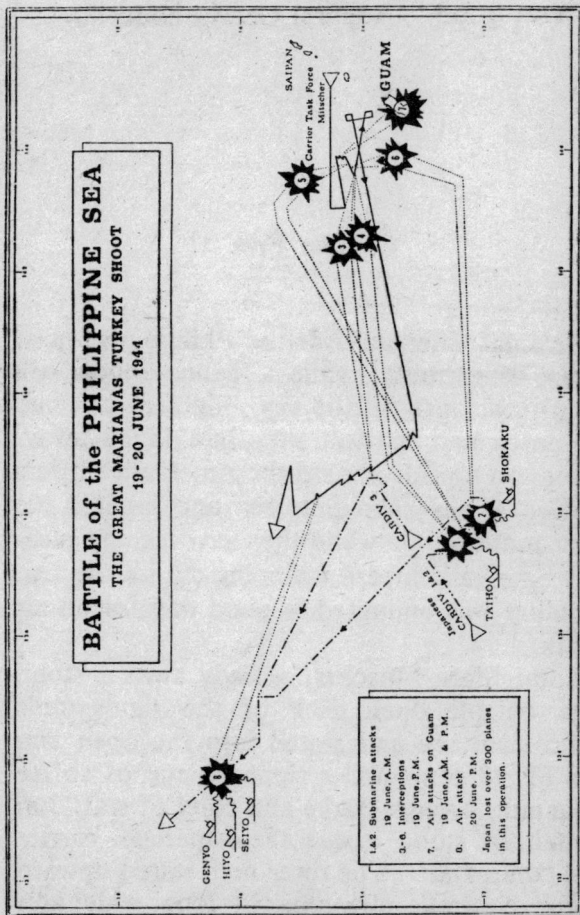

This map shows the route of the four Japanese air units which made attacks on American carriers. Note the starts of Raid I, Raid II, Raid III, and Raid IV.

Chapter Five

Daylight emerged over the Philippine Sea at about 0530 hours, while a paling moon still hung tenaciously in the sky. Night clouds had dissipated and the last stars had faded away. Sailors on topside aboard the American carriers glanced at the calm blue sea and inhaled the fresh morning air while they savored the pleasant nine-knot breeze whipping across the sea. Visibility was unlimited, a good day for an air attack.

Adm. Marc Mitscher, already awake, stood erect on the open deck of the *Lexington*'s island structure and stared into the open sea. The TF 58 commander sipped a cup of coffee while aide Arleigh Burke and chief of staff Jim Whitehead stood beside the American carrier fleet commander. The three men stared upward at the contrails streaking in long wide arcs across the sky—the white trails of U.S. search planes that had left the American carrier decks before dawn.

The Americans had again lost the location of the enemy fleet in the Philippine Sea, not even getting the conflicting reports from the submarines and HF/DF. The Japanese had maintained both radio silence and blackouts since 0200 hours, so both the HF/DF and the prowling U.S. submarines had failed to reestablish contact with the 1st Mobile Fleet.

As dawn rose over the Philippine Sea, every man among the 98,000 sailors and airmen of the huge TF 58 believed instinctively that action would come today. Yet, they felt frustration, even exasperation, for not a man among the TF 58 complement knew the whereabouts of the Japanese. Conversely, the Americans had seen the continual parade of Japanese snoopers all day yesterday and throughout the night. The uneasy American sailors feared the Japanese would strike first because the enemy obviously knew the location of TF 58: 14° north latitude by 143° east longitude, some 115 miles west by southwest of Tinian and only ninety miles northwest of the Japanese island of Rota.

By 0500 hours, more planes left American carrier decks to search to the westward for the Japanese fleet; and at 0530 hours, some of the carriers launched combat air patrols to intercept Japanese planes that might have left their own carrier decks to attack the American fleet. At 0545 hours, Admiral Mitscher got a call from Admiral Spruance.

"Marc, maybe you ought to conduct more

air strikes on those Japanese bases in Guam and Rota. If we punch enough holes in their runaways, we can stop the Nips from getting any help from those airfields."

"We don't have the right kind of bombs," Mitscher answered. "Besides, they refill holes before attacking planes are even out of sight."

"But the Japanese are sure to use the same old tactics," Spruance said; "fly out from a carrier, make an attack, and then go on to land-based airfields. In this case, they'll go to Guam or Rota to refuel and reload. Then they'll try to hit us again before going back to their carriers."

"I don't think it's worth bombing Guam again," Mitscher said, "but we'll keep a CAP of fighter planes around Guam and Rota to stop any enemy planes from coming in or out of those land bases."

"O.K.," Spruance said.

When Mitscher finished talking to the Fifth Fleet commander, he looked at Capt. Gus Widhelm, the TF 58 air commander. "We do have CAP's, don't we?"

"Five squadrons," Widhelm answered, "maybe sixty or seventy planes. They'll stay out four hours before relief."

"Send a couple of squadrons over Guam."

"O.K.," Widhelm nodded.

Mitscher once more stared at the open sea, where the sun now peaked over the eastern horizon, throwing an orange hue into the sky and kindling golden sparkles on the decks of

American carriers. Mitscher could not see Guam from his open deck, but he knew the Japanese island was somewhere to the east, 100 miles away. He agreed with Spruance that Guam could be a problem during any Japanese air attacks, but Mitscher hoped that CAP's around Guam would thwart the Japanese from using the island to launch aerial attacks on the American carriers or recover and reservice any planes that might attack the U.S. carriers.

Mitscher had reason to worry about Guam. Adm. Kakuji Kakuta had worked frantically to help Admiral Ozawa with the impending air strikes against TF 58. Although Kakuta had lost most of his 1st Air Fleet during earlier American air strikes, he still counted 19 serviceable planes on Guam. Fifty more aircraft had left Truk to reinforce Guam and these new aircraft were expected to reach Guam early tomorrow morning, June 19th.

Admiral Mitscher recognized the enviable position of the Japanese. He fully expected carrier-plane attacks from somewhere to the west, but he had no clue on the whereabouts of the Japanese carriers. Further, these same carrier planes could shuttle to land bases on Guam and Rota, rearm, reload, and then attack TF 58 again. Mitscher, however, did have a major consolation: some 450 Hellcat and Corsair planes were available for interception.

At about 0630 hours, while Admiral Mitscher studied reports in the *Lexington's* flag room, Captain Burke handed the admiral a message.

"Admiral, we've picked up a swarm of bogies southwest of Guam. I think the Japanese may be sending aircraft reinforcements up from Truk."

"Jesus," Mitscher said, "it'll be bad enough if carrier planes hit us and then fly on to Guam. But, damn it, we don't want them to hit from Guam, too. Did a CAP reach the Guam area?"

"Yes sir, about twenty-five Hellcats from *Essex* under Cmdr. Dave McCampbell."

"O.K.," Mitscher said, "tell them to intercept those bogies—and send out more interceptors."

"Yes, sir."

Within a few minutes, Cmdr. Dave McCampbell, the U.S. Navy's highest scoring ace with 19 kills so far, got the message to intercept the bogies southwest of Guam. Captain Burke also ordered planes from carriers U.S.S. *Yorktown, Belleau Woods,* and *Hornet* to fly into the Guam area. By 0720 hours, some 40 to 50 Hellcats were on the way to Guam to assist Commander McCampbell. By 0730 hours, McCampbell had closed on Guam and when he looked down, he gaped in awe. Orote Field was a literal beehive with Japanese planes landing and taxiing all over the field.

"I'll be damned," McCampbell hissed. Then he called the flag room of TF 58 on *Lexington* and spoke to Arleigh Burke. "Captain, your suspicions are correct. The Nips have sent aircraft reinforcements to Guam. It looks like they intend to give us a going over from land bases as well as carrier decks.''

"Do what you can there, Commander," Captain Burke said. "Chop up the place and destroy as many of those enemy planes as you can. We don't want any back-door punches if we have to deal with carrier planes from the west."

"O.K., Captain," McCampbell said. Then he called his fellow fighter pilots. "You can see them down there, boys; let's scramble."

Thus began phase one of the great June, 1944 carrier battle in the Philippine Sea.

From 15,000 feet, McCampbell and his fellow Hellcat and Corsair pilots dove into Guam, a small island about five miles wide and 25 long. In 1521, Magellan became the first white man to visit the little island in the Mariana Islands chain. Nearly a half-century later, in 1565, the Spaniards conquered the island. An English ship stopped there in 1742 to find the island teeming with cattle, poultry, and fruit, an agriculture begun by the Spaniards two centuries earlier. When the Americans defeated Spain in the Philippines in 1899, the Spanish concessions included the island of Guam, for President McKinley wanted the island as a coaling station for American ships on the way to the Philippines. Then, in early 1942, the Japanese wrested the island from the Americans during the first months of World War II.

Now, the Americans returned to Guam with

a vengeance. A swarm of Zeros rose to meet McCampbell's Hellcats and the AG 15 leader yelled into his radio. "Skunks (fighter planes)! In pairs, take your pick."

Thus began an air battle that lasted for a half-hour. In the ensuing fight, McCampbell himself got in a quick burst on a zooming Zero, blew out the engine of the enemy plane and watched the plane plop into the sea. McCampbell's wingman, Lt. Bob Hoel, caught another Zero in a quick strafing burst, chopped off the wing with his .50-caliber fire, and watched the wingless Japanese plane flip over and drop like a dead bird, crashing and flaming on Guam itself. Another American pilot spotted a Zero coming from three o'clock. The pilot veered, arched, and came into the Zero's tail before he released a burst of fire that emitted a trail of smoke behind the Japanese fighter plane. The Zero pilot went into a series of aileron rolls, but all for nought. The Zero could not maintain altitude and crashed into the sea.

The Japanese suffered badly during the half-hour of combat, for the pilots lacked the experience of the Americans, and their Zeros were inferior to the American Hellcats. In the lopsided fight, the Americans destroyed 30 Zeros and five bombers both in the air and on the ground.

Surviving Japanese pilots took their planes into hidden revetments, like moles scurrying underground to escape predators. McCampbell and his pilots now hovered over Guam with other naval pilots, waiting for more Japanese planes to expose themselves. But, at 1004 hours, McCampbell got a call from Capt. Gus Widhelm, the TF 58 air commander. "Hey, Rube!" The call, the old circus cry for help, was a request for McCampbell to come home on the double because of trouble. The trouble, of course, was the approach of the Japanese 653rd Air Group.

At 1003 hours, radar operators on battleship U.S.S. *Alabama* had picked up a swarm of bogies on their IFF screens, even while the bogies were still a remarkable 140 miles away. The radar men had immediately called the flag office on *Lexington* and Widhelm in turn had ordered the "Hey Rube" to all airborne aircraft.

The main event would soon begin.

Some three hours earlier, on the bridge deck of carrier *Chitose*, Adm. Sueo Obayashi stood on the bridge and stared at the swarm of planes on the carrier deck. The aircraft engines screamed in deafening whines. Zero pilots and Jill bomber crews sat in their aircraft waiting for takeoff. On the other two carriers of Cardiv 3, *Zuiho* and *Chiyoda*, other Japanese aircraft also whined restlessly, like sea hawks waiting to pounce on unsuspecting fish. Altogether, Obayashi would send out 18 torpedo-laden Jills, 45 Zero fighter bombers, and 16 Zero fighter escorts, a total of 69 aircraft from the 653rd Air Group. Cmdr.

Masayuki Yamaguchi sat in the cockpit of the lead Jill, waiting for the signal to race down *Chitose*'s deck.

Yamaguchi checked his watch: 0800. They were an hour late for takeoff and already two hours behind the original takeoff time of 0600. But, Admiral Ozawa had personally postponed launch time because he wanted as many confirmation reports from the search planes as possible. By 0800 hours, the 1st Mobile Fleet commander was satisfied.

Ozawa's staff had designated the location of the American fleet as 7-1 on their maps and Capt. Toshikazu Ohmae had informed Commander Yamaguchi to make the 7-1 point on his chart and the charts of flight leaders.

So, at 0801 hours, Cmdr. Masayuki Yamaguchi watched the signal man drop his flag. The commander revved his engine and then zoomed down *Chitose*'s deck and hoisted his Jill into the sky. Eight Jills followed, one by one, roaring down the deck and rising skyward into the morning sun. Each Jill carried a 2,000 pound torpedo. Then came a dozen Zero fighter-bombers carrying single thousand-pound bombs, followed by a dozen Zero escort planes with fully loaded .30-caliber strafing guns. The 33 planes arced about the sky until Commander Yamaguchi pointed his Jill eastward and opened to 250 knots. The other *Chitose* aircraft followed Yamaguchi before the complement of aircraft fell into formations of eleven three-plane V's.

From the other carriers of Cardiv 3 came more Zero fighter-bombers, more Jill torpedo bombers, and more Zero escort planes. Soon, the large formation of 69 aircraft was winging eastward. Cmdr. Masayuki Yamaguchi looked at the horde of planes about him, satisfied. He had plenty of aircraft to cause plenty of damage to the American carriers. However, he felt an uncertainty. So many of the 653rd airmen had been hastily trained and few had combat experience. If they met swarms of American interceptors they could be seriously hurt. Yamaguchi prayed for the element of surprise. So far as he knew, the Americans did not know the location of 1st Mobile Fleet and perhaps he could strike before the Americans responded with fighter-plane interceptors.

In the Jills of his 653rd lead formation, crews felt equally apprehensive. Lt. Zunkichi Uda and his gunner, Minichi Ohshoyo, had been fighting in the south and central Pacific for more than two years and they had seen the growing superiority of the U.S. Navy Air Force. Both men continually searched the skies, hoping no American fighter planes jumped their formation.

In a third Jill torpedo bomber, Lt. Masaje Oe and his gunner, P.O. Yashio Nakamuro, also scanned the skies for possible American interceptors. Lieutenant Oe lacked confidence. He had done poorly during the training sessions on low-level torpedo runs. He wondered if he could really hit an American carrier, no matter how big the target, in the face of zigzag-ging manuevers, heavy antiaircraft fire, and possible interceptors. Gunner Nakamuro checked his twin .30-caliber guns in the rear cockpit of the Jill. He occasionally looked through his gun sight. He had never run into American fighter pilots before and he wondered if he could successfully ward off American Hellcats or Corsairs.

Hanging above the droning Jills and fighter bombers were sixteen Zero fighter escorts, not many among a heavy formation of 69 planes. Of course, in the event of interception, the fighter-bombers could salvo their bombs and also act as escort. Lt. Shoichi Sugita, who led the 653rd's escorting Zeros had begun his career several years ago in China.

Sugita had already downed 50 enemy planes, including a dozen American planes in the southwest and central Pacific. Still, he felt un-sure. Could they deal with experienced Ameri-can fighter pilots? Around him were a dozen or more inexperienced fighter pilots, including his wingman, N.C.O. Ryoji Ohhara. Young fighter pilot Ohhara had never been in combat, and Sugita wondered if his wingman would freeze. Like Yamaguchi, Sugita also hoped the 653rd formation surprised the enemy, struck quickly, and escaped before the Americans could mount interceptors against them.

But, Commander Yamaguchi and Lieutenant Sugita would not enjoy the advantage of sur-prise.

By 1000 hours, the Japanese formation had come within 150 miles of point 7-1, the location of the TF 58 carriers. Only a moment later, bogies had shown up on the U.S.S. *Alabama's* radar screen. Then had come the "Hey Rube" order.

Already airborne was a CAP under Cmdr. Charlie Brewer of Air Group 15 from the carrier U.S.S. *Essex*. Brewer counted 35 Hellcats in his patrol complement, whose pilots had extensive experience in the central Pacific naval air war. The AG 15 unit had launched from the *Essex* at 0800 hours, intending to maintain its patrol until noon before relief came from other carriers. At 1005, Brewer got the call from Capt. Gus Widhelm.

"Bogies, about one hundred thirty miles out, at eighteen to twenty thousand," Widhelm said. "Your CAP is closest to them, Commander. Intercept."

"We're on our way," Brewer answered. The VF 15 leader then called his pilots. "Bogies, one hundred thirty miles, directly to the west. We'll climb to twenty-four thousand feet and come down on them from upstairs."

Brewer then jelled his formation of Hellcat fighter planes and zoomed westward at 275 knots to meet the oncoming Japanese formation.

By 1023 hours, when the Japanese had come within 100 miles of flag carrier *Lexington*, every carrier of TF 58 had veered into the wind to launch aircraft. Every ship in TF 58 was on general quarters and all antiaircraft gunners were on battle stations to meet the expected Japanese air attack. Mitscher then ordered every bomber off the decks and to the eastward, out of the potential battle area, while leaving these decks free to launch and recover fighter planes.

More U.S. fighter planes began zooming off carrier decks to join Cmdr. Charlie Brewer. The first came from *Bunker Hill*'s AG 8 under the command of Cmdr. Ralph Shipley, who led 24 Hellcats in four six-plane formations.

At 1036 hours, when Cmdr. Charlie Brewer sighted the lead Japanese formation below him and to the west, he picked up his radio. "I'm going after that Jill leader. Pick your targets and attack in pairs. In pairs. Let's go. Scramble!"

Then, the Hellcat pilots from the U.S.S. *Essex* VF 15 waded into the Japanese.

Even before Cmdr. Masayuki Yamaguchi and his gunner reacted to the diving Hellcat, Commander Brewer opened from 800 feet. Several .50-caliber hits riddled the fuselage of the Jill bomber. Yamaguchi deftly banked away and increased speed to escape further punishment. Brewer did not pursue; there were simply too many other targets. The VF 15 commander arced his plane, came back, and opened on another Jill from 800 feet. This time, his strafing fire hit the fuel tanks. The Jill exploded and plopped into the sea in a cascade of flames. The VF 15 commander then pounced on another Jill, shot off its wing and watched huge chunks of plane flutter away before the aircraft splashed into the sea. Brewer next caught up with a Zero, shot away the plane's wing roots, and then saw the plane crash into the sea.

Now, a Zero dove at the American VF leader and Brewer deftly manuevered his Hellcat. Soon, he was on the tail of the potential attacker and he opened up with several bursts. The Zero pilot manuevered violently, using half-rolls and full barrel rolls. But, Brewer hung with his quarry and finally shattered the fuselage, wing, and cockpit with strafing fire. The Zero burst into flames and went into a tight spiral.

In a matter of minutes, Cmdr. Charles Brewer had downed four Japanese planes and damaged a fifth. By the time Brewer arched his plane back to seek more targets, the enemy planes had scattered and he found nothing.

Meanwhile, Lt. Ken Foltz, Brewer's wingman, dove into a formation of Zero fighter-bombers and quickly tailed one before shooting the Zero down in flames. Then, he arched high in the sky and came down on a second Zero, this one also a fighter-bomber. The Japanese pilot salvoed his bombs and tried to dart away, but Foltz quickly caught up with him in his superior Hellcat. A heavy burst of strafing fire chopped away the tail of the enemy plane and the Zero flipped over and crashed into the sea.

Before Brewer and his pilots were finished,

they had downed 17 Japanese planes! The VF 15 unit might have downed even more, but most of the American pilots had expended their ammo or the Japanese planes had scattered out of sight.

From the start, the fight had been one-sided because of poor Japanese performance. Aside from inexperience among most of the 653rd pilots, their planes were inferior to American planes. Also, Commander Yamaguchi himself had erred in his tactics. Instead of driving his flights straight into the American carriers, he had taken his planes high in the sky to instruct them on the mode of attack against the American ships—something he should have done before they left the ready rooms of their carriers. Yamaguchi's radio communications with his pilots had been monitored by the U.S. communications officer of TF 58, allowing the Americans to pinpoint the location of the Japanese planes. Secondly, Yamaguchi's 15-minute delay, while he instructed his pilots, had allowed Commander Charlie Brewer to get his VF 15 pilots into good position to intercept the Japanese planes that were still quite distant from the American carriers. Further, Yamaguchi had led his flights in a loose formation instead of the tight one that would have allowed maximum fire power from Jill gunners.

Although the Japanese extricated themselves from this first American interceptor attack, Yamaguchi had hardly cleared himself to strike the American carriers. His battered formation had come within 50 miles of the American carriers when a second Hellcat onslaught descended on his 653rd Air Group complement of aircraft. This time, AG 8 pilots from *Bunker Hill* under Cmdr. Ralph Shipley sighted the Japanese formations. The AG 8 leader spotted the Japanese Zero fighter-bombers as they were jelling again after the near disaster with Brewer's AG 15 airmen. Shipley now took up the brawl where Brewer left off.

"Skunks below! Skunks!" Shipley cried into his radio. "Peel off. In pairs!"

Then, Ralph Shipley arced away from his formation with his wingman. As soon as Masayuki Yamaguchi heard the American aircraft above, the Japanese formation leader increased speed. Others in the formation, however, simply scattered instead of salvoing bombs and closing into tight formation to meet the American attackers. The action of the Japanese pilots again reflected their inexperience. Few of them had ever seen combat so they reacted with panic instead of calm.

Shipley dove after a Zero that tried to zoom away, but the Zero could not outrun the American Hellcat. Although the Japanese pilot might have eluded Shipley with his more manueverable Zero, the novice Nippon pilot had failed to consider this advantage. Shipley sent a burst of .50-caliber fire into the streaking Zero and ripped off the tail assembly. The Zero simply fell like a dead bird and plopped into the sea. A moment later, Shipley found a second fighter-bomber also scurrying away. In fact, the Zero pilot had not even salvoed his bombs. So, when Shipley hit the plane with a burst of strafing fire, some of the .50 ammo hit the bomb load. The subsequent explosion blew the Zero and pilot to shreds before the fragments plopped into the sea.

A moment later, Cmdr. Ralph Shipley caught up with a third Japanese plane, a Jill torpedo bomber. While the Japanese pilot manuevered frantically, the rear gunner fired his .30-caliber guns furiously at the trailing Hellcat. The gunner hit the aileron and tail assembly of Shipley's plane, damaging the navigation system. Still, the VF 8 commander got in several good bursts that shattered the elongated cockpit and killed the gunner and pilot. The Jill, out of control, simply spun dizzily downward and splashed into the sea.

Meanwhile, another AG 8 pilot, Lt. Elbert McClusky, downed three Japanese planes in a single attack. McClusky, a navy pilot with four kills, could not believe the mass of targets below him. In a quick pass, he caught one fighter-bomber in the fuselage and almost tore the plane in half before the shattered Jill dropped like a broken balloon and plopped into the sea. Next, McClusky caught a Zero arcing away and the burst of .50-caliber fire tore the plane apart. The Zero flipped over and spun into the sea. Finally, on the same pass, Elbert McClusky caught another Zero that was supposedly escorting a Jill. McClusky's fire chopped off one of the wings and the Zero fell haphazardly into the sea.

Other AG 8 pilots from U.S.S. *Bunker Hill* also scored against the scattering planes of the Japanese 653rd Air Group. More American pilots downed more Zeros and Jills. Before the *Bunker Hill* airmen broke off the engagement, the Americans had knocked some 20 planes out of the sky.

The *Essex* and *Bunker Hill* pilots had downed nearly 40 of the 69 Japanese planes and seriously damaged at least another dozen planes. Killed were Lt. Zunkichi Uda and his gunner, Minichi Ohshoyo. Also down and killed were pilot Masaje Oe and his gunner Yoshio Nakamuro, who had fired his guns even as he burned to death in his flaming Jill torpedo bomber. And among the Japanese fighter pilots, N.C.O. Ryoji Ohhara had been among those meeting death at the hands of the aggressive Hellcat fighter pilots.

Other VF units of U.S. fighter plane had also pounced on the tattered Japanese 653rd Air Group. More Japanese planes went down, more Japanese airmen met death, and more 653rd aircraft suffered damage.

Not a single one of the 69 Japanese planes on this first Japanese air strike had reached the American carriers. One plane had scored a thousand-pound hit on the U.S. battleship *Alabama*, killing 27 men and wounding 47 others. However, the hit had not hurt *Alabama*'s fighting efficiency. Another

Japanese plane had hit and damaged an American destroyer, while a Japanese Jill had scored two torpedo hits on an American cruiser, causing serious damage.

For these meager results, however, Cmdr. Masayuki Yamaguchi had lost all but 18 planes out of the 69 that had left the carrier decks of Cardiv III. And six of these survivors were too badly damaged to return to their carriers.

At 1057 hours, Flagship *Lexington* of the TF 58 unit got an all-clear report. The Japanese air attack had been utterly smashed. A shocked Commander Yamaguchi sent the damaged planes of his 653rd Air Group on to Guam while he himself limped home to his carriers with a dozen planes.

As the elated American pilots returned to their carriers, Cmdr. Ralph Shipley found his stick jammed from the hits by the Jill gunner, and he could not manuever his plane downward to land on the carrier deck. He could do nothing more than radio his position and then bail out. Shipley did not remain in the water long, however, Within a half-hour, the American destroyer U.S.S. *Dewey* fished the Hellcat pilot out of the water.

The loss of Shipley's plane and the loss of eight other American aircraft had been a relatively cheap price for the heavy losses suffered by the Japanese.

Chapter Six

At 0900 hours, June 19th, more than an hour before the first group of raiding Japanese planes ran into the devastating swarms of American fighter planes, Adm. Jisaburo Ozawa again stood on the bridge of _Taiho_. He stared once more at the swarms of planes on the flag carrier's deck, their engines screaming. And Ozawa could hear the echoes of aircraft engines from Cardiv I's other carriers, _Shokaku_ and _Zuikaku_. The three carriers of Cardiv I, the largest carriers of 1st Mobile Fleet, carried totally nearly 200 aircraft among them. This second raid would include most of the aircraft carriers _Taiho_ and _Zuikaku_, while Capt. Mitsuo Fuchida readied planes aboard _Shokaku_ for a later raid.

Cardiv 1 prepared to launch from two of its carriers 128 aircraft: 53 Judy dive bombers, 27 Jill torpedo bombers, and 48 Zero fighter escorts. Over 80 of these would fly off _Taiho_ and the rest from carrier *Zuikaku*. Aboard *Taiho*, Cmdr. Akira Tarui waited somberly in the cockpit of his lead Judy while his gunner, P.O. Norizo Ikeda, sat eagerly in the rear cockpit. Tarui, ranked second only to Captain Fuchida himself among the 1st Mobile Fleet air leaders, watched for the signal to zoom down *Taiho's* long deck.

At 0909, the signalman dropped his flag and Tarui roared down the carrier's deck, straight east and into the now fully arisen morning sun. Behind him came eight more Judy dive bombers before the nine-plane lead formation jelled into triangles of three-plane V's. Tarui, of course, only knew the first launch from Cardiv III had left an hour ago, but had not yet reached target. However, the 601st Air Group leader hoped the first strike would cause enough damage and consternation to allow his own strike to find the enemy in a state of confusion and thus make his job much easier.

For the next 15 minutes, other aircraft left the decks of Cardiv I's *Taiho* and *Zuikaku:* more Judy dive bombers, a horde of Jill torpedo bombers, and hordes of Zero fighter planes. Admiral Ozawa himself stood rigidly on the open island deck of *Taiho* throughout the launch, watching aircraft zoom continually off the decks, arc about the sky, and then close in the standard Japanese V patterns, three planes to a V, three V's to a section, and three sections to a 27-plane squadron unit. Even at 0920, after the last V of planes disappeared to

104

the east, the 1st Mobile Fleet commander remained in his rigid stance.

Capt. Matake Yoshimura, who had been standing next to his commander, also watched aircraft zooming eastward. When the sound of planes had finally diminished to the east, the 1st Mobile Fleet chief of staff looked at *Taiho's* near-empty and almost deserted deck. The signalmen, ordnance men, and aircraft directors had left their posts to disappear into the bowlers of *Taiho's* lower decks to await orders to send off the next strike or to retrieve aircraft from raid two. Yoshimura turned to Ozawa.

"The aircraft have gone off without mishap."

Ozawa did not answer.

"I believe an aide has brought tea and rice cakes to the bridge, Admiral," Yoshimura said. "Perhaps you would like some refreshments."

"Matake," Ozawa finally turned and looked at his chief of staff, "are there any reports that indicate the enemy knows our position?"

"None, Admiral. So far as we know, the Americans are still unaware of our whereabouts. So, our brave airmen should strike the enemy with surprise."

"Very good," the 1st Mobile Fleet commander nodded.

"Some refreshments?" Yoshimura asked again.

Admiral Ozawa ignored the question. He inhaled the fresh morning air, wiped the brow of his narrow face, and then turned to his aide again. "We must succeed with these air strikes if we are to thwart any further advance by the enemy into our western empire."

"We will succeed," Yoshimura said. "We will not fail this time."

Ozawa took one more look at the expanse of water around him and then squinted at the horde of carriers and supporting surface ships spread over the Philippine Sea. Finally, he left the open deck and ducked inside the wheelhouse with his chief of staff.

Already far to the east, Cmdr. Akira Tarui sat stiffly in the cockpit of his two-seater lead Judy. He glanced at the other dive bombers of his three-plane V and at the other V's about him and behind him. He then picked up his radio and called his rear gunner.

"Norizo, are the aircraft in proper formation?"

"Yes, Honorable Tarui," the gunner answered. "The bombers fly at our same eighteen thousand feet and I can see Commander Okimiya's Zero aircraft above us, all in proper formation."

"Very good," Tarui said. "Keep alert. While we do not expect to meet enemy aircraft, no one can be certain."

"Yes, Commander," P.O. Norizo Ikeda said.

The huge air fleet of the 601st Air Group droned on for another several minutes, passing the loitering carriers of Cardiv III, whose aircraft had left on the first raid an hour ago. Tarui looked down at the array of ships: carriers with a battleship and three cruisers on either side of them. Soon, the Cardiv III carriers disappeared to the rear and Tarui now approached the light cruisers and destroyers of the Batjan force forward element that lay 50 to 60 miles east of the carriers on a monotonous patrol.

Then, suddenly, a barrage of ack-ack fire spewed up from the Japanese destroyers. Commander Tarui gaped and then his face reddened in anger. The fools! Why were the idiots shooting at their own aircraft? The 601st commander picked up his radio and called the bridge of carrier *Taiho*.

"This is Commander Tarui. I must speak to Captain Ohmae at once! At once!" he screamed.

"Yes, Commander."

A moment later, Ohmae was on the radio.

Tarui, now flinching instinctively from the bursts of flak around his formations, again screamed into his radio phone. "Captain, we have idiots in our screen destroyers firing antiaircraft guns at our own aircraft. You must stop them. You must stop them at once. We will find enough antiaircraft from the enemy and we have no need to suffer such attacks from our own ship."

"I will call Admiral Ugaki at once," Captain Ohmae said.

But, a full five minutes elapsed before the booming ack-ack fire from the Japanese screen destroyers finally stopped. By then, Commander Tarui had already cleared the destroyer screen. He picked up his radio and called his squadron leaders. To his dismay, he learned that his own Batjan force antiaircraft gunners had downed two of the Japanese planes and seriously damaged seven others that were forced to return to their carriers. Tarui cursed the trigger-happy gunners and his maledictions shocked the Japanese, for Tarui's radio mike was still on.

Now, the 601st Air Group commander continued east.

Admiral Ozawa reddened with anger when he learned that Japanese gunners had fired at their own aircraft. His dark eyes burned when he spoke to Captain Ohmae. "You will learn at once who ordered fire on our air formation to cause these losses and damage. The culprits will be severely punished."

"At once, Admiral," Captain Ohmae said.

"Who is the commanding officer of the destroyer-cruiser screen?"

Captain Ohmae flipped quickly through some papers and then yanked a sheet from the pile. "Capt. Sasi Masate on the light cruiser *Yahagi*."

"You will contact Captain Masate at once and ask him to find out who gave the order to fire on our aircraft. Whether he be a petty officer or Captain Masate, the man will report to me at once."

"Yes, Admiral," Captain Ohmae said.

But, within moments, Admiral Ozawa would find himself plagued by a problem much worse than the miscreant who fired on the Japanese planes.

On June 15, 1944, Adm. Charles Lockwood, commander of the U.S. TF 17 submarine fleet, had laid out a square of the Philippine Sea through which he was certain the Japanese 1st Mobile Fleet must pass. Five submarines had been in the area on June 17–19: U.S.S. *Albacore, Finback, Stingray, Bang*, and *Cavella*. The sub *Stingray* had made the first contact with the Japanese fleet at about 0100 hours, June 18th and the last contact at 0345, June 19th. At 0150, June 19th, submarine *Finback* had reported the searchlight sightings that had conflicted with the HF/DF reports. By dawn of June 19th, U.S. submarines were still within the vicinity of the 1st Mobile Fleet's position in the Philippine Sea, but not close enough to spot the Japanese armada, even on radar.

The Japanese, meanwhile, had failed to take proper defensive measure against submarine attacks, probably because Admiral Ozawa and his staff had continually looked to the east for trouble and not to the flanks. Most of 1st Mobile Fleet's destroyers patrolled far to the van, with only a few tin cans screening the battleships and heavy cruisers that accompanied the carriers. Thus, these heavy surface warships could be as vulnerable as the carriers from any blank submarine attack.

At about 0750 hours, the U.S.S. *Albacore* was running fully submerged, for only a few minutes earlier, the sub's radar screen had reported a swarm of surface ships northeast of *Albacore*'s position in the Philippine Sea. Now, *Albacore*'s skipper, Cmdr. Jim Blanchard, raised periscope and sighted the horde of enemy ships on the horizon. He calculated their speed and course and then went deep, again at full ahead, hoping to close on the ships undetected. Blanchard ran his sub for an hour or so and at 0910, he raised persiscope again for another look. He expressed astonishment. Several big carriers were sailing leisurely eastward with a single destroyer off their starboard flank. Although Blanchard lay a mere 9,000 yards from the carrier fleet and he had upped periscope, the Japanese destroyer never moved from its nonchalant course. Perhaps the Japanese had been neglectful or simply complacent. Whatever the reason, the Nippon destroyer did not react as the U.S. submarine came well into close torpedo range.

Blanchard could not believe his good fortune, for he had expected the Japanese destroyer to charge, flinging depth charges ahead of the vessel. Blanchard easily caught the destroyer in his crosshairs, but he let the tin can pass. He wanted bigger game—the carrier. The *Albacore* skipper slowly altered course and soon came within 5,300 yards of a carrier—and still with no reaction from the Japanese.

"Ready torpedo launch," Blanchard called

110

his torpedo room, "four from the bow and two from aft."

"Ready," the torpedo officer answered.

But suddenly, Cmdr. Jim Blanchard found that his TDC (torpedo data computer) for automatic-fire track had malfunctioned. He could not use the TDC to compute range and speed. However, Blanchard had been a submariner for a long time and he would simply use his seaman's eye to fire his torpedoes; he would fire with an educated guess. At 0912 hours, he called into his JV phone.

"Fire one and two!"

A moment later came a response: "One and two away."

"Fire three and four."

"Three and four away."

"Hard left, hard left, one hundred eighty degrees," Blanchard cried. Only two minutes later, the *Albacore* had come about in a full half-circle. Then, Blanchard ordered torpedoes out of tubes five and six.

Soon, six torpedoes were heading toward *Taiho*, the flagship of 1st Mobile Fleet. From his close 5,300-yard range, Blanchard was sure some of the fish would hit.

But, somebody aboard a Japanese destroyer saw the torpedo wakes and quickly notified *Taiho*. Then, three Japanese destroyers raced in the direction of *Albacore*, firing depth charges as they came on. Blanchard took his sub down, narrowly escaping the first several explosions from depth charges. A moment later, the *Albacore* crew heard a distant explosion, indicating that at least one of *Albacore's* torpedoes had scored on a carrier.

Unfortunately, Blanchard and his crew could not check this suspected hit, for Blanchard could not return to periscope depth for a look. He plunged his submarine to 50 fathoms, while he manuevered *Albacore* frantically to avoid the deluge of Japanese depth charges now raining down on the American submarine. The Japanese, in fact, sent some two dozen depth charges after *Albacore*. Some of the explosions had been close enough to loosen cork insulation on the pipes in some of the compartments, but none of the explosions caused damage. Blanchard successfully snaked his way out of range to escape the Japanese destroyers.

Cmdr. Jim Blanchard and the *Albacore* crew were disappointed and Blanchard cursed the malfunctioning TDC. Had the computer worked properly, he might have scored more hits on the Japanese carrier, especially from the close range of 5,300 yards. Without verification, Blanchard could only note in his log the probable hit on a Japanese carrier; results unknown.

Blanchard and his crew would not learn for many months that *Albacore*'s torpedo hit had been quite fatal.

As the six torpedoes from U.S.S. *Albacore* skimmed toward carrier *Taiho* between 0910 and 0914 hours, Japanese destroyers had given the alarm before plowing after the American submarine. Those aboard *Taiho* had seen the wakes coming toward them and Ozawa had ordered full left rudder to avoid the wakes. But, despite the manuever, one of the torpedoes seemed sure to hit. A daring Zero pilot, Lt. Sakio Komatsu, one of the last pilots to leave *Taiho*'s deck for raid two, sighted the torpedo heading straight for the carrier. The determined pilot dove toward the torpedo, trying to blow it up with strafing fire before the fish hit the carrier. But, the strafing fire failed so Komatsu crash-dived the torpedo, blowing up the torpedo, himself, and his plane.

Komatsu had made the ultimate sacrifice to save the carrier. And, despite the tragic loss of the Zero pilot, those aboard *Taiho* sighed in relief. The carrier had avoided three torpedoes and Lieutenant Komatsu had given his life to destroy the fourth. The Japanese sailors were now certain they had missed possible disaster. On the open deck of the island structure, Ozawa turned to Captain Ohmae.

"You will bring me the name of this brave pilot, for he has shown the true Samurai spirit. His family must know of his courage and sacrifice."

"Yes, Honorable Ozawa," Captain Ohmae said.

But, only a moment later, torpedoes five and six arrived from the nose-diving U.S.S. *Albacore*. The first missed the bow of *Taiho*, but the second hit the carrier on the starboard forward. The hit only shuddered the carrier mildly and neither Ozawa nor anyone else on the bridge believed the hit had caused any real damage.

Capt. Toshikazu Ohmae immediately called the forward hangar deck. "What is the damage? Damage?"

"Nothing serious, Honorable Ohmae," somebody answered. "We have a forward elevator jammed closed and we have some minor flooding. But, repair crews are already at work. We should have the elevator repaired and the flooding sealed before our aircraft return from the strike against the American fleet."

"Fine," Captain Ohmae said.

When the communications officer relayed the report to Admiral Ozawa, the 1st Mobile Fleet commander merely nodded, and he then looked out to sea through binoculars. In moments, those on the open deck had all but forgotten the minor torpedo hit.

However, below, in the forward deck, tragedy would soon follow the seemingly insignificant hit.

Taiho, a big *Shokaku*-class carrier, weighed some 30,000 tons, measured some 300 yards in length and 26 yards in width. Thus, like all the *Shokaku*-class carriers, *Taiho* was long and narrow. She had eight big boilers and four turbines in four engine rooms, giving her 160,000 horsepower. She could plow through the sea at 34 knots. As opposed to American carriers, *Taiho* was quite heavily armed with eight twin-mounted 12.7 cm antiaircraft guns and ten triple-barreled 25-mm antiaircraft guns. Her capacity was 96 aircraft, half fighters and half bombers, with additional room for 12 scout planes. She carried a crew of 3,000, with a thousand of them airmen or direct-air maintenance crews. *Taiho*'s island stucture lay on the starboard, directly forward of two huge stacks. Finally, she could sail for 9,700 miles without refueling.

The huge carrier had been launched in early 1942, but *Taiho* had missed the Battle of Midway and she had seen little hard combat until today, June 19, 1944.

Taiho had just completed launching 84 planes before the torpedo hit that had been considered minor. But, while repair crews quickly sealed the minor flooding and worked on the jammed elevator, a damage-control officer noticed that the torpedo hit had also ruptured two of the vessel's gasoline tanks. The officer ordered the ventilating ducts opened to full in order to blow out the gasoline fumes that were leaking from the ruptured tanks. The tactic, ironically, had an opposite effect. Instead of blowing out the gas fumes, the open duct blowers spread deadly vapors throughout the ship. Not only fumes from the gas tanks, but also deadly fumes from ruptured crude petroleum tanks radiated through *Taiho*'s lower decks. Then, in a further miscalculation, crews pumped loose gasoline overboard, while the blowers of the open ducts sucked still more fumes through the bowels of *Taiho*.

In effect, the open ducts had turned *Taiho* into a gigantic supercharged gas cylinder that only awaited ignition. The ignition finally came. No one knew whether a lighted torch, a match, or some other flame brought on the tragedy, but, at 0930 hours, a tremendous explosion rocked *Taiho* from stern to bow. The explosion heaved the flight deck upward, twisting the deck like someone crumpling paper, and turning the deck into a miniature mountain range. The same explosion blew out the sides of the carrier's hangar decks and blasted holes in the bottom of the ship. The horrendous blast had killed more than 500 men below deck and injured at least another 500 Japanese sailors.

The rocking explosion had thrown *Taiho*'s flag room into total disarray, tossing tables, chairs, maps, charts, and anything else all about the room. Ozawa and Ohmae were thrown off their feet on the open deck and they barely caught themselves from falling to the flight deck below.

"What happened? What happened?" Ozawa cried.

But Ohmae's face was ashen and he could not answer. He stared down at the ruptured flight deck that seemingly had blossomed into a Mount Fuji miniature.

Then, whoop alarms echoed throughout the ship as *Taiho* quickly listed from heavy flooding. Admiral Yoshimura rushed onto the deck, his face twisted in agony as he spoke to his commander. "Honorable Ozawa, a horrible tragedy. The vessel is doomed. There is no way to stop flooding. We must abandon ship."

"Abandon ship?" Ozawa cried, utterly astonished.

"The entire ship is a mass of ruin. We have suffered a heavy loss of men; fire and flooding are everywhere."

"But what caused this? What?"

"No one knows," Admiral Yoshimura said.

Then, Ozawa felt himself falling to leeward as the big, 30,000-ton carrier continued its heavy list to starboard.

"Please, Admiral," Yoshimura persisted, "we must abandon ship."

Ozawa looked down at the ruptured deck where hundreds of sailors scrambled about the hot deck like ants escaping a trampled ant hill. Many were already climbing or diving over the sides, while others threw life rafts and life preservers over the side.

"I have taken the liberty of ordering the ship abandoned," Admiral Yoshimura continued. "You must leave, Admiral."

Ozawa nodded.

A few minutes later, Admiral Ozawa, Admiral Yoshimura, Captain Ohmae, and several others of the 1st Mobile Fleet staff had reached the ruptured flight deck and then climbed into lifeboats that sailors had dropped into the sea. Ozawa stared in awe at the burning, listing carrier and he watched in torment as sailors continued to scramble over the side. Soon, *Taiho* was swathed in huge flames and smoke, creating so much heat that those in the sea closest to the stricken carrier could never be rescued.

Meanwhile, destroyer *Watatsuki* and cruiser *Haguro* steamed quickly toward the doomed carrier to fish sailors out of the Philippine Sea.

Fortunately for Ozawa, destroyer *Watatsuki* came close enough to his foundering lifeboat to throw a line and pull the lifeboat to the side of the ship. Sailors immediately hoisted the 1st Mobile Fleet staff aboard the destroyer. The staff would only remain here long enough to change into dry clothes and to drink some tea. Then, Ozawa ordered a boat to carry him and his staff to the cruiser *Haguro*.

"We will transfer our flag to *Haguro*," he told Admiral Yoshimura. "Did we save anything from the *Taiho* flag room? Anything?"

"A few papers, Admiral," Yoshimura said.

A few minutes later the motor launch reached *Haguro* and transferred Ozawa and his staff to the cruiser's deck. Meanwhile, Ozawa could see the floundering sailors from *Taiho* on the surface of the sea: men swimming about, others aboard life rafts, and still others clinging to debris. Destroyer *Watatsuki* was fishing men out of the water, while in the distance, heavy flames, rising to a hundred feet, spiraled up from *Taiho*; smoke from the stricken carrier rose to a thousand feet.

118

The stricken *Taiho* would burn, belch, and list for most of the day. Then, at 1532 hours, a final, numbing explosion would again rock *Taiho* before the ship capsized, plunged by the stern, and sank to the bottom of the Philippine Sea to a depth of 2500 fathoms. *Taiho* would take more than 700 of her crew and some 14 aircraft to the bottom with her.

Those aboard *Haguro* stood stiffly on the quarter-deck, while a parade of 30 enlisted men stood at attention. When Ozawa and his staff reached the deck of the cruiser, Capt. Miko Hayakawa, skipper of *Haguro*, saluted briskly.

"We are grateful that you are safe, Honorable Ozawa."

"Take me to the plot room," Ozawa answered brusquely.

"Yes, Admiral."

"We will set up our flag organization in your plotting room, Captain," Admiral Ozawa said. "You will expand this ship's communication system so that we can be in radio contact with all vessels of the First Mobile Fleet."

"At once, Honorable Ozawa," the *Haguro* skipper said.

By the time Admiral Ozawa and his staff reached the plotting room of *Haguro*, electricians and radiomen were already working to increase the communication capacity of the Japanese cruiser. When Ozawa entered the plot room, he saw a portrait of the emperor hanging on the wall. He stared at the portrait for a moment and then turned to Admiral Yoshimura.

"Put whatever papers you have salvaged from *Taiho* on the table and we will study them."

"Yes, Admiral."

Ozawa then turned to Captain Ohmae. "You will notify all vessels that our flag is now aboard *Haguro*. Meanwhile, we will continue our air strikes as planned. Cardiv II will launch its strike at 1000 as scheduled, and Captain Fuchida will carry out the last strike at 1100. We cannot delay this air offensive because we have suffered the loss of one of our carriers."

"But who will recover Commander Tarui's aircraft when they return from their mission?" Captain Ohmae asked. "He leads more than one hundred aircraft, with most of them from carrier *Taiho*."

"He will land his aircraft on the decks of other vessels," Ozawa answered brusquely. "Notify all carriers to expect planes from *Taiho* at 1400. You yourself, Captain, will direct the task of sending units of Commander Tarui's returning aircraft to other carriers that can take them. In any event, I am certain that many aircraft from these first two strikes will fly on to Guam. I do not believe we will be unduly restricted in the recovery of aircraft because of the regrettable loss of carrier *Taiho*."

"Yes, Admiral," Captain Ohmae answered softly.

The 1st Mobile Fleet communications officer felt an uncertainty, a sense of doom. He feared the loss of *Taiho* might cause apprehension and confusion among the personnel of 1st Mobile Fleet. And somehow, Captain Ohmae was not sure that he could find deck space to land the eighty planes that had zoomed off *Taiho*'s deck less than an hour ago.

But, Captain Toshikazu Ohmae need hardly have worried about where to land returning Cardiv I aircraft. He could not guess that only 12 of the 69 planes from Raid I would return to the carriers. Nor could Captain Ohmae guess that Cmdr. Akira Tarui would suffer even worse losses on Raid II against the American TF 58 carrier fleet.

Chapter Seven

Cmdr. Akira Tarui, in flight for more than an hour, obviously did not know that Raid I by the 653rd Air Group had ended in near annihilation. Nor did he know as yet of the *Taiho* tragedy. Tarui looked up at the cloudless blue sky and nodded to himself: a good day for an air attack.

Commander Tarui then studied the V's of Zero escorts some 1,000 feet above the bomber formations. He knew that most of his pilots and air crews were inexperienced, and he hoped his airmen did not panic when enemy warships began spewing antiaircraft fire, or worse, when or if American Hellcats and Corsairs tried to stop them. Tarui then looked in front of him, where, several miles ahead, Zero pickets skimmed and banked about the sky like hungry hawks. The van Zeroes would report any potential interceptors and they would report any American surface ships below them.

Then, Commander Tarui relaxed in his cockpit and looked at his altimeter: 18,000 feet—a good height from which to zoom down on the enemy in a dive-bombing run. He called his gunner. "Norizo, stay alert for we will shortly approach enemy waters. Keep a sharp watch for enemy fighter planes."

"Yes, Commander," P.O. Norizo Ikeda said.

Far in the van, in a lead Zero, Comdr. Masatake Okimiya was arching and zooming his plane in a sweeping length of sky as he searched the emptiness for any signs of the enemy. Then, Okimiya leveled off his plane and stared straight ahead. He had been a fighter pilot for more years than he cared to remember, and despondency had gripped him in recent months. He had seen the Americans grow stronger and more dominant. Gone were the days when he and other Nippon pilots could attack and conquer with impunity. For more than a year now, Japan's fortunes had diminished badly in the face of ballooning American power, a strength that had grown by leaps and bounds. Now, the Americans seemingly ruled the skies over the Pacific as they also ruled the battle areas on land and sea.

Okimiya knew that most of his Zero pilots zooming and arching around him had been hastily trained and that they lacked combat experience. The young pilots were eager enough but, like Commander Tarui, Okimiya also wondered what might happen if these young pilots met aggressive, well-trained American fighter pilots. Like every other air leader in the 1st Mobile Fleet, Commander Okimiya also hoped they caught the Americans off guard; they could make their strike and disappear before the Americans retaliated with swarms of interceptors.

And Okimiya understood a sober truth: they must succeed. They must damage badly this American carrier force, for the huge enemy fleet represented an ominous peril to the inland Japanese empire of the western Pacific. The fall of the Mariana Islands would be a severe blow, but not nearly as severe as allowing a huge American carrier fleet to sail throughout the western Pacific with impunity.

Cmdr. Masatake Okimiya looked at his watch: 1042 hours. In fifteen minutes they would reach target.

Among Commander Okimiya's fighter pilots, W.O. Tashio Sakuraba sat uneasily in the cockpit of his Zero. The young Japanese fighter pilot had never met an enemy pilot before and he questioned his own ability to fight the Americans. Sakuraba knew well enough that the Americans had advanced steadily westward toward Japan's inner empire during the past year, continually defeating Japanese air, sea, and land units along the way. Still, Sakuraba had been awed by the huge size of the 1st Mobile Fleet. He could not believe the enemy had anything of comparable size and he believed this Japanese carrier fleet was strong enough to defeat the Americans in this latest confrontation after so many defeats over the past two years.

W.O. Sakuraba looked at his watch: 1046 hours. The first raid from Cardiv 3 was over now. He hoped the airmen of the 653rd Air Group had done considerable damage, had perhaps left the American carrier fleet in a state of disarray, and thus left the Americans too confused to deal with this second Japanese raid.

But, one thing bothered the young Zero pilot. He had not seen any returning aircraft from the 653rd Air Group. Surely, as the 653rd returned westward to their carriers, some elements from this Raid I group should have passed the 601st air formations now flying eastward. But, perhaps Commander Yamaguchi had taken a different route back to the carriers. Or, perhaps the 653rd commander had flown his air crews on to Guam to eagerly refuel and reload for another strike on the enemy.

In the cockpit of his lead Judy, meanwhile Cmdr. Akira Tarui looked at his watch again: 1048 hours. They would be over target soon at the designated IP location on their charts. He picked up his radio and spoke to his pilots.

"Please remain alert. We will shortly reach target. Fighter pilots will keep a sharp watch for enemy interceptors." A pause. Then: "Now, we will maintain radio silence."

In the rear cockpit of the lead Judy, P.O.

Norizo Ikeda stiffened and tightened his fingers on the grips of his twin .30-caliber guns.

Aboard U.S.S. *Bunker Hill, Essex,* and other American carriers, signalmen flagged in returning Hellcat and Corsair aircraft. As the American fighter pilots left their aircraft, they wore elated grins on their happy faces. The deck hands and nonflying officers listened in awe to reports from men like Brewer, Foltz, and McClusky. The deck personnel could not believe that these pilots had nearly wiped out the 65 to 75 Japanese aircraft formation; that the U.S. fighter pilots had left a length of wreckage over the Philippine Sea at a cost of only eight planes, of which four pilots, including Ralph Shipley, had been rescued.

"It's uncanny, just uncanny," Lieutenant Commander Brewer told his group leader, Cmdr. Dave McCampbell.

McCampbell stroked his chin and grinned. "A good show, huh?"

"Just like hitting ducks in a shooting gallery," Brewer said. "They couldn't respond at all. Their formations were too loose and they lacked coordination. I think their pilots were too green."

McCampbell nodded. "Well, the only damage reports came from three of the surface ships and the damage was minor. Not a single one of those Nip planes scored on any of our carriers."

"There weren't any Nip planes left to reach

the carriers," Brewer grinned.

Aboard *Bunker Hill*, Lt. Elbert McClusky gave the same elated account of the battle as did Brewer aboard *Essex*. "It was unreal," McClusky said. "They were just sitting ducks. Most of them didn't try to fight back. They just scattered and ran. Hell, they must know their planes can't outrun a Hellcat or Corsair on the straight and level. Most of them didn't try to maneuver out of the way."

"A real massacre, huh?" a deck officer asked.

"No contest," McClusky shook his head.

"Hell, Ellie got three planes himself," a fellow pilot grinned, "and all on one pass."

"Three planes on one pass?" the deck officer gaped at McClusky.

"Lucky, I guess," McClusky answered.

"We must have knocked out a couple dozen planes with our AG 8 alone," the fighter pilot said. "God knows how many the other groups knocked down."

"Jesus," the deck officer hissed.

Then, the officer ordered decks cleared, for more planes were still coming in. Only Commander Shipley was missing, but the *Bunker Hill* radio room got a report that the AG 8 commander had safely bailed out and a destroyer had rescued him.

At about 1100 hours, the last of the TF 58 fighter planes had alighted on their carrier decks and the air commander, Gus Widhelm, relaxed in the control room of flag carrier *Lex-*

127

ington to drink a cup of coffee. Widhelm had toyed with the idea of recalling the bombers that were loitering to the east, away from the carriers, to keep the decks clear for fighter planes. But, at 1107 hours, radar reports jerked Widhelm from his chair. Radar had again picked up bogies, swarms of them, more than the first time. The new reports had pinpointed the mass of oncoming planes on a 250° course, about 155 miles west of U.S.S. *Lexington*. Widhelm picked up his radio again and ordered a new fighter-plane scramble.

Within five minutes, American Navy fighter pilots reached their planes where deck crews had warmed up engines as soon as Widhelm reported the bogies to all ships.

Aboard *Essex*, Cmdr. Dave McCampbell himself boarded the lead Hellcat. With him came his wingman, Lt. Bob Hoel, and two flight leaders, Lt. Norm Beree and Lt. Gaylord Brown. McCampbell's AG 15 aboard *Essex* had mustered 36 Hellcats, most of the carrier's fighter planes that had not been out on the first interception. From the bridge Lieutenant Commander Brewer shot up a thumb: good luck; hope you have the same kind of success that Brewer and the earlier *Essex* pilots had enjoyed against the first attempted Japanese assault on the American carriers. Brewer's own complement of pilots had gone below to the ready rooms while mechanics and ordnance men reserviced Brewer's Hellcats.

Aboard *Lexington*, Cmdr. Bill Strean of VF

Cmdr. Dave McCampbell, also of AG 15, USS Essex. He was America's leading naval air ace of WW II, with 7 kills alone during Operation Forager.

Admiral Raymond Spruance, commander of U.S. Fifth Fleet.

Admiral Marc Mitscher (L), commander of TF 58, discusses strategy with Captain Arleigh Burke (R), TF 58 chief of staff.

Cmdr. Charles Brewer of AG 15, USS Essex. His overeagerness cost him his life.

Cmdr. Ralph Weymouth (L) confers with Admiral Mitscher (R) after Weymouth led Dauntless attack on Guam that all but finished off the Japanese 1st Air Fleet.

Lt. Cmdr. Paul Buie of USS Lexington (C) and his AG 16 pilots, grin happily after taking a heavy toll of Japanese attacking planes. Buie coined the phrase Turkey Shoot, referring to Japan's heavy losses in Operation Forager.

Lt. Alex Vraciu, also of Lexington's AG 16, holds up six fingers, indicating he shot down an amazing six enemy planes in a single engagement.

Cmdr. James Peters of Yorktown's AG 1 scored two kills during the turkey shoot.

Lt. George Brown of Yorktown's AG 1 bomber unit got his hit on a Japanese carrier but lost his life returning from long combat flight.

Lt. Elbert McClusky of Bunker Hill's AG 8 fighter unit scored four kills during the Marianas Turkey Shoot.

Cmdr. William "Killer" Kane of USS Enterprise was forced to ditch after attack on Japanese carrier. Crew of rescuing destroyer exchanged Kane for Enterprise's ice cream supply.

Lt. Cmdr. Alvin Priel also of USS Enterprise, led the Big E bombers against enemy fleet.

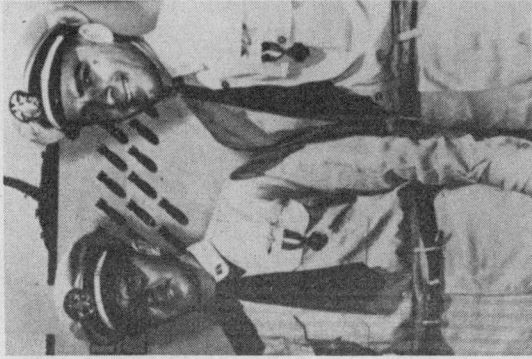

Lt. Ron Gift (L) and Lt. Tom Dries (R) made successful torpedo hits on Japanese carrier.

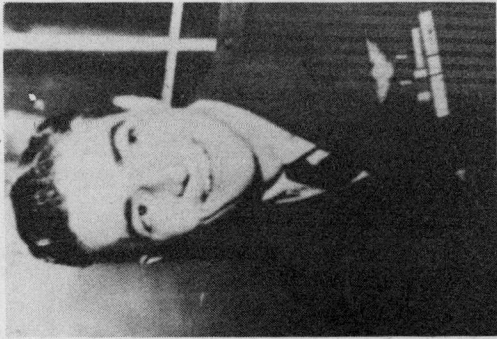

Cmdr. Robert Mehle of USS Monterey successfully held off Japanese fighters to enable the Monterey bombers to fatally hit a Japanese carrier.

Admiral Soemu Toyoda, commander of the Japanese Combined Fleet initiated the A-Go plan to lure American carrier fleet into a decisive sea battle.

Lt. Jim Bennett scored the fatal hit on carrier Hiyo, but lost his life.

Admiral Sueo Obayashi of Japanese Cardiv 3 tried to get off a late afternoon air strike against Americans, but Ozawa made him recall his planes. Had the attack gone off, the Japanese air units may have seriously hurt the U.S. TF 58 carrier fleet.

Admiral Jisaburo Ozawa, commander of Japanese 1st Mobile Fleet, was sure he would defeat the Americans in the decisive carrier battle.

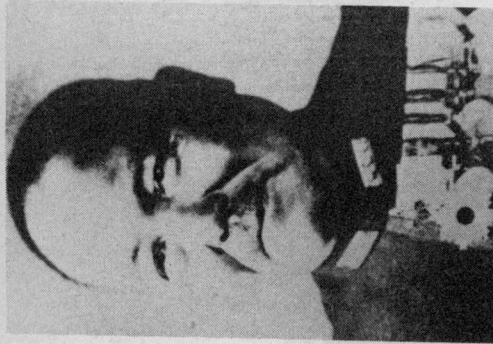

Admiral Matake Yoshimura, chief of staff of the 1st Mobile Fleet, fed Admiral Ozawa glowing reports of Japanese air successes—all of it false.

Captain Mitsuo Fuchida, who commanded the air groups of 1st Mobile Fleet. He was shocked by the ability and aggressiveness of the American naval pilots.

Members of the Japanese 653rd Air Group: standing, L to R, Shoichi Sugita, Zunichi Uda, Massaje Oe';kneeling, L to R, Tyoji Ohhara, Minichi Ohshoyo, and Yoshio Nakamura. All were killed on Raid I except for Lt. Sugita.

Cmdr. Tarui (L), commander of 601st Air Group, and his gunner, NCO Norizo Ikeda (R). Both were killed during Raid II.

Cmdr. Joyotara Iwami, commander of Japanese 652nd Air Group. He luckily missed the American carriers on Raid III and thus he and most of his airmen survived.

W/O Tashio Sakuraba, also of 601st Air Group. He was also killed on Raid II.

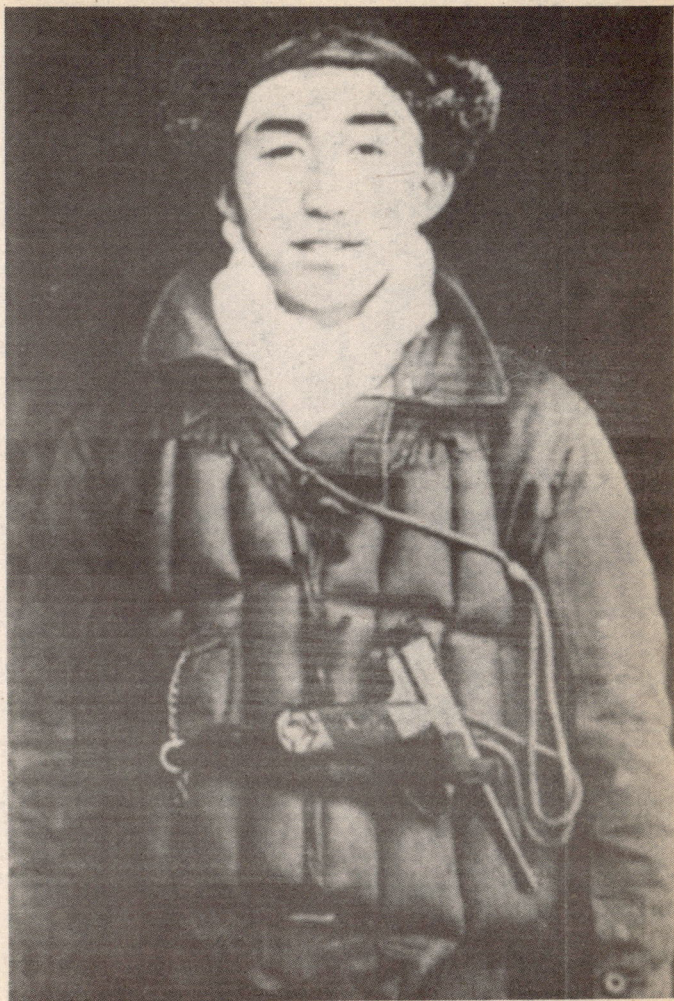

Lt. Takeo Tanimizu, also of 601st Air Group. His segment of planes on Raid III ran into American Hellcat pilots, costing most of his aircraft and men.

Courtesy Toshihiko Ohno

Ensign Toshihiko Ohno, one of the few survivors of the battle.

Lt. Toshihiko Ohno of the 601st Air Group, saw most of the attacking Japanese planes shot down during Raid IV. He landed safely on Saipan only to be whisked into a naval ground unit to fight the losing defense of Saipan.

Admiral Chuichi Nagumo, the commander of the Pearl Harbor attack, saw Japan's navy collapse during Operation Forager. He committed suicide.

Some of the carriers of TF 58, the largest aircraft carrier unit ever assembled.

American naval planes prepare to take off to soften up island of Saipan for the U.S. Marine invasion.

Mitscher's planes attack the Marianas prior to invasion.

Navy gunner remains alert as LCI with marine troops heads for Saipan.

U.S. marines land and establish beachhead on Saipan.

*Aerial view of Guam after American carrier planes pasted
the island and all but wiped out the 1st Air Fleet.*

Anti-aircraft gunners aboard U.S. ships fire furiously at Japanese planes from Raid I.

A Japanese navy bomber scores a hit on American carrier during Operation Forager.

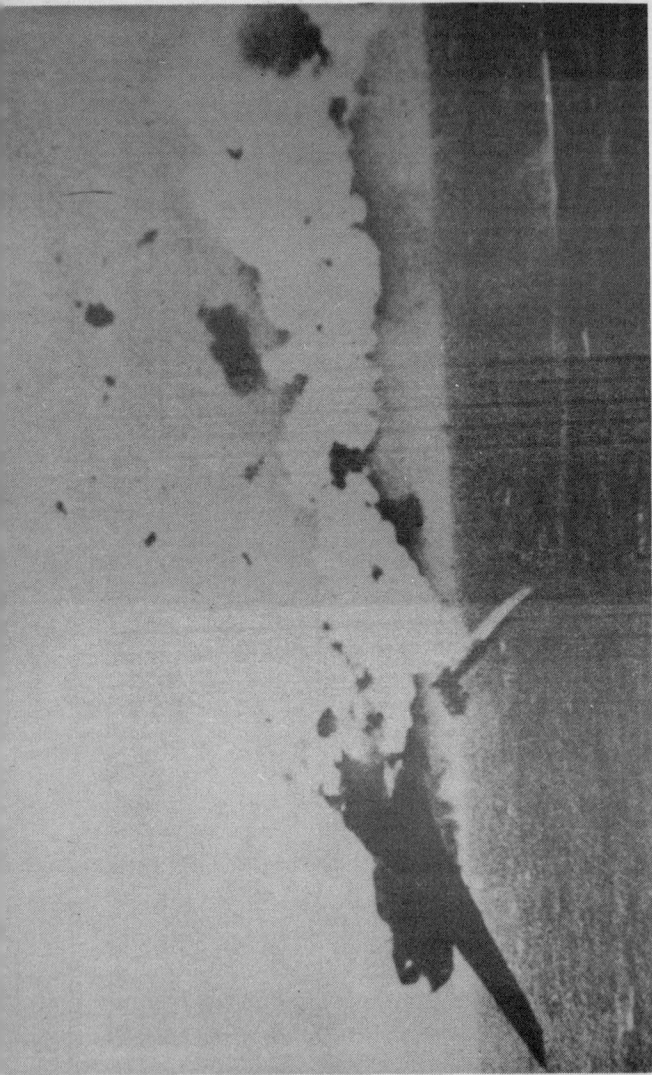

Japanese Jill bomber explodes in mid-air after fatal hit by anti-aircraft fire. The Jill never bog off its torpedoes.

A Japanese Judy dive bomber splashes into the sea, victim of ack ack guns from the carrier USS Bunker Hill (L).

Another Japanese naval bomber attempts to attack an American carrier. The plane was sent down in flames before it could score.

Skies over TF 58 are black from ack ack fire as anti aircraft gunners fire furiously at attacking Japanese planes.

A Japanese Judy on Raid IV plummets into the sea with a trail of smoke. Most of the Japanese planes attempting to attack TF 58 met the same fate.

Carrier plane returns to deck of Enterprise after successful shoot against Japanese planes on Raid III.

Japanese sailors aboard listing carrier Shokaku prepare to abandon ship after fatal torpedo hits from USS Cavella, an American submarine.

Japanese ships maneuver furiously during late afternoon American air attack on the Japanese 1st Mobile Fleet.

American carrier planes leave carrier Hiyo burning (bottom) and leave cruiser Mogami burning (top).

Torpedo scores hit on carrier Junyo during late afternoon attack by American planes.

Japanese cruiser burns furiously after bomb hits by TF 58 aircraft on late afternoon of June 20th, 1944.

Japanese destroyer burns from bomb hits during June 20th strike by American planes.

Crewmen aboard carrier USS Lexington stand at attention during sea burial ceremony for Lexington's dead.

16 climbed into the first of 30 Hellcats on the carrier deck, with aircraft engines screaming in deafening roars in preflight warm-ups. Next to Strean, one of his flight leaders, Paul Buie, led his pilots to another group of Hellcats. Within moments, *Lexington*'s fighter pilots had settled into their cockpits and waited for take-off signal.

From the bridge of *Lexington*, Adm. Marc Mitscher gestured down to Cmdr. Bill Strean in the first AG 16 Hellcat. Strean threw a thumbs-up in return, drawing a grin from the usually sober-faced Mitscher. In the second VF 16 flight, Lt. Cmdr. Paul Buie looked about at his fellow pilots, stopping to grin at Lt. Alex Vraciu, off to Buie's starboard. Buie grinned at the lieutenant and offered a thumbs-up. Vraciu returned the same gesture with his own grin.

The 36 Hellcats from *Essex* under Cmdr. Dave McCampbell got off first. Then, Cmdr. Bill Strean zoomed his 30 Hellcats from VF 16 off *Lexington*'s carrier deck. Behind these two units, more Hellcats and Corsairs roared off other American carrier decks: Corsairs from U.S.S. *Bataan* and *San Jacinto*, and Hellcats from U.S.S. *Yorktown* and *Princeton*.

Soon, American fighter planes covered the sky over the spread-out vessels of TF 58. Then, over 150 American fighter planes roared westward to meet the oncoming Japanese. Soon, Dave McCampbell got a call from Capt. Gus Widhelm.

"Vector at two hundred forty five degrees,

Commander; distance eighty miles."

"Roger," Commander McCampbell answered. He then increased his formation speed to nearly 180 knots true air speed. For the next 10 or 15 minutes he zoomed onward. Then, at 1137 hours, McCampbell spotted the huge formation of enemy planes, now some 45 miles from carrier *Essex* and only ten to twenty miles from the surface-ship screen of U.S. battleships, cruisers, and destroyers. As usual, the Japanese flew in their V formation, three to a V, nine to a flight, and 27 to a squadron. Mc-Campbell estimated that he was about 1500 to 2000 feet above the enemy.

McCampbell called his pilots. "Christ, they've got everything down there: Skunks (fighter planes), Rats (dive bombers), and Fish (torpedo bombers). Lieutenant Brown," he then spoke to one of his flight leaders, "take your flight upstairs to cover us."

"Yes, sir," Brown answered.

"The rest of you, follow me after those bandits," the VF 15 leader said. "We'll attack in pairs. Pick your targets and attack in pairs. O.K., tally-ho."

The first formation of Japanese aircraft, under Cmdr. Akira Tarui, included 18 Judys and 24 Zero fighter planes, with a half-dozen of these fighters in the van of Commander Tarui's lead Judy. The Zeros, one V to each V of bombers, had been arching across the sky, leaving thick contrails of condensation.

At 1139 hours, Commander Tarui saw his

130

escorting Zeroes scoot away and he stiffened in surprise. Then, he heard the screaming planes from above. When he looked up, he saw the oncoming American fighter planes and he quickly picked up his radio. "All pilots, close formations. Close! Hold tight!"

But, Tarui may as well have spoken to the empty sky. Once again, the many inexperienced pilots in his lead Judy squadron could not discipline themselves. Most of them simply arched away and scattered, exposing themselves to the attacking American fighter planes without the benefit of heavy gunnery response from gunners in a tight bomber formation.

McCampbell and five of his pilots, including wingman Bob Hoel, zoomed downward from 24,000 feet. The sextet of Hellcats opened to 350 knots, shuddering the wings of the U.S. Navy fighter planes. But, the swift onslaught proved effective. McCampbell picked out a Judy in the middle of a formation and raked the plane with strafing fire. The Judy fell apart and its pieces tumbled into the sea, along with the Japanese pilot and gunner.

McCampbell then dove through the scattering Judys and arced upward, intent on getting the lead dive bomber of Cmdr. Akira Tarui. But, one of McCampbell's pilots had hit another Judy and the plane exploded. The shattered Japanese aircraft almost blew up in McCampbell's face and he was forced to veer away, thus missing the chance to hit Tarui's Judy. So, the VF 15 commander climbed high, arced, and came down once more on another Judy formation. His first burst of strafing fire punched holes in the dive bomber's fuselage, but did not destroy the plane. The Judy staggered on, escaping destruction. McCampbell next attacked a Zero, but missed the arcing Japanese fighter plane.

Dave McCampbell now zoomed upward once more and again came down to attack a dive bomber. The rear gunner of the Judy fired furious .30-caliber fire at the Hellcat and punched holes in McCampbell's plane. But, the VF 15 commander's strafing fire chopped the Judy apart and the Japanese dive bomber spun downward to crash into the sea.

Then, from an eight o'clock position, McCampbell whirled his Hellcat and finally caught Cmdr. Akira Tarui's lead Judy. The 601st commander rolled and maneuvered his plane as gunner Norizo Ikeda exchanged .30-caliber fire with McCampbell's .50-caliber fire. Norizo Ikeda lost. One burst of .50-caliber fire smashed the elongated cockpit of the Judy and killed Norizo Ikeda. Then, a second burst of .50-caliber fire hit the fuel tank and the Judy burst into flames. Commander Tarui tried desperately to control his aircraft, but to no avail. The plane arced downward and out of control.

Commander Tarui craned his neck to catch a glimpse of his blood-splatered, slain gunner. Then, he shoved back the cockpit canopy and coughed from the smoke. But, he managed to climb out and parachute from the plane. However, Cmdr. Akira Tarui was never heard from again, and he apparently perished in the Philippine Sea.

McCampbell, meanwhile, continued his hunt and laced another Judy with strafing fire. The fire shattered a wing and the Japanese dive bomber teetered precariously. But, when McCampbell tried to send another burst into the damaged Japanese plane, he found he had run out of ammo. He cursed and watched the damaged plane stagger on. The VF 15 commander then climbed high in the sky to direct other pilots of his unit against the Japanese planes. He called his fellow pilots.

"I got their leader. The rest should be easy. Keep after them, in pairs! Keep after them, but stay in pairs."

McCampbell's wingman, Bob Hoel, had some success of his own, when he managed to tail one Zero fighter plane and set the aircraft afire by strafing it. The plane shuddered erratically and then plunged into the sea in a pall of smoke. Hoel then came in to a second Zero at three o'clock high, and his .50-caliber strafing fire shattered the cockpit and killed the pilot. The Zero spun downward, out of control, and plopped into the sea.

In little more than five minutes of action, Campbell himself had downed three planes, including the leader, and damaged two other planes. Lieutenant Hoel had downed two Zeros and the other pilots of VF 15 had claimed the destruction of another 15 Zeros and Judys, while damaging another dozen Japanese planes. For their efforts, AG 15 had suffered the loss of four planes. Two American pilots died and two pilots were injured. One American flyer had suffered a leg wound from a 20-mm fragment and the other injured U.S. pilot had suffered a shoulder wound from a 7.7-mm slug. Both men were rescued.

Once again, the heavily armored Hellcats had weathered the punishment from 7.7- and 20-mm guns, while the lightly armored Japanese planes fell easy prey to the six forward .50-caliber machine guns of U.S. Navy Hellcats.

By the time McCampbell and his VF 15 pilots had macerated the first Japanese formations, the Jill torpedo bombers from carrier *Shokaku* were coming up from the rear. The *Shokaku* planes had been flying below and behind the main formation with their Zero escorts, thus missing the attack by Cmdr. Dave McCampbell and his pilots. They had seemingly avoided the Judy and Zero massacre in the lead formations. But, at 1242 hours, Cmdr. Bill Strean of *Lexington*'s AG 16 group picked up the Jills on the radar screen in his lead Hellcat. The VF 16 commander had caught the Jills on a 265° course and he immediately led his pilots on a west-southwest course.

Strean had also got a call from Capt. Gus Widhelm on the Japanese position. "Vector at 250! Vector at 250!" Widhelm told Strean.

"We've found them and we'll go after them," Strean answered.

Moments later, Strean spotted the Japanese torpedo bombers and he climbed to 24,000 feet before calling his pilots. "O.K., boys, they're down below. I'll direct from up here. Pick your targets and attack in pairs. In pairs!"

The *Lexington* fighter pilots responded, with Lt. Cmdr. Paul Buie leading a flight of 12 planes toward the Japanese aircraft. Buie, from Nashville, Tenn., had already downed five Japanese planes during a year of combat, and he thirsted for a few more kills.

Among Buie's pilots was Lt. Alex Vraciu, a man who had already downed three Japanese planes during the central Pacific conflict. Vraciu, from Chicago, Ill., had learned his trade as a naval fighter pilot from the redoubtable Edward "Butch" O'Hara, one of the Navy's most famed fighter pilots in the Pacific. Vraciu had followed O'Hara in combat scraps over Rabaul, Truk, and other Japanese-held islands. Now, like Buie, Vraciu also wanted more kills.

"Lets scramble," Lieutenant Commander Buie cried again into his radio JV. "In pairs; attack in pairs!"

Buie and his pilots now waded into the again-scattering Japanese planes. Buie himself dove after several Zero fighter bombers. He quickly tailed one and chopped the tail off the Zero. He then blew up a second Zero and shattered the cockpit of a third Zero. Then, Lieutenant Commander Buie climbed upstairs to direct other pilots of his flight on the targets below.

Lt. Alex Vraciu, hovering at 20,000 feet, thought the battle was over when his radar screen suddenly registered a horde of bogies. He arced his plane and soon found a Jill torpedo bomber. The Jill pilot tried to evade, but Vraciu made a quick side run and ignited the Japanese plane with strafing fire that sent the flaming Japanese torpedo bomber into the sea. The Jill gunner was still firing his .30-caliber guns as flames and smoke engulfed the gunner and his plane. Vraciu felt sorry for the young Japanese gunner, who had shown such determination, however futile, even in the face of imminent death.

Less than a minute later, the American fighter pilot caught a Zero fighter-bomber and sent the plane down in flames.

Then, when Vraciu looked about him, he saw an incredible sight. The sky was full of tracer fire, smoke, debris, bits of planes, chattering machine-gun fire, and whining aircraft engines. Vraciu did not sight-see long, however, for he caught sight of a Zero out of formation, a good target. Vraciu quickly followed and hit the plane with a short burst, shattered the cockpit, and killed the pilot before the plane went down. Within the next minute, Vraciu caught two more planes. Another short burst caught one Zero in the fuel tank and the plane blew up in the middle of the sky. A few seconds later, the Chicagoan caught another Zero, shot off a wing, and watched the Zero tumble crazily into the sea. On the same pass, astonishingly, Vraciu caught still another plane, a Judy. He set the plane afire before the flaming Japanese dive bomber crashed into the sea.

Absolutely incredible! Six planes in a matter of two minutes. Lt. Alex Vraciu could not believe his accomplishment.

Other VF 16 pilots had also scored, until the *Lexington* pilots had knocked over 20 Japanese planes out of the sky. As VF 16 headed back toward its carrier, Lt. Cmdr. Paul Buie saw a string of burning, sinking, smoking Japanese planes on the surface of the sea. He called his pilots.

"Goddamn, we've had ourselves a turkey shoot! A real old turkey shoot!"

In the furious few minutes of battle, the Japanese had indeed been the victims of a devastating turkey shoot. Between the AG 15 aircraft from *Essex* and the AG 16 from the *Lexington*, the two units had shot down about 50 Japanese planes.

But, the Americans were not yet finished.

Soon, Corsairs from the U.S.S. *Bataan* and *San Jacinto* as well as Hellcats from the U.S.S *Yorktown* and *Princeton* dove into the scattering, harrassed Japanese Zeros, Jills, and Judys. Swarms of American Corsair pilots shot down 22 more Japanese planes in 20 minutes, while Hellcat pilots shot down more than two dozen.

Still, despite the heavy losses, some of the

Judys and Jills had broken through the American interceptors. One Jill sent two torpedoes into the side of battleship U.S.S. *Indiana*, but the torpedoes did not explode when they hit the belt armor at the waterline. Two Judys went after U.S.S. *Alabama* that had caught an earlier hit during the Japanese first raid. But, *Alabama* ack-ack gunners blew both dive bombers out of the air. Another pair of Jills went for battleship U.S.S *Iowa*, but their torpedoes missed.

Six Judys closed on the carriers U.S.S. *Wasp* and *Bunker Hill*. Despite intense ack-ack fire, four Judys dropped their bombs that exploded in a string of bursts just off the *Wasp*'s port bow, spewing shrapnel all over the deck. The explosions killed one man and injured several others. The other pair of Judys attacked *Bunker Hill*, but their bombs fell short, alongside the carrier's port elevator. However, bursts of shrapnel killed two men and caused minor flooding. Several Jills went after U.S.S. *Princeton* to the north of *Wasp* and *Bunker Hill*, but ack-ack gunners downed two of the Jills and forced the other to veer away without scoring torpedo hits.

By now, all the carriers of TF 58 were swerving and maneuvering frantically in evasive action to avoid hits from Judy and Jill bombers, while ack-ack gunners fired without rest. However, by 1230 hours, all Japanese attacks had ended and ship radar screens showed no more enemy planes. All scrambled CAP's returned to their carriers.

This second Japanese raid had only caused minor damage to several American ships and the loss of a dozen U.S. planes. Destroyers rescued six American fighter pilots, however. For the Japanese, the effort had been disastrous. The 601st Air Group under Cmdr. Akira Tarui had lost 32 Zeros, 42 Judys, and 23 Jills, of which a dozen had been shot down by antiaircraft fire. Among the dead were Cmdr. Akira Tarui, his gunner Norizo Ikeda, and the young fighter pilot Toshio Sakuraba.

Only nine planes from well over a hundred Japanese aircraft flew back to their carriers. Lt. Masatake Okimiya, with a totally shocked look on his face, led these few aircraft westward. Another dozen planes, damaged, sputtered on to Guam. And, when Okimiya reached the 1st Mobile Fleet, he would get another shock—the loss of carrier *Taiho*.

But even worse for the Japanese, the turkey shoot was only half over.

97   12
        +9
        ―――
        21

Chapter Eight

Of all the flyers in the 1st Mobile Air Fleet, perhaps no Japanese aviator showed more dedication than Cmdr. Joyotara Iwami. The Nippon Navy pilot had been at war since 1937, when he first fought against the Chinese off the coast of China. By the time World War II broke out with the United States, Iwami had already flown more than 300 combat missions, mostly during the conquest of China and Indochina.

In December of 1941, Iwami became a squadron leader aboard the carrier *Hiyo* and he had served here for almost three years with only two visits home. By mid-1944, he had risen to the rank of commander and to the leadership of the 652nd Air Group. Although only 30 years of age, Joyotara Iwami looked older, and the airmen under him easily accepted his authority. And, even as Japan's fortunes had worsened during the past two years, even as more and more experienced pilots and crews became victims of America's growing naval strength, and even as the Americans pushed the Japanese ever westward, Iwami had maintained his poise and confidence.

"It is the will of heaven," he told his discouraged bomber crews. "But in the end, God will favor us and we shall prevail."

On the morning of June 19, 1944, in the middle of the Philippine Sea, Iwami believed that Japan's time had come to win the favor of the gods, to win a decisive victory over the Americans. Nine aircraft carriers covered a wide expanse of sea, with some 500 planes crowding their decks and holds. Five big battleships, including two 18"-gun battleships, over a dozen cruisers, and countless destroyers screened the huge 1st Mobile Fleet. In seven years of combat, Cmdr. Joyotara Iwami had never seen such a huge combat armada: not during the years of fighting against China or in southeast Asia, not during those early months of World War II when Japan swept through the Pacific, and not during the ill-fated carrier battles in the Coral Sea, at Midway, or in the hard Solomon Islands campaign.

Iwami knew that the Japanese Navy had been rebuilding its fleet over the past two years. Now, this huge 1st Mobile Fleet with its equally large Batjan support fleet reflected the results of this rebuilding. Iwami believed sincerely that this huge armada surpassed in strength anything the Americans had brought to the

Mariana Islands. Like so many other Japanese military commanders, he could not conceive of the Americans actually having more aircraft carriers, more surface ships, and twice as many aircraft in the Philippine Sea.

At 0950 hours, Cmdr. Joyotara Iwami, commander of the 652nd Air Group, left the ready room of carrier *Hiyo* with his pilots and gunners. Service crews had readied seven Jills and 15 Zero fighter-bombers. Behind Iwami came Lt. Mitso Oshita who would lead the Zero fighter-bombers, each carrying a pair of 550-pound bombs. From the deck of carrier *Hiyo*, Iwami could hear the screaming engines of aircraft aboard *Junyo*, two miles off port. The sister aircraft carrier would launch nine Val dive bombers and 15 Zero fighter planes to escort the Jills, Vals, and fighter-bombers.

Raiding Force III with 46 planes, would be the smallest attack group thus far.

Before Commander Iwami climbed into the cockpit of his Jill torpedo bomber, the operations officer recalled Iwami and his flight leaders to the ready room.

"Commander," the operations officer said, "we have received information from the Six Hundred Fifty-third Air Group commander that they encountered quite heavy antiaircraft fire from the enemy's screen of surface ships. Battleships, cruisers, and destroyers lie some twenty five to thirty miles west of the American carriers. We believe you should alter course."

Commander Iwami only listened.

The operations officer turned to a map pinned on the wall behind him. "We suggest you fly on a northeasterly course to avoid these heavy surface-ship screens. You can then attack the enemy carriers from this position to the north." The operations officer tapped a finger on the chart. "I have made up a new set of charts which we can distribute to you and your flight leaders. These same charts will be issued to Lieutenant Tanimizu aboard carrier *Junyo*,"

Iwami took the charts and distributed them among his flight leaders.

"Only a few minutes ago, at 0945," the operations officer continued, "two seaplanes launched from cruiser *Moyami* reported three enemy carriers and other surface ships at one hundred twenty degrees twenty two minutes latitude north and one hundred forty three degrees forty-three minutes longitude east. We have designated this location of the enemy fleet as a 15Ri position, where you will find the enemy carriers."

"I understand," Commander Iwami said.

Then, between 1000 and 1015 hours, the seven Jills, 15 Zero fighter bombers, nine Val dive bombers, and 15 Zero escort fighter planes took to the air and droned northeast. They expected to be over the American carriers about noontime, or perhaps a little later since they would detour to come into the target areas from the north.

Commander Iwami looked at the six Jills around him and then at the Zero fighter-bombers behind him. He knew that behind the fighter bombers flew the nine Vals. Iwami then looked at his altimeter: 30,000 feet. When he looked upward, he saw some of the 15 escorting fighter planes about 2,000 feet above him. Iwami adjusted his oxygen mask and then called the Zero escort leader.

"Lieutenant, have you seen anything?"

Lt. Takeo Tanimizu stared about him from his lead fighter plane and then answered Iwami. "There is nothing, Commander, nothing. I believe this present course will enable us to reach the American carriers without interference from either enemy interceptors or from enemy surface ships."

"Let us hope so," Commander Iwami answered.

Lieutenant Tanimizu grinned. "We will succeed, Commander, just as the first two formations of attacking aircraft have no doubt also succeeded."

Takeo Tanimizu felt quite confident. He had been aboard *Junyo* for more than three years, and he had won a measure of success during the Battle of Santa Cruz Island. Since then, however, his carrier *Junyo* had seen only limited action in the western Pacific, and Tanimizu had not realized how great and powerful the United States Navy had grown during the past two years. Further, Tanimizu had not realized that outnumbered American pilots with their inferior Wildcat fighter planes of 1942 no longer prevailed today. Now, in mid-1944, well-trained American pilots, with superior Corsair and Hellcat fighter planes, hundreds of them, would challenge the Japanese.

Tanimizu called his 2nd flight leader. "Haji, have you seen anything?"

"Nothing, Takeo," the flight leader answered, "only a beautiful bright sky that reminds me of the sky over Honshu Bay."

"Stay alert," Lieutenant Tanimizu said. "While we do not expect any enemy interceptor planes, no one can tell for sure."

"If I see enemy aircraft, I will let you know."

The planes from the 652nd Air Group droned on about another hour when Commander Iwami got a call from the carrier *Hiyo*'s operations officer. "Commander, only a few moments ago, two seaplanes from *Shokaku* reported three carriers and screening surface ships at fifteen degrees thirty three minutes north latitude, and one forty three degrees fifteen minutes east longitude. This point we have designated on your chart as a 3Ri position."

"Is there some mistake? How can two pairs of search planes report the same enemy carriers at different locations?"

"We believe that the latest report is the more reliable," the operations officer said. "We are sure the enemy carrier force has been sailing due north by slightly northwest. We therefore suggest you mark your chart at this new location; fifteen degrees thirty three minutes north by one hundred forty three degrees fifteen minutes east. Designate the point with the new 3Ri figure.''

"I will do so," Iwami said, "and then alter course to this new location."

"I would suggest that you add the speed of the enemy's course, perhaps 20 knots, to your plotting line. We are sure the enemy carrier forces are moving northward and they will be even further north by northwest by the time you find them."

"A good suggestion," Iwami said.

The Japanese search planes had been tracking the northern segment of TF 58, Adm. Bill Harill's TF 58.4 that included carriers *Essex, Langley,* and *Cowpens.* But, this carrier group was actually moving in a shuttle, northwest and southeast, to protect the north flank of TF 58 from any Japanese end run. So, by the time Commander Iwami arrived at the 3Ri designation he might not find TF 58.4 at all. In fact, some of the flight leaders of the 652nd Air Group did not even get the report from Iwami to alter course, and by the time they came within fifteen minutes of the target area, the Japanese air group had inadvertently split, with 20 planes following Commander Iwami to the new 3Ri point and the other planes under Lieutenant Tanimizu going on to the original 15Ri point.

Meanwhile, the big carrier groups of TF 58 had once more retrieved aircraft after the second scramble against the second attempted attack by Japanese planes. In fact, by 1225 hours, most of the Hellcats and Corsairs had returned to their carriers. Deck crews had begun to lower planes into the hangar decks for refueling and rearming, while they hoisted reloaded and refueled fighter planes from the first interception of Japanese planes. Mitscher wanted to make certain he had planes ready in the event the Japanese sent a third raiding force.

The loitering American bombers, meanwhile, still hovered to the east of the carriers. But, at 1225 hours, the Avengers and Dauntlesses finally got the all clear to return to their carriers.

At the same 1225 hours, Cmdr. Joyotara Iwami had reached the designated 3Ri area and all he found was a patch of empty sea as far as he could see—perhaps a forty-mile radius. Commander Iwami was puzzled. Surely, their search planes could not have miscalculated this badly. But then, an elation swelled inside of him. Of course, the airmen of the 653rd and 601st Air Groups on Raids I and II had probably macerated the enemy fleet quite badly. Any surviving enemy carriers were now steaming swiftly to the east to avoid further punishment.

Iwami noted that his fuel gauge was almost on half and he could not dally to find surviving enemy carriers which were probably far to the east. Besides, more than half of his aircraft had gone off in the wrong direction, apparently failing to get the instructions to alter course to the 3Ri contact. Then, Iwami got a call from Lt. Mitsukuni Oshita who led the Zero fighter-bomber flight.

"Commander," Oshita said, "we have seen nothing. What has happened to the enemy fleet that should be at this 3Ri location as given us by the operations officer?"

"I believe the operations officer gave us the wrong position," Commander Iwami said. "Or, the American fleet has sailed elsewhere, perhaps to the east. We are low on fuel and I believe we have no choice but to return to our carriers."

"As you wish, Commander," Lieutenant Oshita said.

Thus, Commander Iwami veered his 21 planes and headed back to carrier *Hiyo*.

Iwami had missed the American carriers for a quite good reason. The first report at the 15Ri location had been the sighting of TF 58.4 when this fleet unit was sailing south. The second sighting report at the designated 3Ri location had caught the carriers when TF 58.4 was sailing north in its shuttle. Now, by the time Commander Iwami had reached the 3Ri location, TF 58.4 was already sailing south again.

Lt. Takeo Tanimizu, meanwhile, had continued towards the 15Ri position to the southeast. Tanimizu led his 24 planes, 15 Zeros and nine Val dive bombers, eastward toward the 15Ri position, a route that would take him south of the shuttling TF 58.4 and north of the other carrier groups of TF 58. Tanimizu had come midway between the northern and three southern groups when radar operators aboard U.S.S. *Enterprise* picked up bogies. The skipper of Big E ordered an immediate scramble. However, he had barely issued the order when the bogies disappeared from the screen, because the Japanese planes had now flown eastward out of radar range. The Japanese formation had gone northeast of the main TF 58 groups and southeast of Admiral Harill's TF 58.4.

Still the *Enterprise* skipper was apprehensive and he ordered Cmdr. William "Killer" Kane to take 12 Hellcats aloft to maintain a CAP around the carrier. Kane rounded up pilots as service crews warmed up the dozen fighter planes. By 1300 hours, the 12 planes had scrambled.

Because of the bogie reports from *Enterprise*, Adm. Jocko Clark, commander of the TF 58.1 group also ordered a CAP airborne from carrier *Yorktown*.

"We'll scramble sixteen fighter planes at once, Admiral," Cmdr. George Peters of *Yorktown*'s AG 1 told the TF 58.1 commander.

Peters then mustered 15 pilots from *Yorktown*'s AG 1 to man aircraft. By 1310 hours, Peters sat in the lead Hellcat, staring at the men on deck in their array of colored overalls: plane handlers in blue were finishing the last of their chores before takeoff; plane directors in yellow stood by with flags, ready to aid the planes off; green-clad hook men stood by to retrieve any plane that had trouble taking off; and chock men clad in purple coveralls waited to yank chucks away from wheels when signalmen flagged the planes off the flight deck.

Yorktown was now sailing at 30 knots, eastward and into the wind to expedite takeoff. Soon, flagmen signaled takeoff, and Cmdr. George Peters roared down the deck and zoomed off at 90 knots. Fifteen Hellcats from *Yorktown* followed before the 16 U.S. fighter planes circled the carrier and jelled into four plane diamonds. Then, Peters led them to the north of the carrier.

Cmdr. William "Killer" Kane, who had already left carrier *Enterprise*, was already in his CAP with 12 fighter planes of VF 10 when he got word that the bogies on radar screens had disappeared. So, he loitered his planes in four diamonds around the carrier.

Meanwhile, Lt. Takeo Tanimizu, who had only come close enough to the American carriers to get caught temporarily on American radar screens, continued his flight eastward. Like Iwami, Lieutenant Tanimizu was also confused, for he had seen nothing, either. Wasn't the 15Ri location correct? But, unlike Iwami, Lieutenant Tanimizu decided to reverse to a south by southwest course to search for the

American vessels. At about 1300 hours, about the time U.S. aircraft had left the *Enterprise* and *Yorktown*, Lieutenant Tanimizu came across two American battleships that quickly unleashed heavy barrages of antiaircraft fire. Soon, the patch of sky between the battleships and the Japanese planes became saturated with black puffs.

But, none of the ack-ack fire hit any of the 24 Japanese planes because Tanimizu was flying his formation at 24,000 feet. He got a call from one of his flight leaders.

"Takeo, should we not attack these enemy vessels?"

"No, we must find their carriers. We should not waste the bombs of our dive bombers on surface ships. We will search for the American carriers. They cannot be too far away from these surface ships."

"But what if we do not find them?"

"We will fly southward and search for a half-hour," Lieutenant Tanimizu said. "If we do not find the enemy carriers by then, we shall return and attack these surface vessels."

By flying south-southwest, Tanimizu indeed came in the right direction. The Japanese planes had come within 75 miles of carrier *Enterprise* when blips showed up on Big E's radar screen. Bandits! The *Enterprise* communications men immediately called the airborne aircraft from the *Enterprise* and *Yorktown*, reporting to both Kane and Peters the approach of Japanese planes.

"Enemy aircraft to the northeast, bearing on a zero forty seven course; eighty miles distance."

Both Cmdr. William Kane of AG 10 and Cmdr. George Peters of AG 1 immediately jelled their planes into formation and zoomed northward toward the reported location of the Japanese planes.

At about 1300 hours, Lt. Takeo Tanimizu saw the American carriers of TF 58.1 far in the distance. The 652nd Air Group leader grinned. However, he had only flown his formation for another 15 miles before he heard the drone of planes overhead and to the west—the 12 fighter planes from the *Enterprise*. Almost at the same time, Kane saw the Japanese.

"O.K., boys. Skunks, twelve o'clock low," Kane cried into his radio. "Let's get 'em. In pairs; attack in pairs!"

Then, Kane banked his plane and arced down toward the Japanese formation.

Fortunately for the Japanese, Lt. Takeo Tanimizu had a good deal of experience and he understood the need to keep a tight formation. "Dive bombers, close up tight; up tight. Escorts hold close to intercept, if necessary."

Tanimizu thus exhorted the inexperienced 652nd Air Group airmen to hold their tight formations, despite the urge to scatter and run.

Cmdr. William "Killer" Kane, a navy fighter pilot for several years, had served in the Pacific for the past two years. Kane had already downed five enemy planes to become an ace, and now he was looking for more kills. The VF 10 commander dove toward the enemy planes, but he was surprised to see the Japanese keeping tight formation and deftly maneuvering their aircraft. The Japanese fired furiously at the approaching Americans and Kane's Hellcat caught a fuselage full of holes from .30-caliber fire. But, the tough navy fighter plane took the punctures in stride. In turn, Kane managed to arc behind a Zero and opened up with a fusilade of .50-caliber fire that hit the enemy plane. The Zero blew up in midair and then fell in a cascade of smoke and fire before splashing into the sea in a hot sizzle.

Kane and his wingman searched for more planes, but they failed to down any more aircraft, although fellow pilot Bob Shackford did damage two Zeros.

Others among Kane's VF 10 unit, however, had better luck. Lt. Warren Skon of St. Paul, Minnesota, got behind a Zero that zigged and zagged deftly, but the U.S. naval fighter pilot chased the Japanese plane in split esses, waiting for the opportunity to open up. Skon cursed. The Japanese pilot was slippery and capable. However, the American pilot hung with his quarry, chasing the plane to the surface of the sea, where the Zero was finally forced to level off and run. Now, Skon got a bead and opened up with chattering strafing fire. Heavy .50-caliber tracers chopped the plane apart until the Zero burst into flames and then rolled twice before splashing into the sea.

Lt. Bob Shackford, still hanging with Commander Kane, suddenly saw a Zero hovering some 1,000 feet above him. At first, Shackford thought the plane was from his own VF 10. But soon, the plane tore down at him and Kane with a stream of .30-caliber fire that punched several holes in both aircraft. Kane veered away and Shackford stiffened before he arced upward and then came in behind the Zero. Now, the Zero tried to get away. But, the Hellcat was too fast. Shackford loosed a fusilade of .50-caliber fire that ripped the plane to pieces before the Zero flipped over and crashed into the sea.

By the time Cmdr. Bill Kane's air unit had completed its dogfight with the Japanese fighter pilots, the Americans had knocked down four planes and damaged several more. But, on this occasion, the Japanese pilots seemed more adept, aggressive, and determined than the pilots from the first two raids. Kane himself had lost two Hellcats, although both pilots were subsequently rescued by American destroyers. He might have lost more, save for the tough hides of the navy fighter planes. So, the pilots from AG 10 had not experienced the turkey shoot the American pilots on the first two interceptions had enjoyed.

Still, the Japanese were not home free. As Lt. Takeo Tanimizu continued on toward the American carriers, his formation suddenly ran into Cmdr. George Peters and the 16 Hellcats from *Yorktown*'s AG 1. The Japanese planes had come within 20 to 25 miles of the zig-zagging TF 58.1 carriers. But, the Val dive bombers of the Japanese 652nd Air Group would now need to run through the gauntlet of American fighter planes.

Cmdr. George Peters cried into his radio. "If we don't break them up, they'll give those carriers a good going over. In pairs! Attack in pairs!"

Now, from 20,000 feet, Peters banked his plane and zoomed toward the lead Japanese Val at 25 knots. A few moments later he came into a trio of dive bombers. The Japanese pilots had apparently failed to see Peters because they had held to their straight formation with eyes on the American carriers. When Peters opened up from 800 feet with strafing guns, he caught the starboard plane of a three-plane V. The Val blew up from a dozen fatal hits. Only then did the other two Japanese bomber pilots react. They zoomed off in two directions and disappeared before George Peters could find either of them.

But, other *Yorktown* pilots shot down two more Vals and damaged two more. The *Yorktown* pilots also shot two more Zeros out of the air.

Still, at least a dozen of Lieutenant Tanimizu's Vals and Zeros reached the carriers of TF 58.1. A heavy barrage of ack-ack from the carriers' antiaircraft gunners as well as ack-ack fire from screening American destroyers drove off most of the Japanese planes, damaging several more in the process. But at least three Zeros and three Vals reached the carriers. Fortunately for the Americans, the Japanese pilots showed little accuracy.

The Zeros came in strafing, forcing men on deck to take cover. But, they did not cause any damage. Tanimizu cursed because the fighter bombers had not come close enough to do any real harm.

But, the Vals scored some hits. Half of the 18 550-pound bombs dropped by the Japanese dive bombers missed the carriers by a wide margin, exploding harmlessly into the sea. However, the other bombs scored.

Two bombs exploded just off the port quarter of carrier *Enterprise* and sprayed shrapnel over the deck, wrecking a hook line and wounding a dozen men. Another bomb struck the fantail of carrier *Bataan*, killing a half-dozen men, chopping a hole in the deck, and destroying three planes. Two more 550 pounders exploded off the starboard of *Hornet*, with shrapnel punching holes in the hull and starting minor flooding. However, *Hornet*'s damage-control crews quickly sealed the flooding. Finally, one bomb blew up off the bow of U.S.S *Bataan* and shrapnel hit the underside of a Corsair just taking off. The plane wobbled and then skidded off the deck and into the sea. Thus, the Japanese air units of the 652nd Air Group had downed another plane, albeit indirectly. However, the American pilot escaped the lost Corsair and a destroyer quickly fished him out of the sea.

Lieutenant Tanimizu had lost seven planes in this raid, slightly less then a third of his aircraft. In turn, his pilots had destroyed three American planes and damaged some carriers, although nothing really serious. Thus, Tanimizu had made out much better than those on the first two Japanese air attacks. By 1400 hours, Lt. Takeo Tanimizu was droning back to his carrier with a half-dozen planes, while a dozen more planes, damaged, flew on to Guam.

Bogies had disappeared from all American radar screens by 1400 hours. The all clear again whined through the decks of the American carriers, the third all clear of the day.

Chapter Nine

Despite the all clear at 1400 hours on this June 19, 1944, the Dauntlesses and Avengers, now airborne for hours, still loitered east of the American carriers, and the airmen felt absolutely bored and frustrated. The pilots and crews of the U.S. Navy bombers grumbled like stranded commercial airline passengers in an unending holding pattern over a crowded LaGuardia Airport.

The bomber pilots, using JV radio communications, pressed Cmdr. Ralph Weymouth, the group leader of U.S.S. *Lexington*'s AG 16 bomber unit. "When are we going home, Commander?" "How the hell long are we going to stay up here?" "We'll rot in this goddamned sky." "When are we going back to our carriers?"

To the barrage of complaints from the irritated AG 16 pilots, Commander Weymouth offered the same answer. "I don't know. The

Nips have been trying to hit our carriers all day; one formation after another."

Weymouth himself called *Lexington* several times and spoke to Capt. Gus Widhelm, the air commander of TF 58. But, Widhelm only offered the same stock answer: "Pretty soon," or "The Nips are still coming over."

Throughout the late morning and early afternoon, Weymouth had heard the almost continual reverberation of ack-ack fire and the echo of whining planes to the west. As the Japanese sent one group of aircraft after another to attack TF 58, Weymouth's only consolation had been the assurance from Captain Widhelm that none of the carriers had suffered damage, and most of the Japanese planes had been shot down.

At about 1400 hours, when the echo of ack-ack fire to the west stopped again, Cmdr. Ralph Weymouth once more called Captain Widhelm. "Well? Can we come home?"

"We've got search planes to the west," Widhelm said. "If we don't get any more bogies in the next twenty or thirty minutes, we'll call you back."

"Jesus, they can't have any more planes left," Commander Weymouth grumbled.

"I don't know where the hell they're coming from," Widhelm said.

"O.K.," Weymouth sighed, resigning himself to his holding pattern. But, when he looked at his fuel gauge, he scowled. He was low on gas and he would probably need to

159

salvo his bombs if he hoped to remain airborne for another hour. He looked at his panel map. Guam lay about 60 miles away. Hell, some of those Japanese planes might be making for Guam to refuel and rearm so they could attack the carriers again. The AG 16 commander, on his own, decided to lead his own dozen SBD Dauntlesses from *Lexington* and the nine SBD Dauntlesses under Lt. Comdr. Alvin Priel from *Enterprise* to attack the Agana and Orote airfields on Guam. He called Priel.

"What do you say? How about hitting those Guam airfields. A lot of those attacking Nip planes probably flew on to that island. The place must be jammed with aircraft. We'll only have to salvo bombs pretty soon to conserve fuel."

"Do we have permission?" Lieutenant Priel asked.

"I'll take the responsibility," Weymouth said.

"O.K. Commander," Alvin Priel answered. "Lead the way."

Then, Weymouth called the flight leader of the 11 Hellcats on CAP to protect the bombers. "Commander," he said to Lt. Comdr. Ron Mehle, the VF 28 commander from carrier *Monterey*, "we'll need to salvo bombs pretty soon to conserve gas. So, we're going to hit Guam with our bombs. Stick with us."

"We'll hang over you, Commander," Mehle answered Weymouth.

Within 20 minutes, the 21 American Navy

bombers, along with their 12 Hellcat escorts, arrived over Guam. Weymouth found the two airfields jammed with aircraft, just as he suspected. Some were replacements sent up from Truk, but most of them were damaged or errant planes that had made Guam after the disastrous attempts to attack the TF 58 carriers. No Zeros rose from the fat target area to intercept the Americans. But, Japanese ack-ack gunners quickly threw up spews of heavy flak at the approaching planes.

Still, Cmdr. Ralph Weymouth and the other bomber pilots braved the furious antiaircraft fire and dove on their targets—the Agana and Orote fields, and the planes scattered about the two airfields.

Weymouth came in low and hit the runway with a thousand pounder from the bomb bay and the two 500 pounders from his wing. Two bombs chopped big holes in the airstrip and the third bomb exploded between two parked Betty bombers, destroying both planes. As the AG 16 commander zoomed away, other Dauntlesses from *Lexington* also came in to unleash trios of bombs on the Orote runway. The array of explosions ripped more holes in the runway and destroyed more parked planes: Jills and Zeros that had earlier escaped American interceptors in the dogfights west of the American carriers.

As fire and smoke belched from the AG 16 attack, Lt. Cmdr. Alvin Priel led his nine Dauntlesses from the *Enterprise* over Agana Field. This second rain of 500- and thousand-pound bombs chopped more holes in the second Guam runway and destroyed more grounded planes. By the time the last Dauntless dive bomber had left Guam, the Americans had destroyed 16 planes on the ground and left both Orote and Agana fields punched with holes.

But, the quite determined Guam antiaircraft gunners took a toll. One glide-bombing Dauntless had just dropped bombs when the plane caught a burst of flak that ignited the gas tank and blew the plane in half. Pilot and gunner died in a flaming crash. A Hellcat pilot tried to strafe Orote Field, but a burst of flak chopped off a wing. The Hellcat flipped over and crashed to the ground. A third plane, another Dauntless, caught a burst of flak after arcing away from its glide-bomb run. The heavy flak chopped off the tail and the plane simply dropped like a rock, hit the ground, and exploded.

In fact, the American had lost six planes to ack-ack fire during the attack on Guam. A seventh plane, the Dauntless of Lt. George March, also became a statistic. March had dropped his bombs successfully, but as he pulled away from Orote Field, his plane took a hit in the engine. March got safely out to sea, but the engine rapidly lost oil pressure and then blew a gasket. Luckily March inflated his life raft and both he and his gunner clambered out of the plane after March ditched in the sea.

Fortunately, a four-plane flight of Hellcats

from *Bunker Hill* spotted the raft with the two American airmen and the planes orbited the raft, indicating they had reported its position. The Hellcats hung around in the event some Japanese Jakes or Zeros showed up to strafe March or his gunner. Before dark, an American floatplane rescued the two men.

Although losses among the American attackers on Guam had been relatively heavy, the U.S. planes had done considerable damage. Besides potholing the runway and wrecking planes, the Dauntless pilots had also destroyed an aviation fuel dump.

When Adm. Marc Mitscher learned that Cmdr. Ralph Weymouth had taken upon himself the decision to attack the Guam airfields with the loitering Dauntlesses, the TF 58 fleet commander responded with a rare grin.

"At least the man was thinking. How did he make out?"

"Our bombers left both the Agano and Orote fields in shambles," Capt. Arleigh Burke answered, "and they knocked out a bunch of grounded Japanese aircraft."

"How about losses?"

"We did suffer a half-dozen aircraft losses from intense antiaircraft fire," the TF 58 chief of staff answered, "but Weymouth and the others sure put Guam out of business for a while. If any more Nip formations try to hit us, they won't be able to fly on to Guam for a while, and they sure as hell won't be able to send any planes out from Guam."

Admiral Mitscher nodded and then stared from the bridge of the *Lexington* to the other carriers around his flagship. "We must have a lot more Dauntlesses and Avengers just flying around like bees without a hive." He looked at Captain Widhelm. "We may as well put them to work, too. Order some of the other planes to hit the enemy airfields on Rota and Saipan."

"Yes, sir."

"All the bombers have CAP's, don't they?"

"Yes, Admiral."

"O.K. their CAP's can escort them, just like the CAP escorted Commander Weymouth and the others to Guam."

"I'll send them off at once," Captain Widhelm said.

Soon, more Dauntlesses and Avengers roared eastward, this time over the Japanese air bases at Rota and over Aslito Field on Saipan. The American bomber crews did not find as much antiaircraft fire on Rota and Saipan as the earlier American air units had found on Guam. But, neither did they find as many aircraft. However, the U.S. Navy bombers successfully chopped up the runways on the Mariana Islands with 500- and thousand-pound bombs.

Marines fighting their way inland on Saipan watched the navy planes lace Aslito Field and the combat troops felt a mixture of disappointment and anger. Why the hell were those navy planes bombing that field instead of giving these marines more ground support? The gyrenes here had only heard nebulous, fragmentary reports on the Japanese air strikes against TF 58. They had not realized the extent of these strikes; nor did they realize the danger posed by the air strikes from the 1st Mobile Fleet, if TF 58 air units did not stop them.

In fact, the craters the American planes had put onto the Saipan runway, like the craters American airmen had put into the airfields on Guam and Rota, could not have come at a more opportune time. The horde of planes that comprised the Japanese Raid IV was on its way to attack the American carriers.

Aboard *Haguro*, the new flag of 1st Mobile Fleet, Adm. Jisaburo Ozawa had watched the last group of planes take off from carriers *Shokaku* and *Zuikaku* of Cardiv I, and from *Hiyo* and *Ryuko* of Cardiv II: 19 Judys, six Jills, 27 Vals, 12 Zero fighter-bombers, and 30 Zero escort fighters. The aircraft had left between 1100 and 1130 hours, and by 1145 hours the horde of planes had disappeared to the east.

At about the same time, about a dozen planes from Raid I were returning to their carriers. Ozawa was not unduly worried about the small number of planes, for he naively assumed that most of the planes from the 653rd Air Group under Cmdr. Masayuki Yamaguchi had simply flown on to Guam or Rota to refuel and rearm.

Ozawa's only regret at the moment was the loss of his flag carrier *Taiho*. He could not guess that within a half-hour, he would suffer another stunning regret.

While carrier *Taiho* waited to plunge to the bottom of the Philippine Sea, a second big carrier from Cardiv 1, *Shokaku*, loitered at a position of about 12° north and 137° east. The big carrier, a sister ship of *Taiho*, had the same four boiler rooms and 160,000 hp, the same 96-plane capacity, the same 3,000-man crew, the same 257.5-meter length and 26-meter width, and the same 9,700-mile range without refueling.

Carrier *Shokaku* had been in World War II since the beginning of the Pacific conflict, a part of the 5th Aircraft Carrier Division since 1940. She had been among the three big carriers that had launched planes during the attack on Pearl Harbor on December 7th. After Pearl, *Shokaku* had joined the mobile fleet supporting Japanese ground forces that had swept through the western, central, and southwest Pacific in early 1942.

By April of 1942, *Shokaku* had shifted her combat role to the Indian Ocean where her planes and aviators had supported naval attacks against Ceylon, Assam in India, and Allied shipping in the Indian Ocean. *Shokaku*'s aircraft had been part of the air fleet that had sunk the British heavy cruisers H.M.S. *Cornwall* and *Devonshire* off Colombo, Ceylon. Her aircraft had also sunk the British carrier *Hermes*. Then, this proud Japanese carrier had resumed her combat activities in the southwest Pacific.

Shokaku had participated in the Battle of the Coral Sea on 7–8 May, 1942. Although the Japanese had failed here, *Shokaku*'s aircraft had sunk the destroyer U.S.S. *Sims* and the tanker U.S.S. *Noehso*. Her aircraft had also participated in the strikes against American carriers, strikes that eventually sank the old carrier U.S.S. *Lexington* in the Coral Sea battle. However, in the same battle, American planes from the old U.S.S. *Yorktown* aircraft carrier had damaged *Shokaku*'s flight deck and the Japanese carrier had returned to Yokosuka for repairs. She had thus missed the Battle of Midway.

"Perhaps if we had been in the Midway battle," said Capt. Hajima Fukaya, the *Shokaku*'s skipper, after the war, "*Shokaku*'s presence might have changed the course of the Battle of Midway."

Shokaku was repaired in time for the Guadalcanal campaign and the big carrier fought in the Battle of Santa Cruz Island. *Shokaku*'s airmen had sunk the old U.S. carrier U.S.S. *Hornet*. However, the big carrier had almost lost her own life in the same battle when American naval planes scored telling hits on *Shokaku*, causing serious fires and wrecking the carrier deck. Luckily, *Shokaku* had no planes aboard at the time, planes whose exploding gas tanks on deck or in the hangars could have caused fatal damage to the carrier.

Once more *Shokaku* had returned to home waters in Japan for repairs. Then, *Shokaku* saw limited action as did most other Japanese carriers during the U.S. Navy advance across the central Pacific. But, in the spring of 1944, still under the command of salty old Capt. Hajima Fukaya, *Shokaku* became a part of the huge 1st Mobile Fleet.

However, times had changed. Young, inexperienced, and hastily trained men now comprised the bulk of *Shokaku*'s air crews, with the few experienced veterans acting as flight or squadron leaders. Captain Fukaya, discouraged, could not share the enthusiasm and optimism of his young airmen, for the old salt knew that these men would be no match for the new American combat giant. Still, Fukaya had prepared his airmen and deck crews as best he could.

While the U.S. submarine pack from TF 17 remained in the vicinity of the 1st Mobile Fleet during June 19th, U.S.S. *Albacore* had finished off the carrier *Taiho* that now listed and burned. At about midday of June 19th, U.S. submarine *Cavella* under Lt. Comdr. Herman Kossler was shadowing the Japanese warships. Kossler had been chasing elements of the 1st Mobile Fleet for most of the night of June 18–19 and during the entire morning of June 19th. Kossler had occasionally raised periscope to study the enemy fleet, and he had seen aircraft flying constantly into the skies over the Philippine Sea. Kossler guessed the planes were Japanese and the aircraft were apparently going out on air strikes. Kossler had also seen aircraft landing on the carrier decks, and he believed they were planes returning from air strikes or returning from reconnaisance flights.

At 1210 hours, Kossler again raised periscope and this time he saw in front of him, no more than 10,000 yards off, the huge carrier *Shokaku*. Kossler could not believe that enemy destroyers had not borne down on him as soon as he raised periscope. As the *Cavella* skipper came closer to the carrier, he saw clearly the bedspring-shaped antenna on the carrier's foremast and the large Japanese ensign on her island structure. He lowered periscope and looked in astonishment at his executive officer.

"The picture is too good to be true."

"What is it?"

"A Nip carrier, a large one, and less than ten thousand yards away. She's got two cruisers ahead of her port bow and only one destroyer about a thousand yards off her port beam. There's not a goddamn thing screening the vessel between us and the carrier."

"How the hell could they be so stupid?" the executive officer asked.

"I don't know," Kossler said, "but we'll get as close as we can and then launch torpedoes."

The executive officer now looked through the periscope himself. "Looks like they're launching and recovering planes."

Kossler nodded. "Probably too busy to notice anything else. O.K., let's go in on a zero twenty-six bearing and fire torpedoes."

"Aye, sir," the executive officer said.

Shokaku, of course, was not recovering combat aircraft, for most of her combat planes were off on Raid IV. In fact, activities aboard the carrier had diminished to almost nothing except for the activity of some deck hands who had directed a few Jake search planes that occasionally landed or took off from the carrier. Captain Fukaya himself stood nonchalantly on the open island structure bridge with his aide, while both men sipped tea. The *Shokaku* commander knew that real activity would not resume until the aircraft from Raid IV under Captain Fuchida returned to their carriers, and that would be at least two hours from now.

As Kossler closed with the U.S.S. *Cavella*, the Japanese screen destroyer, *Urakaze*, made no attempt whatever to interfere with the gliding submarine. Kossler, in fact, came within 1,500 yards of the big carrier and the executive officer grew anxiously fearful.

"Jesus, Herm, how long can our luck hold out. We're practically in the lap of that carrier. We'd better fire torpedoes and get the hell out of here."

Lt. Comdr. Herman Kossler nodded.

In fact, the U.S.S. *Cavella* had come within 1,200 yards of the big carrier before Kossler finally attacked. *Cavella*'s TDC was operating perfectly and Kossler would not need to use a seaman's eye. At 1220 hours, he again raised periscope.

"Ready tubes one and two," he called the torpedo officer.

"One and two ready."

"Fire!"

"One and two away," the torpedo officer answered.

"Ready tubes three and four."

"Ready."

"Fire away!"

"Three and four away," came the response from the forward torpedo room.

As soon as the third and fourth torpedoes went off, the Japanese destroyer *Urakaze* veered sharply to starboard and roared forward, her stack heaving heavy puffs of smoke. Still, Kossler waited until he launched two more torpedoes before he yanked down the periscope and cried to his control officer. "Dive! Dive!"

In moments, U.S.S. *Cavella* plunged deep. And, before the Japanese destroyer dropped depth charges, Kossler and his submariners heard three deafening explosions. Three of the torpedoes had apparently hit the carrier. The American crew might have cheered wildly, but seconds later came the first booms of deapth charges from destroyer *Urakaze*, bursts that had come dangerously close to U.S.S. *Cavella*. More depth-charge explosions followed, dozens of them, for several more Japanese destroyers had joined *Urakaze* to find and destroy the U.S. submarine. The crew of *Cavella* winced from the almost continual explosions and the sailors jerked from the constant shudder of the submarine, that bounced, rattled, and shook from the countless depth-charge booms.

U.S.S. *Cavella* fought for her life as she dodged and escaped depth charges for nearly three hours. Somebody kept count and before the attack ended, he had counted 106 depth-charge explosions. Finally, at about 1500 hours, the sailors aboard *Cavella* heard prolonged, monotonous rumblings—the death rattles of *Shokaku*. Kossler and his crew were quite certain they had badly damaged or perhaps even sunk the Japanese carrier.

By 1520 hours, Kossler finally escaped the Japanese destroyers, for now the depth charges became faint echoes in the distance. Still, the *Cavella* commander would stay deep until dark, and until he had left the Japanese fleet far behind.

The U.S.S. *Cavella* crew had guessed right on the results of their torpedo attacks. Four of *Cavella*'s torpedoes had struck *Shokaku* within a minute, and each explosion had shuddered the huge ship. Three hits set off a series of internal explosions on the carrier that erupted fires and serious flooding. One of the explosions knocked out two boiler rooms and flooded a third engine room. Almost immediately, *Shokaku*'s speed dropped to a few knots and the big carrier fell out of formation.

On the bridge, Capt. Hajima Fukaya gaped as whoop alarms echoed throughout the ship; and he coughed from the heavy smoke that poured from the bowels of the carrier. He turned to his aide.

"How badly are we hit? How badly?"

"I do not know, Captain."

But, a moment later came a call from the damage-control officer. "Honorable Captain, the torpedo hits were disastrous. We have fires throughout the lower decks and flooding in all areas, especially the bow. Some of the lower decks are already under water. There is no way to contain the flames and flooding. I believe we must abandon ship."

"Abandon ship?" Fukaya cried. "Surely, we can save her."

"There is no way," the damage-control officer insisted. "Three of the boiler rooms are out and we cannot even maintain a five-knot speed with our sole remaining boiler. And even this boiler may explode at any moment from uncontrolled fires. I implore you, Captain, issue the order to abandon ship."

"All right," Captain Fukaya sighed. "I will do so."

By the time *Shokaku*'s commander gave the order to abandon ship, the vessel was already on a ten- to fifteen-degree list. And, by the time sailors began clambering or jumping over the side, the big carrier had tilted to a precarious 30-degree list. The big ship then began settling by the bow where the torpedo hit had opened the worst hole.

Fires spread rapidly throughout the ship and huge palls of smoke now rose from every part of the carrier. Still, more than 2,000 men from *Shokaku*'s crew escaped the stricken vessel.

173

Destroyers rescued most of them, including Capt. Hajima Fukaya.

From the plot room of cruiser *Haguro*, Adm. Jisaburo Ozawa gaped in utter shock when he heard of the fatal hits on *Shokaku*. He shuttled his glance between his chief of staff, Adm. Matake Yoshimura and his communications officer Capt. Toshikazu Ohmae.

"How could this be? How? We have already suffered the loss of *Taiho* and now we have suffered the grievous loss of another carrier."

Neither Yoshimura nor Ohmae answered.

"Where was the screen? Where?" Ozawa screamed. "Why were they not protecting the flanks against enemy submarine attacks?"

The aides did not answer, but the fault lay with Ozawa himself. The 1st Mobile Fleet commander had left the bulk of the Batjan force far ahead of his carriers instead of maintaining the usual Hochi horsehoe pattern with as many screening vessels as possible on the flanks. Captain Ohmae remembered vividly his suggestion to use the Hochi pattern because the Philippine Sea crawled with American submarines. However, Ozawa had spurned the suggestion.

"No, danger will come from the east, not the flanks," Ozawa had said.

However, Captain Ohmae was not about to remind Admiral Ozawa of the admiral's rejection of the Hochi pattern that had contributed to the loss of the two carriers.

Now, Ozawa glared at his communications officer. "Captain, you will order at least four destroyers around each of our remaining carriers, with at least three on the extreme starboard and port flanks. You will order a picket destroyer to shuttle at least two miles on the flanks. Is that understood?''

"Yes, Honorable Ozawa," Captain Ohmae answered.

"You will issue the order at once to the Batjan force commander."

"I will contact Admiral Ugaki immediately," Captain Ohmae said.

Ozawa now sighed heavily and fell into a chair near the plotting table. He dropped his head in his hands, drained by this second tragic loss. But, Ozawa's troubles were far from over.

Chapter Ten

Now, the last group of Japanese planes was on the way toward the American fleet: 94 planes that included 19 Judy dive bombers, 27 Val dive bombers, six Jill torpedo bombers, 12 Zero fighter bombers, and 30 Zero escort fighters. The planes had left the carriers *Junyo, Hiyo,* and *Ryuho* shortly after 1100 hours on this broken-cloud morning of June 15, 1944. Rear Adm. Tajaki Joshima of the Japanese Cardiv II had received a report that the American fleet lay at the 15Ri position.

As yet, no one in the Japanese 1st Mobile Fleet, from Admiral Ozawa down to the lowest seaman, knew that American Hellcat pilots had shot down most of the Japanese planes on the first three raids. In fact, Ozawa had reports that three carriers had been sunk and six more American carriers had been set ablaze—all false reports. Ozawa assumed his first three aircraft formations had simply flown on to airfields in Rota or Guam.

In the lead Judy of the 601st Air Group, Captain Mitsuo Fuchida stared from his cockpit at the Judys on either side of him. Then, he squinted straight ahead at the patch of sea below the broken clouds. When he finished, he called his gunner.

"Have you seen signs of enemy aircraft or ships?"

"No, Honorable Captain."

"Stay alert."

"Yes, Commander."

For several more minutes, Captain Fuchida stared about him: to the fore, above, the sides, and the sea below. But, he still saw nothing. The 1st Mobile Air Fleet commander, now personally leading the 601st Air Group, frowned in surprise. The American fleet reportedly lay a mere 375 miles away and he would reach target in ten or fifteen minutes. Yet, neither Fuchida nor his airmen had seen any sign of enemy interceptors and no ack-ack fire from screening American surface ships. Surely, the Americans knew this massive formation of over 90 aircraft was heading for TF 58. Fuchida stared ahead for about two minutes and then picked up his radiophone.

"This is Tenzen B-2 leader to Tenzen F-2 leader. Please come in."

"I read you, Honorable Captain," Lt. Toshohiko Ohno answered.

"Have you seen any sign of the enemy?"

"None, Captain," Ohno replied. "Neither I nor any of the other fighter pilots have seen either enemy aircraft or surface ships. I have three Mitsubishi fighter aircraft far to the van, but they have reported nothing."

"Strange," Fuchida said. "We must be approaching target by now."

The veteran Mitsuo Fuchida, who had been on the initial Pearl Harbor attack, the Battle of Midway, and in other air battles, could not understand. He knew that the Americans always responded to incoming air attacks with interceptors or surface-ship guns long before the Japanese formation could reach its target. This had been especially true when the Americans had developed their long-range radar equipment.

"You are certain you have seen nothing?" Fuchida asked Ohno again.

"Perhaps the first three groups of aircraft from our carriers have already destroyed the enemy fleet."

Fuchida did not answer, for he believed the idea preposterous. He had been at war too long and he knew that no Japanese efforts could wipe out an American carrier fleet the size of TF 58. And, since the American Navy had introduced the Hellcat and Corsair fighter planes in 1943, Japanese Zero pilots had lost their superiority. And worse, over the past two years, the Japanese had lost many of their experienced pilots. Now, men like Ohno and so many others, with minimal training and little combat experience, could hardly wipe out an American carrier fleet.

No, something was wrong. Captain Fuchida checked his readings and frowned. They were only 12 miles from the 15Ri position. Where were the Americans? Fuchida picked up his radio again. "We will descend below the clouds in one minute and fly on a straight zero zero four course to the reported position of the enemy carrier fleet."

A moment later, the horde of Japanese planes from the 601st Air Group fell through the broken clouds and leveled off at 1,500 feet above the surface of the sea. Then, the Japanese air armada droned almost straight eastward for several minutes. But, Fuchida saw nothing but a broad expanse of empty sea; not a sign of an American carrier or any other American ship. The 601st leader called the carrier *Junyo*, flag of the 1st Mobile Fleet's Cardiv II.

"This is Tenzen leader, Tenzen leader," Captain Fuchida said. "I must speak to the communications officer."

A moment later, operations officer Chika Najajima answered. "Yes, Captain?"

"There is no sign of the enemy fleet at the reported 15Ri location," Fuchida said. "Was there some mistake?"

"Either the other air groups have destroyed the American carrier fleet or any surviving enemy carriers have retired in a crippled state toward Saipan," Commander Najajima said. "I would suggest, Captain, that you continue on your eastward course. If the enemy has indeed retired to Saipan waters, you may still find him.''

"But such a course will take us beyond the fuel range from our carriers."

"You may simply fly on to Rota or Guam, as I believe that many of our other air units have done this," Najajima said. "The First Air Fleet has no doubt recovered many of our aircraft and they can recover your Six Hundred First Air Group."

"I will do so," Capt. Mitsuo Fuchida said.

The 94 Japanese bomber and fighter planes simply continued on, droning at their 1,500-foot altitude above the sea. The massive formation had come within 45 minutes of the islands of Rota and Guam when Fuchida picked up his radio and again called Lt. Toshohiko Ohno.

"Lieutenant, you will take half of your fighter escorts and our twenty-seven Achi dive bombers to Rota. I will take the remainder of the Six Hundred First Group to Guam."

"Yes, Captain."

Within a few minutes, the squadrons of aircraft broke into two groups, one heading for Rota, north of Saipan, and Captain Fuchida heading for Guam itself, directly to the east.

The Japanese had not been mistaken in their patrol-plane reports on TF 58. One of the fleet divisions, TF 58.2 under Adm. Al Montgomery, had been at the 15Ri position. However, following the attacks by Japanese Raid III, Montgomery had sailed quickly in a northeasterly direction while he recovered planes from his four carriers: U.S.S. *Bunker Hill, Wasp, Monterey,* and *Cabot*. Meanwhile, his screen of three cruisers and a dozen destroyers had loitered west and south of the retiring U.S. carriers.

At 1144 hours, Lt. Toshohiko Ohno, who was leading his planes northeast to Rota, stared routinely from his cockpit. Suddenly, he gaped, for he saw the array of skimming American cruisers and destroyers on the sea, with the big carriers of TF 58.2 faintly visible to the northeast. Ohno eagerly picked up his radio.

"The enemy carriers ahead! The bombers will attack at once."

Then, the 27 Japanese Vals accompanied by a formation of 12 dive bombers, roared ahead, toward the carrier U.S.S. *Wasp*. At the moment, the American deck crews were recovering planes from recent dogfights with the third group of Japanese planes from the 1st Mobile Fleet. A lookout on cruiser U.S.S. *Mobile* was the first to report the approaching Japanese planes and he quickly called the cruiser's bridge. *Mobile*'s skipper, Capt. Lou DuRose, called Admiral Montgomery in the TF 58.2 flag carrier U.S.S. *Bunker Hill*.

"They're coming again," DuRose said, "another couple dozen Japanese bombers. I don't know why the hell nobody gave you a radar report."

"Holy Christ," Admiral Montgomery grumbled, "where the hell are they getting all those planes? They're like an endless swarm of locusts."

"Yes, sir," DuRose said.

Then, gunners on cruiser *Mobile* opened up with ack-ack fire at the approaching Val dive bombers. Soon, other cruisers and destroyers of TF 58.2 also sent up antiaircraft fire. However, the swarms of Japanese planes broke through the heavy flak, split into two groups, and headed for carriers *Wasp* and already harrassed *Bunker Hill*. Once more, carrier helmsmen veered and swerved to avoid enemy planes, while ack-ack gunners again fired furiously at the oncoming enemy aircraft.

As six bombers headed for *Wasp*, ack-ack fire caught one Val in the fuselage. The belly blew out of the Japanese dive bomber and the plane burst into flames, flipped over in midair, and plopped into the sea. The second Val caught a flak burst that chopped away the left wing. The plane rolled over uncontrollably, veered downward, and also crashed into the sea. The third Val escaped the heavy ack-ack fire and loosed four 500-pound bombs. But, the *Wasp* helmsman successfully swerved hard to port and the bombs exploded harmlessly into the sea. The next two Vals also missed, while ack-ack gunners caught the sixth Val, blowing the plane to shreds.

Now, three Vals came after *Bunker Hill*, the TF 58.2 flag carrier. Once more ack-ack gunners fired furiously at the approaching planes and knocked one of them out of the air.

However, the other two Vals successfully unleashed 500-pound bombs. Most of them missed, but one hit the flight deck and chopped a hole in the forward section. A second bomb struck the catwalk and turned the length of walk into twisted metal. The next three Vals coming over *Bunker Hill* unleashed more 500 pounders. Two bombs hit, but did not cause extensive harm.

This damage to the two carriers would be the extent of that done by Japanese bomber crews in Raid IV. Admiral Montgomery had frantically called the fighter pilots of both his CAP and the Hellcat pilots coming in to land.

"We're under attack! Under heavy attack again!"

Soon, forty Hellcats zoomed from several directions. In moments, the American fighter pilots were diving on V formations of Vals and Zero fighter planes. A shuddering staccato of .50-caliber fire rattled from strafing guns, while five-inch rockets whooshed from wings. The Vals and Zeros fell out of the sky like birds caught in the multiple shotgun blasts. Japanese planes exploded in midair, burst into flames, broke in two or disintegrated to shreds. One after another of the Japanese planes plopped into the sea. Only three Vals and four Zeros escaped the Hellcat onslaught. The seven surviving planes ducked into a cloud bank and headed for Rota.

Lt. Toshohiko Ohno was utterly stunned. This had been his first real heavy combat with

American pilots and he suddenly realized that his Zero fighter planes and his novice pilots were no match for the superior Hellcat and the superior American pilots. Now, as he droned northeastward, he suspected the truth. The other air groups of Raids I, II, and III had not sunk and burned American carriers and then flown on to Mariana Islands bases. No, they had probably been wiped out just like his own formation had been wiped out, except for the seven survivors.

Not only Ohno, but the other airmen were also shaken by the deadly lesson in aerial warfare from the honed U.S. Navy fliers. Only Lieutenant Ohno and one other pilot had managed to score kills against the Hellcat pilots, downing two American planes. But, the victory was small consolation for the heavy losses.

Now, the shocked Lieutenant Ohno led his seven planes eastward, hoping to find safety. However, when he called Rota, he found that the airfield was under attack by American planes. So, he called Saipan, whose operations officer allowed him to come into Aslito Field.

"We shall land on Saipan," Ohno radioed the pilots of the other six planes.

When the formation reached Saipan, Ohno and his companions came in low amidst a barrage of ack-ack fire from both American destroyers off the coast of Saipan and from U.S. Marine ack-ack batteries on the beach. The heavy flak blew one of the Zeroes apart and badly damaged another that crashed on landing. Ohno and the other Zero pilot, along with the three Val crews, managed to land safely on Aslito Field that had already been potholed from American bombardments. Ohno and his fellow airmen sighed gratefully for their safe landing, but they had really flown from the frying pan into the fire.

Lieutenant Ohno would find himself whisked into command of an artillery unit of Adm. Chuichi Nagumo's 1st Naval Defense Command. Ohno would thus fight on Saipan until the bitter end.

Meanwhile, Capt. Mitsuo Fuchida droned on toward Guam with the Judy bombers, six Jills, 12 Zero fighter-bombers, and 15 Zero fighter escort planes of the 601st Air Group. Fuchida had been low on gas and he sighed in relief when he saw the island of Guam ahead. He picked up his radiophone and called 1st Air Fleet headquarters.

"This is Tenzen Two leader, Tenzen Two leader. We could not find elements of the American fleet and we request permission to land and refuel."

"Orote Field has been attacked and cannot recover aircraft," the 1st Air Fleet control officer answered. "Agana Field is also too badly damaged to recover aircraft. We can only suggest that you jettison your bombs and come in from the westward to the emergency clearing at the north end of the island. Recovery crews will stand by."

But, unfortunately for Captain Fuchida, everything went wrong.

Radar men aboard carrier U.S.S. *Hornet* picked up the swarm of bogies on their radar screen. The radar men immediately called *Hornet*'s skipper, Capt. Bill Sample, who in turn called TF 58 flag carrier *Lexington* and spoke to Capt. Gus Widhelm.

"We've got a horde of bogies on our screen that are heading for Guam, according to our best calculation."

Widhelm, of course, had been directing American interceptor pilots to flights of Japanese planes all day. Monitoring for Captain Widhelm was Lt. Charles Sims, a man who understood Japanese fluently. Sims had translated messages from the 1st Mobile Fleet operations room and Japanese air-group commanders all day, especially from Commander Najajima, the Japanese operations officer. Now, once more, Sims tuned into the Japanese radio band and heard Fuchida's radio communication with Guam, where the 601st Air Group wanted to land some 50 planes on Orote Field.

Sims thus verified the *Hornet* radar report that the Japanese planes were indeed heading for Guam. When Sims relayed his translated message to Widhelm, the TF 58 air commander immediately contacted Lt. Everett Hargreaves of *Hornet*'s AG 2. He was on CAP just west of Guam.

"There's a swarm of bogies heading for Guam."

"We'll get on them, Captain," Hargreaves answered. A moment later, with Hargreaves in the lead, 12 American fighter planes from *Hornet* zoomed southeast toward Guam.

Capt. Gus Widhelm then called Cmdr. Dave McCampbell of VF 15 from the carrier *Essex*. McCampbell and nine fellow fighter pilots had been airborne since 1300 hours and they had already engaged two flights of enemy planes on this harrowing day. Still, when Widhelm told McCampbell about the enemy planes heading for Guam, the VF 15 leader did not hesitate.

"How many bogies are there?" McCampbell asked.

"I don't know," Widhelm answered, "but I understand there's got to be at least fifty of them."

"Then we'll have good hunting," Cmdr. Dave McCampbell said.

Next, Gus Widhelm called Cmdr. Ralph Shipley of *Bunker Hill*'s VF 8. "Fifty Japanese planes are heading for Guam. You'll have to take your boys out again."

"We'll launch at once," Commander Shipley answered.

Within minutes, 12 Hellcats roared off the deck of *Bunker Hill*.

By 1500 hours, all American fighter planes were approaching Guam to the horror of Capt. Mitsuo Fuchida, who was just ready to land his Jills, Judys, and Zero fighter-bombers on the emergency clearing on Guam. Fuchida doubted that the 15 ill-trained Zero pilots in the escorting Zeros could do much against 40 odd American Hellcat pilots.

The Japanese 1st Mobile Air Fleet commander was in a circling pattern with his bombers and fighter-bombers when the first American planes appeared. The Japanese were in no position to run for they were too low on fuel, and they had nowhere else to go. Fuchida frantically radioed the 1st Air Fleet headquarters.

"Enemy planes! Please attack with antiaircraft fire and please send up fighter planes to aid my own fighter pilots on interception."

But, the 1st Air Fleet had no planes on Guam to send up and their antiaircraft fire was sporadic and ineffective.

Lt. Everett Hargreaves came in first with 12 Hellcats, quickly taking on the 15 Zero escort planes. The Japanese soldiers and sailors on Guam stared in awe as the roar of engines, whine of planes, chatter of machine guns, and whoosh of rockets echoed across the sky above the island. But, they winced painfully at the obviously uneven fight. The Hellcats were superior to the Zeros and the American pilots outclassed the raw, mostly inexperienced Japanese pilots. Within moments, Zeros were falling out of the sky. Some arced like burning comets before splashing into the sea or crashing on the island. Others disintegrated in midair. Some burst into flames and fell like cascading fireballs into the sea or on the island of Guam. A few Zeros managed to duck into clouds to avoid the massacre. Only one Hellcat fell out of the sky.

Meanwhile, the VF 15 pilots under Cmdr. Dave McCampbell waded into the circling Judy bombers and Zero fighter bombers. Japanese antiaircraft gunners fired furiously at the oncoming U.S. Navy Hellcats, but the continual American attacks on Guam all day had apparently demoralized them. The ack-ack gunners showed none of the accuracy they had shown earlier against Comdr. Ralph Weymouth's attack. Meanwhile, Judy aircraft gunners fired furiously from their rear canopy positions at the oncoming American planes. But their fire, too, was ineffective. McCampbell and his *Essex* pilots dove on the Japanese bombers, tailed them, or closed from the lateral with whooshing rockets and chattering machine guns.

One of McCampbell's pilots, Lt. Russell Reiserer, enjoyed the most uncanny success of his career. Within a minute, he broke into the Japanese landing circle of a string of five Judys and knocked one after another of the bombers out of the air. One plane exploded, another lost a wing, a third lost its tail, the fourth lost its engine, and the fifth disintegrated from two rocket hits.

Reiserer's wingman, Lt. Bill Blair, called Reiserer on the radio. "Holy Christ, Russ, have you got something to tell your grand kids. I never saw anything like that."

"I was lucky; I just caught them right,"

Reiserer answered. "But, there's a lot more around, so help yourself."

"What about you?"

"I'm finished; out of ammo and rockets," Reiserer answered. "I'll patrol upstairs and warn you if any Nip Zeros show up."

"Roger," Blair answered.

Lt. Bill Blair quickly zoomed into a circling Judy, loosed a pair of rockets, and caught the Japanese bomber in the engine with a hit that tore away the cowling and smashed the engine. The engine gasped once and then stopped. The Japanese pilot tried to glide his plane to a landing, but another burst of .50-caliber fire hit the gas tank. The plane exploded before it hit the ground and erupted in a ball of fire.

Other *Essex* pilots under Commander McCampbell and his VF 15 pilots also enjoyed success in this continued Mariana Islands turkey shoot. Circling Zero fighter-bombers and Judy dive bombers took telling strafing and rocket-fire hits. The Japanese planes, lacking even the maneuverability of Zero fighter planes, were indeed helpless turkeys. Lt. Bill Blair got his second score when he sent a spew of .50-caliber strafing fire into another Japanese plane. The hits shattered the elongated cockpit, killing pilot and gunner, before the plane spun downward and crashed. Cmdr. Dave McCampbell got his seventh kill of the day when a stream of strafing fire from his Hellcat guns tore a wing off a Judy before the bomber cartwheeled and plunged into the sea.

Within a few minutes, the VF 15 pilots had knocked nearly 20 enemy planes out of the air.

Capt. Mitsuo Fuchida had been one of the fortunate ones. He had been the first to land on Guam and he had already left his plane when American fighter planes appeared over the island. But, even as the Judys taxied toward dispersal areas, Hellcat pilots swept over the island with rattling machine-gun fire, punching holes in the Japanese light bombers. Fuchida and other Japanese airmen had barely escaped into shelters.

But, other descending Judys of the 601st Air Group did not enjoy the same good fortune. Cmdr. Ralph Shipley and the other pilots from U.S.S. *Bunker Hill*'s VF 8 continued to sweep over Orote Field as soon as they arrived. Shipley and his pilots shattered Judys that were trying to land. Some exploded on the runway. Others blew up along the taxiways, and still others burst into flames before they touched down on the runway.

Only 19 Japanese planes escaped the holocaust at Guam. These survivors, bombers and fighters, simply wandered aimlessly to the east of Guam if they had not already landed on Orote Field. Some of the Japanese planes still airborne landed bumpily on Rota's potted airstrip while others managed to return and land on Guam after the American pilots were gone. A few ran out of gas and crashed into the sea. Thirty-five other planes of the 601st Air Group trying to make Guam had either been shot out of the air or destroyed on the ground.

The fourth raid from the 1st Mobile Fleet had been another disaster.

At 1530 hours, Cmdr. Dave McCampbell called into his radio. "O.K., break off. They've got nothing left to hit. Let's get back to our carriers."

"What about a run over the airfield?" Lt. Bill Blair asked.

"Jesus, Lieutenant," McCampbell answered, "we've been airborne all day. You'll be lucky if you get home. No! Head for the carrier. I'll call air control and let them send a few TBM's to finish the job."

"Roger," Lieutenant Blair said.

When the drone of American planes faded to the northwest at 1545 hours, Capt. Mitsuo Fuchida and Adm. Kakuji Kakuta himself came out of the 1st Air Fleet shelter on Guam. The two men ogled at the devastation around them: smashed and burning aircraft wherever they looked. Potholes in the Orote runway and the Agana runway, and even some buildings burning from American rocket hits. For a full minute the two men simply stared soberly.

Then, two runners came up to Admiral Kakuta and bowed before him.

"Well?" Kakuta barked. "What is the damage?"

"Quite bad, Honorable Kakuta," one of the runners said. "We have less than two dozen planes operable here on Guam."

Kakuta nodded and then sighed. "Do what you can," he said softly.

"Yes, Honorable Kakuta," the runner said before he moved off.

Then, Kakuta turned to Capt. Mitsuo Fuchida. "I can only offer you my sympathies, Captain." The admiral then screwed his face. "We simply do not have enough experienced pilots; not enough aircraft, and not enough supplies. We continue to be overwhelmed by the Americans."

"I understood, Admiral, that you could mount five hundred land-based planes from the First Air Fleet to support the First Mobile Fleet," Captain Fuchida said. "It was our belief that such aircraft would help us to destroy both the American carrier fleet and the American invasion forces on Saipan."

Kakuta scowled. "Five hundred dreams, Captain, five hundred dreams! Seventy aircraft," he gestured, "they only sent me seventy aircraft to replace the heavy losses we suffered from the American air attacks. What can the First Air Fleet do with seventy aircraft?"

Captain Fuchida did not answer. He only stared again at the crackling fires and spiraling smoke in and around Orote Field. The 601st Air Group had been macerated in this futile fourth raid that would "Complete the destruction of the American carrier fleet," as Admiral Ozawa had announced boastfully. Fuchida felt a shudder race through his thin frame. He suspected the same truth as did Lieutenant

Ohno: the other raiding groups from the 1st Mobile Fleet had suffered the same fate as the 601st Air Group now. The Japanese would need more aircraft if they were to stop the Americans, but Capt. Mitsuo Fuchida had no idea where such planes could come from.

Chapter Eleven

The Americans were not yet finished with the Japanese at Guam. After the fourth attempted raid from the 1st Mobile Fleet, Adm. Marc Mitscher grew quite irritable—four potential enemy air attacks in four hours. How many more Japanese air formations would the bastards send after TF 58? And why didn't his own search planes find the Japanese fleet, even after reports from submarines *Albacore* and *Cavella?* While the TF 58 commander continued to send out search planes, he also decided to keep his rear clean. Despite the almost all day earlier attacks on Guam, Rota, and Saipan, and despite the most recent donnybrook over Guam, Mitscher decided to launch still another strike on Guam.

Cmdr. Ralph Weymouth had just returned to his carrier *Lexington* and gone to the rec room for coffee, when he got a call from air commander Gus Widhelm.

"Ralph, the admiral wants you to hit Guam again."

"Jesus, there can't be anything left there," Weymouth complained.

"It doesn't matter; he wants another air attack anyway."

"O.K., we'll go back," Ralph Weymouth answered.

Capt. Gus Widhelm also contacted *Yorktown* for an Avenger unit to join Weymouth, and the TF 58 air chief contacted *Enterprise* for a Dauntless unit. By 1630 hours, Cmdr. Ralph Weymouth had zoomed off *Lexington*'s deck with 12 loaded and refueled Dauntlesses. Lt. George Brown zoomed off *Yorktown*'s deck with 12 Avengers, and Lt. Comdr. Alvin Priel, who had also been over Guam earlier in the day, took off from *Enterprise* with a dozen Dauntless dive bombers.

Already circling over the Guam and Rota areas were Hellcats from *Hornet*'s AG 2 under Lt. Everett Hargreaves and Hellcats from AG 15 under Cmdr. Dave McCampbell. These units, after they had macerated Commander Fuchida's formations that were landing on Guam, got the word to maintain a CAP. So, they had not returned to their carriers as Mc-Campbell wanted.

However, shortly after the decision to attack Guam again with bombers, Capt. Gus Widhelm decided to relieve this CAP with a new combat air patrol that could also escort the bombers. He called for a relief CAP from carrier *Essex* and another from carrier *Bunker Hill*. Although Cmdr. Charlie Brewer had been out for most of the day, he quickly mustered 16 Hellcats from VF 15 and zoomed off the deck of the *Essex*. Meanwhile, Lt. Elbert McClusky zoomed off the deck of *Bunker Hill* with 16 Hellcats from VF 8. The two fighter-plane leaders had been involved against the Japanese Raid I early in the day. McClusky, especially, was anxious to get another swipe at the Japanese, because the enemy planes that did elude the American interceptors in the day-long raids, always seemed to single out U.S.S. *Bunker Hill* for punishment.

Meanwhile, on the shattered island of Guam, Adm. Kakuji Kakuta, commander of the 1st Air Fleet, had received some promising news from Iwo Jima. A squadron of Zero fighters and a squadron of Jill torpedo bombers, 32 planes total, were on the way to Guam and should be arriving at any moment.

"We will have reinforcements," Admiral Kakuta told Capt. Mitsuo Fuchida. "Two squadrons of aircraft should be here by dark."

"That is encouraging news," Fuchida said.

"We will refuel and load these aircraft this evening to strike the American carrier fleet at first light in the morning. Thankfully, our construction crews are already making emergency repairs to the Agana and Orote runways that were damaged two hours ago by the Americans."

Fuchida squinted up at the empty, late-

197

afternoon sky that was almost fading to a dark blue. "Let us hope the Americans make no more attacks today."

Admiral Kakuta shook his head. "The enemy will not launch air strikes this late in the day."

But, the Americans were on the way, flying due east with 36 bombers and 32 escorting Hellcats. In the meantime, the 16 Jills and 16 Zeros coming down from Iwo Jima had almost reached Guam as they flew directly south.

At 1825 hours, just before sunset, would come the last big air fight on this harried June 19th day in 1944.

At 1820 hours, Cmdr. Ralph Weymouth had been scanning the darkening skies around him. He could see the fellow navy bombers hanging in close formation; and above him, he could see the diamonds of Hellcat fighter planes, the escort. Then, Weymouth looked at his instrument panel and gaped in surprise. His radar showed a horde of bogies directly to the east— just about over Guam. He quickly picked up his JV and called Lt. Cmdr. Charlie Brewer.

"Bogies at twelve o'clock—straight ahead about fifteen miles. They're just about over Guam. Try to take them out so we can make our bomb run."

"Will do, Commander," Charlie Brewer said.

Moments later, Weymouth saw the fighter planes zoom off. Brewer reached Guam just as several Japanese Jills from Iwo Jima were landing on the hastily patched Orote runway. But, in his haste to hit the fat targets landing on the runway, Lieutenant Commander Brewer had neglected to use caution. He should have climbed high to maintain a CAP while the Dauntlesses and Avengers came in with their bomb loads to rake the field and the alighting Jill torpedo bombers. Instead, he decided to make strafing runs. Brewer cried into his radio.

"O.K., boys, let's get them."

A moment later, Brewer peeled off from the lead diamond of Hellcats, his wingman, Ens. Tom Carr, following him down. However, all 16 Zeros from Iwo Jima pounced on the four-plane flight under Lieutenant Commander Brewer. The odds were simply too high and the Zeros had the advantage of height. The Zero pilots, with aggressive determination, unleashed torrents of .30-caliber and 20-mm fire from 600 yards against the quartet of Hellcats.

Brewer managed to come over Orote runway and loosen a barrage of .50-caliber fire on one of the Jills that had just landed, punching holes in the torpedo bomber and forcing the suddenly flaming Jill to swerve off the runway and scud into the surrounding sand dunes. Wingman Tom Carr, meanwhile, had unleashed a stream of .50-caliber and five-inch rockets on a taxiing Jill; Carr had badly shot up the Japanese plane, but the aircraft did not explode.

Suddenly, from high in the sky, Lt. Elbert McClusky frantically called Brewer. "Above you! Above you! A horde of skunks!''

But, the warning came too late. The Japanese machine-gun and 20-mm fire shattered Charlie Brewer's cockpit and hit the VF 15 commander. The Hellcat wobbled and then crashed at the end of the Orote runway, killing Brewer. Seconds later, a flood of machine-gun fire raked Ens. Tom Carr's Hellcat, almost chopping the Hellcat in half while the American fighter plane flew at a very vulnerable low-level height. The navy fighter plane flipped over and smashed into the ground with a grinding thud. The crash killed Carr and totally demolished his plane.

The other two pilots of the lead Hellcat flight survived the countless .30-caliber holes in their fuselages, and they managed to arc away to zoom upward and out of range.

Soon enough, the other fighter planes from carriers *Essex* and *Bunker Hill* pounced on the 16 Zeros, scattering the Japanese formation with heavy .50-caliber fire and swishing rockets. Still, the Japanese pilots from Iwo Jima seemed more experienced and aggressive than those pilots in the raiding groups from the 1st Mobile Fleet.

The dogfight that followed between the U.S. Hellcats and the Japanese Zeros during the waning hours of daylight cost the Americans six of their fighter planes, including the loss of Brewer and his wingman, Tom Carr. In turn, however, the American Hellcat pilots had downed eight Zeros and a half-dozen of the Jill torpedo bombers trying to land on Guam. Lt. Elbert McClusky scored his fifth and sixth kills of the day when he first shot down a Zero and then blew apart a Jill trying to arc into Guam for a landing on Agana airstrip.

By 1815 hours, the Hellcats had finished their melee with the Japanese planes and now Cmdr. Ralph Weymouth zoomed over Orote Field with his Dauntlesses. Fortunately, the Hellcat escorts had eliminated or driven off the threats from Zeros, and Weymouth faced only antiaircraft fire. The AG 16 commander successfully dropped his two 500 pounders and one 1,000 pounder on Orote runway to gouge out three deep holes. Other Dauntlesses followed to dig more craters into the runway. Thus, in a matter of minutes, the dive bombers from U.S.S. *Lexington* had undone the hours of repair by the Japanese repair crews on Guam.

Lt. Cmdr. Alvin Priel, meanwhile, took his dozen Dauntlesses over Agana airstrip and the 12 American dive bombers once more turned the runway into a length of deep potholes. During the same bombing attack on Agana Field, Priel's unit had also destroyed two Jill torpedo bombers.

Finally, Lt. George Brown made low-level sweeps with his Avengers from *Yorktown*. He led six of the AGI Avengers over Orote Field, while the other six Avengers zoomed over Agana Field. The Avengers carried four 500-pound bombs instead of the usual torpedoes, since they were hitting a land target and not surface ships at sea. The Avengers successfully shattered parked aircraft, set an ammunition dump afire, and wrecked three buildings. Fire and smoke rose over Guam.

The American bomber attack, however, had not been without casualties. Three Dauntlesses and one Avenger fell victim to Japanese antiaircraft fire.

At 1820 hours, 20 minutes after the attacks began, Cmdr. Ralph Weymouth picked up his JV. "O.K., we've done all we can. It's getting dark. Let's get back to our carriers or we won't even be able to see them, much less land on them."

"I'm with you," Lt. George Brown answered.

By 1840 hours, the drone of aircraft faded to silence and a deathly stillness hung over Guam. Both Admiral Kakuta and Captain Fuchida looked in dismay at the blazing Guam air base. Not only had the Americans chopped up the runways again, but they had shot down eight Zeros and six Jills, while destroying another half-dozen Jills on the ground. The other eight Zeros and few remaining Jills successfully landed on the emergency landing field for the second time that day.

And, in fact, neither Adm. Kakuji Kakuta nor Capt. Mitsuo Fuchida had realized how badly the day had gone for the Japanese. June 19, 1944, had been a disaster for the 1st Mobile Fleet and the Japanese Naval Air Force in general. The Japanese had thrown 555 planes into the raids and searches from their carriers and the Mariana Islands. When all results were in, the Japanese would count 315 planes lost on the four raids from the Japanese carriers. In addition, among the planes on the Mariana Islands of Guam, Rota, and Saipan, the Japanese had lost another 150 planes on the ground and in the air. The toll then was 465 aircraft. And only a handful of Japanese planes had returned to their carriers. By dusk of June 19, 1944, 1st Mobile Fleet possessed only 130 operable planes. Only a little more than a dozen planes remained operable on Guam, and none on Saipan and Rota.

The Americans had thrown more than 600 planes into the air battle of June 19th, including the bombers that hit Rota, Saipan, and Guam on several attacks during the day. The American efforts had cost them 23 fighter planes and six bombers, including the loss of 20 pilots and seven air crewmen killed, while four officers and 27 enlisted men had been killed aboard ship during the Japanese air strikes.

By the time total darkness descended over the Philippine Sea on June 19, 1944, the skies were empty of planes. The turkey shoot was over. But, the great carrier battle between the American TF 58 fleet and the Japanese 1st Mobile Fleet would resume with a new vigor after a 23-hour respite.

The June 19th air battle had been the

greatest air battle of the Pacific war so far. The forces included three times as many planes and four times as many carriers as those involved in the Battle of Midway. The air actions had even surpassed the number of planes involved in any single day's action between the Germans and British during the Battle of Britain. From 1023 to 1845 hours on June 19th, fierce action had continued almost unabated. So many ships and planes had been involved that the Japanese had been able to mount countless formations of planes on the hour, and the Americans had been able to counter with endless formations of fighter planes to repulse each new Japanese air attack.

The lopsided results of these air battles could be attributed to several factors. First, the American pilots, better trained, had been more aggressive and capable. Next, Hellcat and Corsair fighter planes had been far superior to the Japanese aircraft, including the once indomitable Zero fighter planes. And finally, the Japanese had failed to keep their attack aircraft in tight formation to muster maximum fire power against intercepting fighter planes.

On the evening of June 19th, Admiral Ozawa discussed the day's operations with his staff. But, since cruiser *Haguro* did not have an adequate communications system, Ozawa remained ignorant of his heavy aircraft losses. His incoming reports were fragmentary and exaggerated.

"Our pilots report considerable success, Admiral," said chief of staff Matake Yoshimura, who held several sheets of paper in his hand. "They report at least six American carriers and several surface ships left burning and listing. We have received a signal from carrier *Zuikaku* that indicates that Captain Fuchida's last raiding group left a carrier and battleship in sinking condition. It appears our brave airmen have sunk at least four enemy capital vessels, and perhaps even more."

Ozawa nodded.

"Our fighter pilots also report heavy scores against the American Grummans (Hellcats)," Yoshimura continued. "They estimate the American aircraft losses at about one hundred and fifty Grummans. We have done extremely well this day, Admiral."

"And what of our own losses?"

Admiral Yoshimura looked through some reports in his hand and squeezed his face. "Unfortunately, we have lost some one hundred aircraft, Honorable Ozawa, but as yet, we do not have an accurate count."

"These losses are regrettable," Ozawa said. "Still, when we consider the losses we have dealt the enemy, our airmen have not sacrificed their lives in vain."

"It is our understanding that most of our aircraft have flown on to airfields in Guam, Rota, and Saipan," Admiral Yoshimura said. "We have received word from Admiral Kakuta of the First Air Fleet that large numbers of planes have landed on Guam and Rota. The admiral reports that Guam is jammed with aircraft.''

Kakuta was accurate about the Guam fields jammed with planes, but the 1st Air Fleet commander had neglected to tell the 1st Mobile Fleet staff that almost all of these planes were shot up or destroyed.

"Have we taken count of the number of aircraft that are still aboard our carriers?" Ozawa asked.

"We have only an estimate," Yoshimura said, "but the count is about one hundred fifty aircraft." Yoshimura paused and then continued. "What are your thoughts, Admiral?"

Ozawa now studied the map on the plot table and then turned to Yoshimura. "If the reports from our airmen are correct, then we can assume we have left the enemy carrier fleet in disarray. We must press our advantage. We will sail on a northwesterly course through the evening, refuel tomorrow, and then return east to strike on the morning of the twenty first. We will coordinate such attacks with our aircraft now at the Mariana Islands fields."

"Yes, Honorable Ozawa," Admiral Yoshimura said.

At 1850 hours, the evening of June 19th Ozawa mustered his huge fleet and set a course northwest to rendezvous with his oilers for refueling.

And, although the 1st Mobile Fleet had lost two carriers and had acknowledged the loss of at least a 100 planes, the sailors of the 1st

206

Mobile Fleet still felt eager and confident during the evening hours. The loss of a hundred planes and their aviators did not depress the Japanese. These dead warriors had gone to a glorious reward, especially with the heavy losses they had supposedly inflicted on the Americans.

As Ozawa mustered his fleet to sail northwestward to refuel, Adm. Marc Mitscher discussed with his own staff the next move of the Americans. He stood in the flag room of U.S.S. *Lexington* with chief of staff Arleigh Burke, air commander Gus Widhelm, and other members of the TF 58 staff. After the successful turkey shoot that day, and after the heavy destruction of Japanese air bases in the Mariana Islands, the Americans were anxious to find and destroy the Japanese fleet.

"Our crews can get some rest tonight," Mitscher said, "and we can attack that enemy carrier fleet in the morning. They've got to be somewhere west of here, and we'll alter course as soon as we've recovered all planes for the night. He looked at Widhelm. "Gus, how long will that be?"

"Everybody should be in by dark," Widhelm said, "maybe nineteen-thirty hours at the latest. Those aircraft that just hit Guam are the only planes still out."

"O.K.," Mitscher said. "As soon as they're back we alter to a two hundred sixty-degree course, west by northwest. Pass the word."

"Shall we launch night searches?" Captain

Widhelm asked. "If search planes find the enemy fleet sometime during the night, it'll make it easier for our airmen to find the Japanese."

"Admiral Spruance has made the same suggestion," Admiral Mitscher said, "but I don't think it's a good idea. The airmen are dog-tired after all those donnybrooks today."

"But, Admiral," Captain Burke now spoke, "we have no idea where that enemy fleet is at the moment. We do have several trained night-fighter Avenger units and they weren't in action today."

But Mitscher still disagreed. "I don't like the idea of an air crew getting lost during the night on that big expanse of ocean. No, we'll launch search planes as early as possible so they can be coming back during daylight."

"Yes, sir," Captain Burke said.

Admiral Mitscher now looked at Captain Widhelm again. "What about the Japanese bases on the Mariana Islands? If we sail west, could they be a menace to the Saipan operation?"

"According to all reports, we've pretty much finished them off. I doubt if the Japanese can get a dozen planes off their base on Guam, and they've got absolutely nothing on Rota and Saipan."

"We'll leave Harill's TF 58.4 behind to protect and support the marines on Saipan," Mitscher said. "The rest of us will sail west."

"Yes, sir," Captain Arleigh Burke said.

However, all planes had not returned to their TF 58 carriers until nearly 2000 hours. Only then could the American fleet turn to the westward and begin its sail on the 260-degree course. Mitscher increased speed to a fast 23 to 25 knots in the hope of closing the range on the enemy. However, Ozawa had a two-hour head start. Even though the Japanese sailed at a leisurely 17 to 18 knots, Mitscher was not likely to close on Ozawa in time to launch morning air strikes.

Dawn of June 20th broke fair and clear with the usual golden sunrise that always appeared on a clear day over the Philippine Sea. The wind blew at a soft, pleasant ten to twelve knots from the east, a wind direction that would prevail for most of the day. The sea was calm, with a steady barometer of 29.85 and a pleasant temperature of 75 degrees that would rise only to 85 during the rest of the day.

At 0530 hours, six Avengers roared off the decks of TF 58 carriers to search for the 1st Mobile Fleet, whose last location had been reported by the submarine *Cavella* when she had fatally torpedoed carrier *Shokaku* at about noon yesterday. The six Avengers, equipped with the lastest radar, had been the third search launch since 0330 hours. The planes would fan out in a 325-mile arc. But the Avengers, like the search groups before them, came only within 50 miles of the 1st Mobile Fleet, again missing a sighting.

Adm. Jisaburo Ozawa had also launched

planes at dawn to find the American fleet, with his first launch coming shortly after midnight. At the same 0530 hours, the morning of June 20th, nine Jake floatplanes catapulted off the decks of Japanese cruisers, the fourth search launch since midnight. The Japanese Jakes covered another wide arc, but they found nothing. At 0645, Adm. Sueo Obayashi of Cardiv 3 launched six more planes to search a section of the sea in a ten- to 50-degree arc. One of the Japanese planes finally got a clue. At 0713 hours, the Jake crew spotted two American carrier planes, although the Japanese observers did not find any American carriers or surface ships.

As soon as Captain Ohmae got the report, Admiral Yoshimura suggested to Admiral Ozawa that the sighting of the American planes indicated that the American fleet had come to the westward to close and attack the Japanese fleet.

"In view of the heavy damage our pilots scored yesterday," Yoshimura told Ozawa, "I would suggest we retire to home waters. We still have no word on our aircraft that reportedly flew on to the Mariana Islands bases, and we do not have enough fighter aircraft among our carriers to intercept successfully any large American air attack."

"No," Ozawa said, "I do not believe the Americans know our location, and as soon as we locate the enemy again, we can launch a new air strike in the morning without fear of an attack from the enemy."

"Yes, Admiral."

Throughout the morning, both American and Japanese search planes continued to seek out the other's fleet. Meanwhile, both fleets continued westward, with TF 58 sailing a few knots faster than the 1st Mobile Fleet. However, because of the two-hour head start the previous evening, Ozawa's fleet remained out of American carrier range.

At 1300 hours, June 20th, Ozawa transferred his flag from cruiser *Haguro* to carrier *Zuikaku*, where communications were much better. Ozawa got a shock when he arrived on the carrier and learned the horrifying truth: most of his aircraft from yesterday's raiding groups had been shot down, and the reported damage to the American carrier fleet had been highly exaggerated. Admiral Ozawa also learned that both the airfields and most of the aircraft on the Mariana Islands bases had been destroyed. Adm. Matake Yoshimura again urged Ozawa to give up the fight and head for home waters.

This time, the 1st Mobile Fleet commander did not disagree. "We will do so, but first, we will refuel from our tankers."

By midafternoon of June 20th, Ozawa's combat ships finally rendezvoued with the oilers to refuel. However, his ships were in disarray as carriers, battleships, cruisers, and destroyers mulled about haphazardly in the patch of Philippine Sea to await their turn to fuel up. No Japanese reconn pilots had seen another American plane since that morning, and no reconn pilots had found the American fleet. So, the Japanese believed they were far to the west of the Americans, and they had disregarded proper protective measures.

On the American side, Adm. Raymond Spruance, commander of the Fifth Fleet, believed the American search planes would never find the enemy. He was sure the enemy fleet was probably barreling far to the west and north after the disastrous plane losses the previous day. He called Admiral Mitscher.

"Marc, I don't think you'll ever find the Japanese. They're simply too far west. They'll soon be within Philippine Island waters where they can draw from land-based aircraft for support. We can't take a chance on that. I suggest that you give up the search and return to Saipan."

"But those cripples hit by our submarines may be lagging behind and we can at least finish them off."

"I don't know," Spruance balked.

"Let me continue on until dark," Mitscher pleaded. "If we don't find the enemy by then, we'll turn back."

"O.K., 'til dark," Admiral Spruance said.

Shortly after the radio communication between Spruance and Mitscher, two American Hellcats, radar equipped, at 1505 hours, ran into a pair of Jakes, adversary search planes. The Jakes veered quickly away when their pilots saw the American planes and the Hellcat pilots gave chase. By 1538 hours, the Americans had come to their range limit of 325 miles and they were about to give up the pursuit and return to their carriers. But then, the Hellcat pilots saw ripples on the water, far below and just off the port, distance 30 miles. The two American pilots closed and saw the sprawling Japanese 1st Mobile Fleet, with most of the ships loitering about randomly as they waited to refuel from Japanese oilers.

One of the American pilots, Lt. Bill Velte, radioed the *Lexington* flag room at 1540 hours. "Enemy carrier fleet below us—huge, and at least two groups of carriers, one heading west and the other east. They seem to be refueling."

Then came a radio message from Velte's companion, Lt. Russ Nelson. "We can see heavy cruisers and destroyers with a northern carrier group, and more surface ships with a southern group of carriers. We're getting a bearing on them now."

"Snap it up," Capt. Gus Widhelm said impatiently.

At 1605 hours, both Lieutenant Velte and Lieutenant Nelson radioed the same position of the Japanese fleet: 14° 13' north latitude, by 134° 30' east longitude.

"They'll need to regroup into formation before they can sail west again," Velte said, "and that should take them some time."

Capt. Gus Widhelm nodded and quickly notified Admiral Mitscher of the sightings.

"That enemy fleet will be delayed for quite a while because the capital ships are in the process of refueling. If we keep after them at twenty-three knots, we should be plenty close enough to hit them the first thing in the morning."

Mitscher studied a chart on the flag-room table and then looked soberly at Widhelm. "Gus, we can't wait until morning. The enemy fleet will be too far into Philippine Islands waters by morning. They'll be able to call on land-based planes and do us a lot of damage. No, we'll need to launch planes now."

"Now?" Captain Widhelm gasped. "My God, if we launch planes now, we'll have to recover in total darkness. It'll be at least 1900 or 2000 before they get back. Anyway, the enemy fleet may be out of range because we'll have to turn into the wind to launch aircraft. We'd be pushing our planes to their range limit; and that on top of coming back after dark."

"We'll turn about immediately after launch and sail west at full ahead," Mitscher said. "That should close range to shorten their flight distance home." He paused and then looked hard at Widhelm. "Send out the word, Captain; I want at least a hundred aircraft out at once."

"Yes, sir," Widhelm answered softly.

Both Arleigh Burke and Gus Widhelm looked at each other but said nothing. However, the same thought struck both of them. If they sent out a hundred aircraft this late in the day, and on such a long flight, they could lose most of the planes and airmen before the flyers returned safely to their carrier decks.

But Adm. Marc Mitscher would not waver. "Sure, it's going to be tight," he told his subordinates, "but we can make it." He paused and then looked again at Widhelm. "Launch 'em!"

BATTLE OF THE PHILIPPINE SEA

AMERICAN CARRIER STRIKES, SUNSET, JUNE 20, 1944

CARRIER DIVISION 1:
SHOKAKU (CV), MYOKO,
HAGURO AND DESTROYERS

Cumulus Mass

12—15 Nautical Mi.

HORNET (CVL)
YORKTOWN (CV)
BATAAN (CVL)
BELLEAUWOOD (CVL)

AG'S 1, 2, 24, 50

AG'S 16, 10, 51

CARRIER DIVISION 2:
JUNYO (CV), NAGATO,
HIYO (CV), MOGAMI,
RYUHO (CVL) AND DESTROYERS

LEXINGTON, (CV), ENTERPRISE (CV)
SAN JACINTO (CVL)

OILERS AND ESCORT

Approximately
50 Nautical Mi.

AG'S 8, 31, 28, WASP (CV), CABOT (CVL), MONTEREY (CVL)

AG 14
WASP

CARRIER DIVISION 3:

CHITOSE (CVL)
TAKAO
ATAGO
MUSASHI
AND DESTROYERS

CHIYODA (CVL)
HARUNA
KONGO
CHOKAI
AND DESTROYERS

ZUIHO (CVL)
KUMANO
CHIKUMA
SUZUYA
TONE
YAMATO
AND DESTROYERS

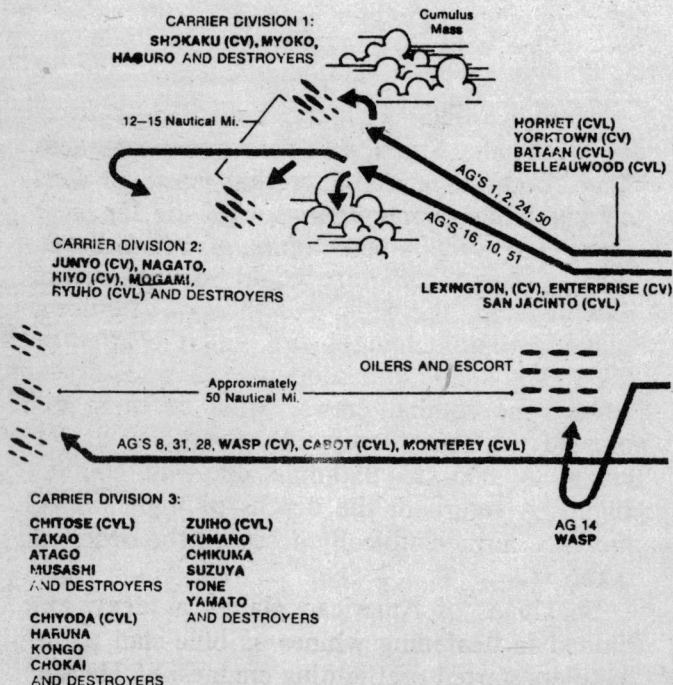

Here is a map showing the American TF 58 air attacks on Japanese First Mobile Fleet on late afternoon of June 20th.

216

Chapter Twelve

When Mitscher's order reached the carriers of TF 58, the American aviators were stunned. True, bombers and fighters had been on alert all day, while search planes sought the Japanese fleet. However, by 1600 hours, no one believed that any combat aircraft would take off before morning. So, the order for the late-afternoon strike abruptly changed the elated chatter of the turkey shoot to a sudden uneasy soberness among the combat crews. Most of them expressed the same complaint: the admiral was crazy. A 300- to 350-mile one-way combat flight? A return in the depths of night? Still, the U.S. airmen stoically accepted the order to take off.

Deckloads of American planes suddenly exploded in deafening whines as blue-clad plane handlers started preflighting engines: 85 Hellcat fighters, 77 Dauntless dive bombers, and 55 Avenger torpedo bombers from U.S.S. *Bunker*

Hill, Monterey, Yorktown, Lexington, Enterprise, and seven other carriers. And, as the carriers quickly turned 180 degrees into the wind to launch planes, pilots and crews hurried to ready rooms for briefing.

By 1610 hours, pilots and crews were racing toward aircraft as they had never run before. They wanted to get off as fast as possible to win precious minutes for the long flight. They carried chart boards under their arms and pistols at their hips, while oxygen masks dangled from their helmets. By 1620 hours, the 12 TF 58 carriers had completed their turns to launch planes.

Ship captains had relayed Mitscher's pep talk over PA systems, a speech that had ended with the short exhortation to "Give 'em hell, boys." But, the pep talk could not raise the adrenaline level of the sober combat crews.

Aboard *Bunker Hill*, the VF 8 leader, Cmdr. Ralph Shipley, sat quietly in his Hellcat. He considered a dusk attack too dangerous, but he would go anyway. Next to Shipley, Lt. Elbert McClusky sat in the cockpit of his own Hellcat with the same uneasy feeling. He was not on a turkey shoot now, or even on a relatively easy mission to Guam.

Inside the lead Dauntless of AG 8, bomber leader Ron Mead sat in the cockpit with a sober face. In the rear cockpit, Mead's sober gunner stared at the sky around him. The sun was already sinking toward the western horizon and both pilot and gunner believed the same thing:

they'd be lucky to reach the enemy carriers by dark.

An almost ghoulish silence prevailed on *Bunker Hill*'s deck, save for the screaming aircraft engines. The idea of flying so far and returning at dark staggered the imagination of the airmen as well as the unusually quiet deck crews.

At 1624 hours, Cmdr. Ralph Shipley and Lt. Elbert McClusky zoomed down *Bunker Hill*'s deck in a diagonal tandem before the two pilots soared upward and arced in a 180-degree turn to the westward. Ten other Hellcats followed the first pair. Moments later, Cmdr. Ronnie Mead with Lt. Ken Musuck as wingman, also zoomed down the deck of *Bunker Hill*. Fourteen Dauntlesses followed them. Then, the dive bombers also arced in the sky, jelled into formation, and roared westward.

Aboard U.S.S. *Monterey*, Lt. Cmdr. Robert Mehle of AG 28 felt a numbness as he sat in the cockpit of his Corsair and waited for the takeoff signal. Mehle could not believe the order for a three-hundred-mile combat flight this late in the day. He sat tensely until the yellow-clad signalman dropped his flag. Then, Mehle zoomed down the deck and into the air. Eleven Corsairs followed him.

Lt. Ron "Rip" Gift, the young Avenger pilot who had led the initial air strike on Guam before the Saipan landings, now zoomed down *Monterey*'s deck in his lead torpedo bomber. Lt. Tom Driess, Lt. Bob Bennett, and nine other Avengers followed the VB 28 squadron leader into the air. The 12 TBM torpedo bombers all carried bombs instead of torpedoes as they jelled into three four-plane diamonds and then headed westward.

Cmdr. James Peters, commander of *Yorktown*'s AG 1, sat again in the cockpit of his Hellcat for the fourth time within the past 36 hours. He had talked endlessly after the turkey shoot, but now he felt an agonizing doubt. How could they fly that far this late in the day? How could they land in the dark? Still, he waited grimly, determined to do whatever they asked. The signal flag finally dropped and Peters roared off carrier *Yorktown*. Eleven other Hellcat pilots followed him.

Behind the Hellcats, Lt. George Brown had waited on the same *Yorktown* flight deck in his torpedo-loaded Avenger, a tinge of shock on his face. His crew, radioman Ellis Babcock and gunner George Platz, felt the same sense of horror. Besides the twin torpedo load, the Avenger also carried an auxiliary gas tank for the long flight. Brown and his crew had done well in the attack on Guam, but none of these men relished this mission. They had never flown 300 miles on a combat mission, and they had never landed on a carrier deck in the dark.

Behind Brown, Lt. Ben Tate also waited, and behind Tate, Lt. Warren Omark waited. Omark's crew, radioman Jim Prince and gunner Robbie Ranes, sat mute, not even talking to each other.

Brown's Avengers would be among the few American planes that carried torpedoes. As Lt. George Brown raced his Avenger down *Yorktown*'s flight deck, a single thought lay in his mind: "Get a carrier! Get a carrier!"

Moments later, the eleven other Avengers of AG 1 zoomed off the carrier deck after Brown.

Aboard *Lexington*, Cmdr. Bill Strean, commander of VF 16, sat in his lead Hellcat and waited for takeoff. Beside him waited Lt. Cmdr. Paul Buie, who had spent all day yesterday in combat. Buie must now make a long escort flight far to the west. But, he accepted the task philosophically, however distasteful it was to him. He looked about at his fellow pilots and when he saw Lt. Alex Vraciu, Buie almost frowned. Vraciu had scored six kills yesterday; surely he had done enough during the hectic turkey shoot. But, Vraciu sat calmly in the cockpit of his Hellcat, also resigned to the dangerous task ahead.

Soon, Paul Buie roared down *Lexington*'s deck and took off. By 1624 hours, eleven other Hellcats had also left the carrier's deck.

Also on *Lexington*, Cmdr. Ralph Weymouth had been sitting in his lead Dauntless, waiting to take off with Lt. Jim McClellan in the Dauntless behind him. Weymouth and McLellan had already been out three times to hit Japanese Mariana Islands bases, and now they would fly out on an almost impossible task. In the rear cockpit of Weymouth's lead plane, gunner Harry Kelly sat uneasily in the loaded beast. He did not like the auxiliary gas tank, for the belly tank reminded Kelly that he was going on a long flight during this late afternoon, and that he would not come back until well after dark—if he got back at all. Kelly felt tense and apprehensive. When he looked about the deck, some of *Lexington*'s deck crews gave him a thumbs-up signal—success. But Kelly only scowled.

"Thumbs up, hell," the gunner thought. "What they really meant was so long, sucker."

But, Harry Kelly pondered this discouraging and bitter thought for only a few seconds before the Dauntless suddenly jerked forward and roared off Lady Lex's deck. Fifteen more Dauntlesses followed Weymouth's lead bomber.

Aboard U.S.S. *Enterprise*, Lt. Comdr. William "Killer" Kane had not said a word since the order came for the late-afternoon strike against the Japanese fleet, except to brief his pilots and crews in the ready room. Kane had successfully convinced the ship's doctor to let him fly, and he still wore his special helmet over the bandage on his head. But now, he felt a tinge of regret for pressing the medics to give him the O.K.

Kane's idea of flying combat had been yesterday's delightful turkey shoot, not a long, dangerous flight to the westward with the possibility of neither finding the enemy nor finding his way home in the dark. "Killer" Kane now waited soberly in the lead Hellcat of

VF 10. To the west, he could see the sky growing dark and he suspected that total darkness might descend over the Philippine Sea by the time he reached target. Nonetheless, he gritted his teeth, determined. When the yellow-clad signalman dropped his flag, Kane roared off the deck of *Enterprise*. Lt. Bob Shackford followed. Then, ten more Hellcats zoomed off the flight deck of Big E.

Now, Lt. Comdr. Alvin Priel waited for the takeoff signal. Priel would lead 16 Dauntlesses from *Enterprise*, with all planes carrying one-thousand pounders in the bomb bay and two 500 pounders under the wings of the beasts. Priel was not sure he would make the 300 miles and back even with the auxiliary gas tank. But, the lieutenant commander was a by-the-book man and he accepted any job. As he zoomed off the deck of Big E, he charged himself with determination. He would get a Japanese carrier today or die in the attempt.

Right behind Priel, Lt. Vannie Eason roared down the deck and took off with the same determination. Fourteen Dauntlesses followed.

From other carriers of TF 58, other Hellcats, Corsairs, Dauntlesses, and Avengers also roared off carrier decks. By 1635 hours, after a phenomenally short twelve minutes, 216 aircraft from Mitscher's huge task force had taken off the carriers. Then, the carriers quickly came about 180 degrees to steam westward at flank speed. Mitscher wanted his carriers to close as much as possible to shorten the range for his aircraft that must return in the dark. Among the TF 58 aircraft themselves, all the Hellcats, Avengers, and Dauntlesses carried extra gasoline tanks for the long flight.

Mitscher had issued the same order to all air commanders: "Cripple them; slow them down, so we can finish them off in the morning." Then, Mitscher had ordered Gus Widhelm to ready another 200 aircraft for a strike in the morning.

Before 1700 hours, the various American air groups rendezvoued, but not in one huge formation. The group leaders had no time for the air units to do so and waste fuel. Still, all air groups droned westward at about the same 290° course at the same 130- to 140-knot speed to conserve fuel. Most of the U.S. airmen on the mission were young, from age 19 to their early 20's. The majority of them had only been out of aviation-cadet or crew-training school a few months, and they were edgy, continually scanning the skies or the sea for possible interceptors. Many of them vividly remembered the turkey shoot and the devastating fate of Japanese airmen who had made similar long flights yesterday—and without the need to return in the darkness. Now, these American aviators wondered if perhaps they would be deluged with Zero interceptors and suffer the same fate as the Japanese aviators yesterday. Or, perhaps they would tire badly from the long flight, slowing their reactions. The loss of precious seconds could allow Zero fighter pilots, fresh off their carrier decks, to shoot the Americans out of the sea.

And of course, the TF 58 American airmen could not shake from their minds the worst fear of all—splashing or ditching into the black, empty sea where they might be lost forever; where they would die slow, horrible deaths from exposure.

At 1715 hours, while the 216 aircraft from TF 58 droned westward, two searching Japanese Kates sighted a pair of TF 58 carriers at a distance of 325 miles to the eastward. When Captain Ohmae brought the report to Ozawa, the admiral frowned.

"It is too late to make an air strike now, but perhaps we can launch a night torpedo strike," Ozawa said. "The aircraft can then continue on to Guam. You will notify Admiral Obayashi of Cardiv III to dispatch such an after-dark strike and you must remind him to escort these torpedo planes with three radar-equipped aircraft."

"Yes, Admiral."

"You will also contact Admiral Ugaki of the Batjan force and order him to prepare for a night action against the enemy fleet."

But, the orders for night action did not reach Admiral Ugaki for more than two hours, by which time the 1st Mobile Carrier Fleet would be under attack. Further, the torpedo planes from Obayashi's Cardiv 3 would fail to find the American fleet, even with their radar-equipped scout planes.

By 1820 hours, oncoming dusk had left a romantic setting over the Philippine Sea. The sun, a big orange ball dipping over the horizon, had left a brilliant color on the high cirrus clouds that drifted at 10,000 feet in the sky. Surface visibility was excellent. The wind had abated and the sea had calmed. A thin sliver of a pale moon had risen in the sky. Japanese sailors aboard the carriers and surface ships might have appreciated the pretty view. But, at 1825 hours, Japanese CAP pilots reported the horde of American planes approaching from the east.

Ozawa grimaced when he got the report. His fleet was not in a disposition to defend itself against air attack or in a position to launch planes. The surface ships of the Batjan force were not in the van to unleash heavy anti-aircraft fire. Fortunately, however, the ships had already refueled and had been reforming into three groups. *Zuikaku*, last of Cardiv I's carriers, wallowed at a 16° 20' north, 133° 30' east position. Carriers *Junyo, Hiyo*, and *Ryuho* of Cardiv II, with the surface-ship screen, loitered about 15 miles southwest of Cardiv I, while carriers *Chitose, Chiyodo*, and *Zuiho* of Cardiv III, with its own supporting surface ships, wallowed some 30 to 35 miles southwest of Cardiv II. The oilers and their escorts lagged behind, still some 50 miles to the east of Cardiv III.

By 1835 hours, at dusk, 42 U.S. aircraft, including bombers and escorting fighters, headed for the carriers of Cardiv III. Aboard *Chiyoda*, the lookout saw the approaching planes and gave the alarm. A moment later, *Chiyoda*'s signal flags went up: "Repulse air attack!" *Chiyoda*'s ack-ack gunners quickly manned guns and opened up with a barrage of antiaircraft fire. Cmdr. Ron Mead, however, grimly led his AG 8 aircraft. The 34-year-old naval-academy graduate had been at war for two years, but this was the first time he had ever seen such a big enemy target.

"O.K., boys, take your pick and make it quick."

By his calculations, Ron Mead had determined that his AG 8 from *Bunker Hill* had already flown 315 miles and he could only afford one pass to save enough fuel for the return to U.S.S. *Bunker Hill*. So, Mead and his Dauntless pilots could only take one shot. Mead dove his Dauntless at *Chiyoda* at a 70-degree angle, strafing with .50-caliber guns and whoosing rocket fire before finally releasing his bombs from 2,000 feet. Mead, however, completely missed the zigzagging carrier when *Chiyoda*'s helmsman made a quick turn to port.

Other Dauntlesses came diving after Mead and into the same carrier, while other American bomber pilots went after the screening battleship and two cruisers. But, the Japanese helmsmen proved quite adept. In addition, the heavy antiaircraft fire had blackened the sky so thickly with dark puffs of exploding flak that the dive-bomber pilots could not pin-point their targets. Finally, the U.S. pilots were obviously tired from the long flight of over 300 miles and the fears of returning in the dark, so they had lost their sharpness.

Bunker Hill's AG 8 only scored near misses on *Chiyoda* that killed some of the crew and shuddered the ship violently. However, the carrier suffered only minor damage. Similarly, all bombs from AG 8 had missed the Japanese battleships and cruisers.

As the AG 8 Dauntlesses retired, several Japanese fighter planes roared after the American dive bombers. Lt. Ken Musick caught a stream of .30-caliber fire that ripped holes in the wing of his Dauntless and loosened the ailerons. Still, Musick straightened his bomber and roared away, although the plane vibrated violently.

Before the Zeros attacked again, Cmdr. Ralph Shipley, Lt. Elbert McClusky, and other VF 8 fighter pilots roared to the rescue. In a furious two-minute dogfight over the zig-zagging carrier *Chiyoda*, the Japanese showed extreme skill and determination, but only shot down two of the Hellcats. In turn, Commander Shipley shot one Zero out of the sky and Lieutenant McClusky shot another Zero into the sea. Other VF 8 pilots also scored, over-coming the Japanese pilots despite the long flight from the east. Only one of the Japanese fighter planes survived to return to its carrier. The Japanese fighter pilots had not shot down a single one of Cmdr. Ron Mead's Dauntlesses.

And Adm. Sueo Obayashi's Cardiv 3 still faced plenty of trouble. Moments after the *Bunker Hill*'s Ag 8 aircraft completed their run on *Chiyoda*, Lt. Ron "Rip" Gift of *Monterey*'s VB 28 came roaring after *Chiyoda* and the screen battleship *Hurana* with his wingman, Lt. Tom Dries. Each torpedo plane from *Monterey* carried GP bombs instead of torpedoes. Despite heavy ack-ack fire, Gift scored two hits on *Chiyoda*'s aft, setting the carrier afire, wrecking her flight deck, destroying a Jill and Zero on her deck, killing 20 Japanese sailors, and wounding 30 more. Lt. Tom Dries, off Gift's starboard, scored a bomb hit on battleship *Hurana* that flooded a magazine.

Then, Lt. Bob Bennett and his wingman, Lt. Hank Edwards, also came roaring into *Hurana*, but their bombs missed. However, heavy flak shattered Bennett's cockpit, killing the gunner and radioman and wounding Bennett in the chest. Another flak burst tore apart pieces of the fuselage. Still, Bennett managed to arc his plane away. Edwards, meanwhile, escaped the barrage of ack-ack without a scratch to him or his crew and without a hit on his Avenger.

As other Avengers roared into Cardiv 3's vessels, the Avenger pilots scored near misses on the cruiser *Mayo* that ignited several small fires. However, repair crews on the *Mayo* quickly doused fires and minor flooding while her complement remained on battle stations.

Lt. Gift cursed under his breath. If he had carried torpedoes, he could have done better. But, the long flight had ruled out torpedoes and he had been forced to carry GP bombs instead. Further, the same long flight had allowed him only one pass over target. They could not use too much fuel if they expected to complete the long flight back to their carrier.

As Gift and his *Monterey* Avenger crews headed away from Cardiv 3, the Americans successfully escaped heavy antiaircraft fire. However, two Zeros closed toward the American torpedo planes. But, Lt. Comdr. Roger Mehle himself caught one with raking .50-caliber fire that tore off the wing of the Zero before the Japanese plane cartwheeled into the sea. The second Zero caught a cross fire of strafing fire from the flank and tail. The Zero simply fell apart and the pieces plopped into the sea.

A swarm of aircraft from U.S.S. *Cabot*'s AG 31 also attacked Cardiv 3, but failed to score anything more than minor hits and near misses. *Chiyoda* was swinging in full circle and the pilots of AG 31 could not get an accurate bead on the carrier to hit with torpedoes. Meanwhile, carriers *Chitose* and *Zuiho* had not even come under attack.

To the north, Lt. George Brown, leading 12 Avengers from *Yorktown*'s AG 1, roared after the other carrier groups. As four Avengers veered after carrier *Zuikaku*, Lieutenant Brown and the other eight Avenger pilots veered southward to hit Adm. Tajaji Joshima's Cardiv 2 carriers. As Brown came down on carrier *Hiyo* with a formation of four Avengers, he called his other pilots.

"We'll spread out and hit from four directions."

"Roger," Lt. Warren Omark answered.

"We read you," Lt. Ben Tate said.

Lt. George Brown led the attack on the now zigzagging carrier whose antiaircraft gunners sent out furious fire. As Brown came toward the carrier, his aircraft caught several ack-ack hits that knocked out part of the plane's right wing and started a fire in the elongated cockpit. Radioman Ellis Babcock and gunner George Platz shoved back the canopy. Babcock then booted Platz out of the plane before the radioman bailed out himself, taking the packaged rubber life raft with him. Brown, meanwhile, continued his dive, despite wounds to his chest. He leveled off at nearly sea level and loosed a torpedo that hit the aft of *Hiyo* with a shuddering explosion. Then, despite wounds and the heavy damage to his plane, Lieutenant Brown arced his aircraft upward and escaped further flak fire.

Meanwhile, Lt. Ben Tate roared after *Hiyo*, skimmed along the sea, and let go his torpedoes. The torpedoes missed. However, a third Avenger in this lead quartet, piloted by Lt. Warren Omark, skimmed his torpedoes from a mere 400 feet. The zigzagging Hiyo could not escape a second hit that struck

231

squarely and ignited a magazine. The subsequent explosion started huge fires in the bowels of the Japanese carrier; and the same blast tore a huge hole in the hull that flooded all engine rooms, killed all power, and started *Hiyo* on a quick 20-degree list. The carrier was obviously doomed.

Battleship *Nagato* and cruiser *Mogami* now circled about the stricken *Hiyo* while destroyers hurried alongside to rescue the crew of the Japanese carrier.

Even as *Hiyo* belched fire and smoke, Cmdr. Roger Weymouth roared toward Cardiv II with 16 Dauntlesses from U.S.S. *Lexington*. He picked up his JV and called his fellow pilots. "We'll fly over their carriers, bank around, and come in from the west. We'll make our run from out of the sun and then start home."

"O.K.," Lt. Warren McClellan answered.

As Weymouth and his pilots veered and came into the Cardiv II aircraft carriers from the west, several Zeros zoomed down on the Dauntlesses from above. Gunner Harry Kelly fired furiously from the rear cockpit of Weymouth's lead Dauntless and knocked a wing off the Zero. The Japanese plane then tumbled crazily into the sea.

Meanwhile, Lt. Cmdr. Paul Buie and his Hellcat pilots sped to the aid of Cmdr. Weymouth and the other Dauntless pilots from *Lexington*. Buie tailed one Zero, fired a heavy burst of .50-caliber fire squarely into the plane, and blew the Zero apart. But, Buie's wingman caught a heavy burst of .30-caliber fire from an aggressive Zero pilot. The tracers shattered the Hellcat's cockpit and killed the pilot before the Hellcat spun out of control and crashed into the sea.

Lt. Alex Vraciu, meanwhile, scored a kill when he caught a Zero trying to arc away. Vraciu's .50-caliber fire and whooshing rockets tore the wing off the Japanese plane before the Zero cartwheeled into the sea.

Buie and his VF 16 pilots from the *Lexington* had shot down four planes and driven off other interceptors to allow Weymouth and the AG 16 bomber pilots to make their attack. Weymouth, leading the pack, scored two hits on the carrier *Junyo* that chopped a pair of holes in her carrier deck. Other AG 16 pilots scored three more hits on the Japanese carrier.

But, there were losses. Lt. Jim McClellan caught a heavy spew of .30-caliber fire that almost chopped his Dauntless apart and set the dive bomber afire. The hits killed McClellan's gunner and McClellan could not control the plane. The Dauntless arced in a wide semicircle and then glided toward the sea. Fortunately, McClellan managed to skim along the water and ditch before he successfully escaped the plane, inflated a rubber raft, and climbed aboard. He now had a fish-eye view of the battle, along with radioman Babcock and gunner Platz from Lieutenant Brown's Avenger. All three men now watched carrier *Hiyo* belch fire and smoke, listing, before the Japanese carrier went down.

The attack on *Junyo* infuriated the Japanese and another formation of Zeros jumped the AG 16 Avengers from *Lexington*. But, Lt. Cmdr. Paul Buie and his Hellcat pilots again intervened. In another donnybrook, the Americans shot down six Zeros, but lost three of their Hellcats.

The AG 16 formation then assembled and headed eastward for the long ride home.

After the *Lexington* attack, aircraft from U.S.S. *Enterprise* entered the fray. Cmdr. Bill "Killer" Kane of VF 10 spotted carrier *Ryuho* that had now sailed several miles west of the sinking *Hiyo* and the damaged *Junyo*. Kane called into his JV.

"Dead ahead on a two-hundred-sixty-degree bearing, enemy carrier. Hellcats get upstairs to protect the Dauntlesses. Bombers will attack!"

"We read you," Lt. Cmdr. Alvin Priel answered.

Then, Priel dove toward the snaking *Ryuho* whose gunners fired furious flak at the approaching Dauntlesses. But, Priel got through the ack-ack fire and loosed two 500-pound bombs from the wings and the 1,000 pounder from the bomb bay. The first two missed, but the 1,000 pounder scored on the fantail and the shattered explosion erupted smoke and fire. *Ryuho* veered sharply to port, but other AG 10 Dauntless pilots roared into the carrier and scored eight more hits about the bow of the aircraft carrier. Flames shot 200 to 300 feet into the air from an ignited magazine.

Then came Lt. Vannie Eason, leading another four-plane formation. Eason successfully hit the target with two bombs that erupted another ball of fire that rose some 200 feet into the air. Eason's companions also scored hits. Still, the rugged *Ryuho*, though battered and afire, was never in danger of sinking.

As Priel mustered his Dauntlesses for the long flight home, a swarm of Zeros came in at three o'clock high to intercept. But, Cmdr. "Killer" Kane and his Big E Hellcat pilots successfully broke into the Zero formation to thwart any attempted Japanese fighter attack on the Dauntlesses. Kane himself caught a Zero with a fusilade of .50-caliber and rocket fire that cut the Japanese plane apart. The shattered Zero wobbled for several hundred feet and then plunged into the sea. Kane's wingman, Lt. Bob Shackford, got two kills when he shot off the engine of one Zero and the tail of a second. In fact, Kane's VF 10 shot down eight Zeros to a loss of two Hellcats. Priel and his Dauntless crews thus escaped successfully.

But, as Kane and his fighter pilots zoomed east to catch up to their Dauntless charges, Kane caught a burst of flak in the right wing and the Hellcat shuddered violently. He now carefully nursed his plane homeward, hoping to keep up with the rest of the VF 10 aircraft.

Meanwhile, U.S.S. *Wasp*'s AG 14 attacked the Japanese oilers and their supporting destroyers. The *Wasp* airmen set afire and sunk the tankers *Seiyo Maru* and *Hayashi Maru*, while causing serious damage to oiler *Genyo Maru*. As the *Wasp* aircraft retired, Zeros jumped AG 14. However, the Zeros only knocked down one Hellcat while losing a Zero of their own. The bombers escaped unscathed.

By 1935 hours, in the rapidly darkening day, the Americans had ended their attacks on the 1st Mobile Fleet. American AG's 1, 2, 24, and 50 had hit Cardiv 1, causing damage to cruisers *Myok* and *Haguro*, but not hurting carrier *Shokaku*. AG's 16, 10, and 51 had struck Cardiv II, sinking *Hiyo*, damaging *Junyo*, and damaging cruiser *Mogami*. AG's 8, 31, and 28 had hit Cardiv III, damaging two cruisers, two destroyers, and carrier *Chiyoda*. *Wasp*'s AG 14 had sunk two oilers and badly damaged another.

Perhaps the score was not impressive, considering the attack by more than 100 U.S. bombers and over a 100 fighter planes. But, the Americans had done much better in this single attack than the Japanese had done in four attacks on the previous day.

But, if the American bombers had not scored impressively against the 1st Mobile Fleet, although sinking a carrier is impressive, the American fighter pilots had scored extremely well. The American pilots had all but wiped out whatever remained of Admiral Ozawa's 1st Mobile Fleet aircraft. During the attack on the Japanese fleet, U.S. Hellcat and Corsair pilots, as well as Dauntless and Avenger gunners, had destroyed or seriously damaged 65 Japanese planes to a loss of 20 American planes.

By 1945 hours, June 20th, after the last American plane disappeared to the east, Adm. Jisaburo Ozawa counted only 35 combat-ready planes left in his 1st Mobile Fleet; only 35 planes out of 430 that had been aboard the hangar and flight decks of his carriers on the morning of June 19th. Admiral Ozawa was certainly out of business.

Ozawa's face reflected his dejection as he stood on the open bridge of *Zuikaku* with Captain Ohmae and Admiral Yoshimura. The two subordinates said nothing. There was nothing to say. The Americans had beaten them soundly. Finally, Ozawa spoke in a low, soft voice.

"We will form in proper disposition and set sail for home waters. The battle is over."

"Yes, Honorable Ozawa," Captain Ohmae said.

"You will relay these instructions to all ship commanders at once."

"Yes, Admiral," Ohmae said again.

But, if the Americans had won a victory in the great carrier battle on the Philippine Sea in mid-June of 1944, the U.S. airmen still faced a serious and perhaps insurmountable task. Nearly 200 American planes and their crews and pilots, low on fuel, must now fly hundreds of miles to reach their carriers, even as darkness settled over the Philippine Sea. Many of the U.S. aircraft sputtered, shimmered, or strained from heavy damage. Many of the pilots, gunners, and radiomen suffered from severe wounds.

Every airman aboard the returning U.S. planes felt the same dreaded fear: would they get safely to their carriers, or would they be swallowed up and lost forever in the dark expanse of the Philippine Sea?

Chapter Thirteen

The long flight home: miles of murky sea below, darkness overhead, endless blackness to the east. And soon, an extensive weather front that had been moving south all during the day had reached and covered the Philippine Sea. There was not even moonlight to aid the American airmen in finding their carriers. In the total night, at 1945 hours, pilots and crews of the American air formations could barely see the shadowy silhouettes of wingmen.

Aboard his Dauntless, Lt. Cmdr. Ron Mead stared into the darkness ahead and picked up his radio to call his gunner. "Are the other planes with us?"

"Yes, sir," the gunner answered.

"If you see any stray off, be sure to call me."

"Aye, sir," the gunner spoke again.

Mead strained his neck to see the Hellcats hanging over him like huge black shadows. The escorts as well as the bombers of Mead's AG 8 were holding tightly together. But, when Mead looked at his gas gauge, he frowned. The needle had fallen below the half mark and his carrier deck still lay over 200 miles to the east. Mead knew he must maintain the slow 140-knot speed if he hoped to conserve enough fuel to reach his carrier. He prayed that *Bunker Hill* was making straight westward at full ahead to close the gap.

Mead didn't know it, but the carriers, despite their full ahead, were still 250 to 300 miles to the eastward.

Lt. Cmdr. Ron Mead flew on for another fifteen minutes. Then, certain he had come out of range from the Japanese fleet, he called his other pilots. Nine Dauntless pilots reported O.K., but three were missing. Four other bomber pilots reported an array of damage: shot-up tails, shattered wings, oil leaks from flak hits, and a badly damaged fuselage. All the AG 8 bomber pilots reported less than a half-tank of gas and few of the airmen aboard the damaged Dauntlesses believed they could make it home.

Lt. Ken Musick was especially pessimistic. "The left wing is shot to hell," he told Mead. "We're shaking like a cement mixer and I don't think I can keep up."

"Hang on, hang on," Mead said. "Stay in formation."

Then, Mead called Cmdr. Ralph Shipley, who led both the Hellcat escorts and the

Bunker Hill planes themselves. "We're not doing so good, Ralph."

"Neither are we, Ron," Shipley answered. "We lost two planes over target and at least a half-dozen other fighter planes are badly damaged. I'm not sure they can make it home. Just myself, McClusky, and a few others are in good shape. But, if we move along at this reduced speed, and if we don't run into Zeros, maybe the others can make it. Meanwhile, keep the tight formation."

"Will do," Mead answered.

But, Shipley and Mead had barely finished their squawk-box talk, when Lt. Ken Musick called Mead. "We're done, Commander. I can't keep the plane airborne. The vibrations are brutal. We'll be falling apart in a couple of minutes, and I'll have to ditch."

"O.K., Lieutenant," Mead said. "Stay in the flight route. I'm sure somebody will rescue you sometime in the morning." He paused. "Good luck."

"Aye, sir," Musick answered. Then, Musick cut the engines, slowing the vibration dramatically, before he glided the damaged Dauntless toward the sea. A moment later, he skimmed across the water to a stop. Musick and his gunner quickly scrambled from the plane and moments later they sat inside an inflated raft. Now, the two men prayed for rescue, for death came slowly and torturously on the open sea.

In the cockpit of the lead Corsair from

Monterey's AG 28, Lt. Cmdr. Roger Mehle also stared into the eastern horizon ahead of him. When he looked about him, he saw but a half-dozen Corsairs still in formation with him. Several planes from *Monterey*'s AG 28 were missing. Mehle did not know if these pilots had been shot down over target, had ditched in the sea, were lagging behind, or had simply lost JV communications and could not respond to the AG 28 commander.

Mehle then looked under him and he caught the tight diamonds of Avengers. But, with his limited vision, he only saw a half-dozen torpedo bombers. Mehle knew that the Avengers from *Monterey*'s AG 28 had run into heavy ack-ack while they damaged a Japanese battleship, cruiser, and carrier. He only hoped that most of them made it home. He picked up his JV and called Lt. Ron "Rip" Gift.

"Rip, what are your losses?"

"Not bad, Commander," Lieutenant Gift answered. "We've still got most of our Avengers. Two are missing. Bobby Bennett and Jim Edwards. I haven't been able to contact them, but none of our bomber crews saw them go down. Maybe they're just straggling."

"Let's hope so," Lt. Cmdr. Bob Mehle said.

Far to the rear of the AG 28 formation, Lt. Bob Bennett moved along his shattered Avenger at a mere 120 knots. His head ached from shrapnel wounds. A dizziness had engulfed him. His radio had been shot away. Behind him, in the shattered, elongated cockpit, both his gunner and radioman were dead. Bennett soon lost clear vision and he saw ahead of him only a bleary darkness, nothing more. He squinted hard, but he saw nothing in the cloud-covered sky. Then, his engine sputtered. He tried to study his gas gauge, but with fuzzy vision, he saw only the needle near the empty mark. Flak had apparently opened his gas tank that now lost fuel at a rapid rate.

For fifteen minutes, Bennett droned on, the engine sputtering. But then, the plane wobbled and lost altitude. A formation of four Hellcats came suddenly behind the badly damaged Avenger and two of the fighter pilots peeled off to follow Lieutenant Bennett down. They could see that Bennett was half-conscious and bleeding profusely. They could see him blinking his eyes, apparently from restricted vision. One of the fighter pilots tried to contact the Avenger pilot over the JV radio, but Bennett could not answer. In the darkness, the Hellcat pilots hurried alongside the bomber, but the plane from AG 28 suddenly splashed into the sea. The Hellcat pilots buzzed the rapidly sinking Avenger and then came around for another pass. But, they only saw the last of the Avenger go under. Nobody on the surface of the sea.

"He's gone," one of the pilots radioed his companion. "We can't hang around or we'll be down ourselves."

"Roger," the second fighter pilot answered.

Then, the two Hellcat pilots zoomed upward to rejoin their Hellcat formation.

Lt. Jim Edwards had better luck. When his Avenger sputtered its last, he successfully ditched his bomber on the sea. Moments later, he, his gunner, and his radioman scrambled out of the sinking plane. They quickly inflated their life raft and climbed aboard. Then, on the vast, dark empty sea they prayed that someone would rescue them.

Far ahead, Lt. Ron Gift called his fellow Avenger pilots of AG 28. He got positive responses from Lt. Tom Dries and nine other Avenger pilots who still droned eastward without serious problems.

Behind these first two groups, both *Yorktown*'s AG 1 Hellcats and Avengers droned in tight formations, with the Hellcats hanging above the Avengers. Cmdr. James Peters counted only six Avengers and he wondered what had happened to the other six torpedo bombers. He was certain that his Hellcat pilots had driven off or shot down any Japanese interceptors, and Peters could only conclude that antiaircraft fire had shot down the AG 1 bombers. Or perhaps, luckily, the other AG 1 Avengers were simply lagging behind.

Peters squinted into the darkness, frowning. Like the other American air-group commanders, he hoped that *Yorktown* had closed enough range to recover AG 1 aircraft before his Hellcats and Avengers ran out of fuel. Peters also worried about landing in the dark for many of his pilots had never trained in night landings. When he was sure he came out of Japanese radio range, Cmdr. James Peters called his pilots over the JV.

"Stay tight, stay tight. Keep close to the bombers and stay alert. It's goddamned dark out there and you could lose the formation or run into another plane." He paused. "Damage; please report damage."

Peters got positive replies from nine other Hellcat pilots, but no response from the other fighter pilots. The AG 1 Hellcats had either been shot down over target or were lagging behind. Peters then called his bomber unit. Strangely, a flight leader answered instead of Lt. George Brown, the VB 1 commander.

"Where's Brown?" Peters asked.

"His ship was hit bad, sir," the Avenger pilot said. "He must have fallen behind. Lieutenant Omark and Lieutenant Tate are also missing."

"Damn it," Peters huffed.

"Maybe they're just late getting away from target," the flight leader said. "They may still catch up."

"O.K.," Peters answered. "Keep your Avengers tight and maintain one hundred forty knots. If we're lucky, we'll make it back to *Yorktown*."

"Yes, sir."

Far behind the AG 1 formation, the badly injured George Brown nursed his battered Avenger eastward. His crew had bailed out and Brown himself felt pain and dizziness from shrapnel wounds. Still, he could see another Avenger at his side, the aircraft of Lt. Ben Tate. As he hurried home, Tate had spotted Brown's plane, badly shot up and blackened from fire. When Tate pulled alongside the battered Avenger, he saw that Brown was seriously injured and bleeding profusely as he sat grimly at the controls of his aircraft. Tate settled next to Brown to guide the injured pilot back to *Yorktown*'s deck.

As the two planes droned easterly, Tate carefully watched the wounded Brown, and he continually talked to Brown on the radio. Both aircraft hung a thousand feet above the surface of the sea.

"Stay close, George, stay close," Tate called into his JV.

"Will do," Brown answered, gasping from pain.

"You're doing fine, but you've been losing altitude; keep your nose up. Keep your nose up."

But, despite all efforts, Brown was too injured to control the plane and the aircraft itself was too badly damaged to respond. Brown occasionally wandered off and Tate searched for him through the broken clouds that now hung close to the surface of the sea. Tate stiffened anxiously whenever he lost Brown and he sighed gratefully whenever he found Brown again.

"You're doing fine, George, just fine," Tate said again.

But, in the deepening darkness and thickening clouds, Lt. George Brown continued losing altitude or he continued wandering away. Once more, Brown vanished into a cloud bank and this time Lieutenant Tate failed to find him. Tate searched frantically for several minutes, darting and arcing about the darkness until he could spend no more time loitering because he was too low on fuel. He set a course for TF 58 and hurried eastward, hoping he could find *Yorktown*'s carrier deck before he ran out of gas.

Meanwhile, Lt. Warren Omark had been delayed after the bomb run on the Japanese carrier because two Vals had attacked him. Omark had taken evasive action while his gunner, Joe Prince, shot at the Vals with his turret guns, and radioman Bobbie Banes fired at the same Japanese aircraft with his tunnel guns. They had driven off the Vals but, a moment later, a Zero approached them. Again, Lieutenant Omark maneuvered frantically to evade. Then, Omark increased speed to catch up to the rest of the AG 1 Avengers. Instead, Lt. Warren Omark ran into the straggling Lt. George Brown whom Tate had lost earlier.

Even in the darkness, Omark and his crew recognized that Brown was seriously injured. He bled badly and he appeared semiconscious. They also noted that Brown's plane was badly damaged. Omark picked up his JV.

"We're with you, George; just hang on and follow me. We'll maintain a one hundred twenty-knot speed to get you back.

"O.K.," the badly wounded Brown answered, gasping and nodding.

"Prince," Omark called his gunner, "keep the lieutenant in sight. If you see him lag or wander off, call me immediately."

"Yes, sir," the gunner answered.

For nearly an hour the two Avengers continued eastward in tandem. When Lt. George Brown occasionally lost altitude or wandered off, gunner Prince immediately called Omark who searched for Brown and steered the injured Avenger pilot back on course. Finally, however, Brown wandered off course again and this time, Omark could not find him. He searched for ten minutes, darting in and out of the overcast, but to no avail.

"You're sure he fell to starboard, Prince?" Omark asked.

"Yes, sir," the gunner said. "I think he passed out and went down. He's gone, sir, gone."

"Probably," Omark answered. "Well, we can't hang back any longer or we won't get back ourselves."

Thus, despite the efforts of Tate and Omark, Lt. George Brown disappeared on the way back to the U.S.S. *Yorktown*. Brown was never seen or heard from again, so he had obviously perished in the Philippine Sea.

As the formations of AG 16 Dauntlesses under Cmdr. Ralph Weymouth droned eastward in the total darkness, the *Lexington* air commander stared at the other dive bombers hanging about him. Weymouth had already broken radio silence to take count, and he had found two bombers missing. He had clearly seen the Japanese Zeros riddle Lt. Warren McClellan's plane before the aircraft went down in a trail of smoke. Weymouth assumed that McClellan had perished, but the AG 16 commander hoped that the other missing Dauntless crews had ditched in the sea with every possibility of rescue sometime tomorrow. When he came within an hour of his carrier's supposed location, he frowned for he had not heard from *Lexington*. Then, Weymouth picked up his JV and called Lt. Cmdr. Bill Strean. "Commander, what are your casualties?"

"We've got six missing," Strean answered. "We lost three planes over target, and I hope the other three Hellcats are only lagging behind."

"How's the fuel supply?"

"I've checked with the other pilots," Strean said. "We'll have enough gas to get home at this reduced one hundred forty-knot speed."

"Hang tight and let's hope we hear from *Lexington* soon."

"O.K., Commander," Strean answered.

But, while the formation from *Lexington*'s AG 16 continued on, pilots and crews grew increasingly anxious as gas gauge needles continued dropping toward the empty mark. They saw only darkness to the east, with no sign of their carrier, and they saw only thick clouds about them to further obscure their view.

Behind the AG 16 Formation, Lt. Cmdr. Alvin Priel droned eastward at the head of nine other Dauntless bombers from AG 10. The *Enterprise* bomber commander had lost two Dauntlesses over target. Four other AG 10 Dauntlesses had been too seriously damaged to continue the long flight home. One after another the quartet of dive bombers had ditched on the dark sea. Priel searched about him and he barely made out the shadows of Hellcats overhead.

AG 10 had come within an hour of the expected location of carrier *Enterprise*, but Priel had yet to hear from the carrier, or even from the AG 10 Big E leader, Cmdr. Bill "Killer" Kane. Several times, Priel was tempted to call Kane, but he hesitated. Instructions called for Kane to make the first break in radio silence.

Priel did not know that Kane had fallen behind the AG 10 formation because of heavy damage to his Hellcat. Kane's radio communications had been shot away and the AG 10 commander could not even report damage or loss of speed. Kane had dropped his plane far behind the AG 10 formation. In fact, Kane had pushed his aircraft no more than a 100 knots for more than an hour, thus lagging even further behind while his aircraft engine coughed and gasped, and while the plane itself rapidly lost altitude.

At about 1950 hours, Kane skidded along the surface of the sea, successfully ditching the plane and escaping the sinking Hellcat. Now, as Kane's air unit continued on to the east, the AG 10 commander found himself in his rubber raft, alone on the dark, remote surface of the Philippine Sea. He prayed that rescue would come before he died from sharks or exposure.

Meanwhile in the lead plane of the AG formation, Priel looked at his watch: 2010 hours. Surely, they were far out of Japanese radio range. Why hadn't "Killer" Kane called? Priel debated with himself for another minute, and then broke radio silence. "AG Ten F leader come in, come in. This AG Ten B leader; AG Ten F leader, please come in."

Nobody answered.

"This AG Ten B leader; AG Ten F leader, please come in," Priel called again.

A fighter pilot flight leader finally answered Priel. "AG Ten F leader is not with us, Commander. He's not with us."

"What happened to him?" Priel asked.

"I don't know, sir," the flight leader said. "We didn't notice him missing until we came well away from target. We can only assume he's down somewhere. What do you want us to do?"

"Just hang close," Priel said. "If we don't hear from our carrier soon, I'll contact them."

"Aye, sir," the flight leader answered.

Now, Lt. Cmdr. Alvin Priel squinted again into the eastern darkness. He had come well over 200 miles from target, but he still saw no sign of his carrier; nor signs of any ships. Priel stiffened for a moment. Maybe the carriers had failed to close to the westward as planned. Maybe they were still too far east to recover planes before the Dauntlesses and Hellcats ran out of fuel. The thought frightened Priel and he shuddered.

Priel looked still again at the dark shadows around him, the surviving Dauntlesses and Hellcats from *Enterprise*. He licked his lips. Why hadn't they heard from the carrier? Why? Priel looked at his watch again: 2015 hours. If he didn't hear from the *Enterprise* within the next few minutes, he would call the carrier himself. But, even this idea frightened him. Suppose nobody answered?

At the same 2015 hours, the evening of June 20th, Adm. Marc Mitscher had chain-smoked three cigarettes as he paced the deck of *Lexington*'s island structure. He squinted continually into the darkness to the west and northwest, but thus far, he had seen nothing. Capt. Arleigh Burke and Capt. Gus Widhelm, the TF 58 air commander, stood behind Mitscher with equal apprehension.

Among the three officers, perhaps Widhelm felt the most compassion for the airmen making the long flight home in the dark, and especially for any man who had ditched in the sea. Widhelm himself had once spent 48 hours on the sea during the Battle of Santa Cruz

Island, more than a year and a half ago. He had been shot down, escaped his plane, and then scrambled into his life raft. He had then wallowed on the sea, watching damaged Japanese ships sail by him, northward. Widhelm had been fortunate because on the second day alone, a PBY had spotted his raft and rescued him from the sea. Widhelm vividly recalled the dryness in his throat, the eerie loneliness during the dark night, the harsh thirst, and the ache in his head from the hot sun during the day. He remembered the sharks that had circled his raft, waiting for an opportunity.

Finally, at 2020 hours, a call reached *Lexington*'s flag room from Cmdr. Ralph Weymouth. A communications officer rushed to the open deck with the message.

"Sir, from the AG Sixteen commander," the officer told Admiral Mitscher. "He says they sank two carriers and they set afire two other *Zuikaku*-class carriers. He hasn't any idea how many planes we lost, but he thinks we've lost at least a couple dozen among the various air groups."

"What about fuel?"

"Very low, sir," the aide answered softly. "Commander Weymouth reports that his own AG Sixteen aircraft barely have enough fuel for another half-hour. He's anxious to know if he can reach our carriers within the next fifteen or twenty minutes."

Mitscher scowled. "Are we still at full ahead, Arleigh?"

"Yes, Admiral," the chief of staff answered, "still at thirty-two knots."

Mitscher knew well enough that American pilots were nursing their last drops of fuel to reach the American fleet. So, the ships of TF 58 needed to speed westward as fast as possible to close enough range for aircraft recovery. Mitscher looked at the communications officer.

"Stay in radio contact with Commander Weymouth, and tell Commander Weymouth we're closing range as fast as we can. We'll let him know when he reaches the carriers." Then, he gestured emphatically. "I'd also like you to go to the radar room and tell them to stay alert. As soon as they pick up our planes on their screens, they're to track the aircraft all the way in. Then, call Weymouth and tell him to inform his pilots that they should use their own YE or YJ radar-beacon gear."

"Yes, sir," the communications officer said.

Mitscher now turned to Captain Burke. "Have the vessels spread themselves out, Arleigh? We don't want any aircraft running into each other when they try to find their own carriers in the dark."

"We've already spread them out for fifteen miles, Admiral," Burke said. "Our planes should have plenty of room to maneuver. We'll also get Desron Fifty out ahead of us on a twenty-five- or thirty-mile north–south axis. They'll look for any planes that have to ditch."

Mitscher nodded. They had done all they could, but perhaps these efforts would not be enough. The heavy cloud cover had left a total darkness over the TF 58 carrier fleet, and Mitscher could not even see the horizon because of the pitch black.

Capt. Gus Widhelm shared Mitscher's apprehension. "I'm not sure those pilots can find their carriers, Admiral, even with the help of radar. We may have two hundred planes coming back, and there may be nothing but confusion."

"We'll see," Mitscher said.

Then, at 2025 hours, radio reports started flooding fleet-carrier radio rooms. The voices of group and squadron leaders sounded crackly, uncertain, anxious, urgent. The airmen had obviously been under an intense strain for hours. They had gone through heavy antiaircraft fire, they had fought off Zeros, and they had seen fellow airmen go down over target or on the way home. Many of these pilots were themselves injured, as were many airmen; and, planes were damaged.

"Planes are down all the way back to the Jap fleet," Lt. Cmdr. Alvin Priel told his communications man on carrier *Enterprise*. "I don't know how many more will ditch before we get home. Can we find the carriers? Can we find the carriers?"

"Read your radar; read your radar."

"It's too confusing," Priel answered. "Bogies are jumping all over the screen. There's too many carriers and surface ships down there. Somebody's got to flag us in."

"No way, Commander," the communications officer said. "We can't even see the end of the deck in this darkness."

The TF 58 staff had failed to consider Lt. Cmdr. Alvin Priel's question. The YE and YJ radar aboard the returning planes could not pinpoint their own carriers among the maze of vessels that constituted the TF 58 task force. In fact, the radio blips could not even distinguish the difference between carriers and surface ships. The problem was conversely worse aboard the ships. Radar screens on the carriers and on the surface ships of TF 58 showed swarms of bogies on their screens, and then more bogies, as one air group after another came into radar range. No communications man aboard any American ship had any idea which air group belonged to which particular carrier.

When an aide came to the bridge of the *Lexington* to report this apparently insurmountable problem to Admiral Mitscher, the TF 58 commander frowned irritably. Of course. With so many ships around and so many planes aloft, who knew which planes belonged where? Mitscher left the open bridge deck and hurried to the plot room. He fell into a leather chair and stared at the radar units where bogies blipped about the screen in huge, haphazard, numerous winks. There was no way to decide which planes belonged where.

"It's an impossible task, Admiral," Capt. Gus Widhelm said.

Mitscher sat in his chair, stroking his chin and glancing between the map on the wall and the radar screen. The TF 58 commander was obviously pondering the problem with a deep intensity. Nobody spoke. They only looked at their fleet commander. Mitscher finally rose from his chair and stared again at the map and then at Captain Burke.

When the admiral looked at Burke, the chief of staff spoke. "We've probably lost fifteen or twenty planes over target and God knows how many on the way home. And I don't know how we're going to get those planes on carrier decks, Admiral."

"Arleigh," Mitscher answered soberly, "there's only one thing we can do. Order all carriers and surface ships to turn on lights."

"Turn on lights?" Burke gasped. "My God, Admiral, with lights on, this fleet will look like a penny arcade for any Japanese submarines or night aircraft that might be in the area."

"I don't know how many airmen we lost today," Mitscher said, "but I'll be goddamned if I'm going to lose any more than I have to. Anyway, those combat crews have been taking their chances for two days; we can take some ourselves."

Burke looked anxiously at Captain Widhelm. "Gus?"

"The admiral is right," Widhelm answered softly. "It's the only chance those airmen have to land on their carriers."

Mitscher stared again at Burke. "I want glow

257

lights on every carrier to outline the flight decks. I want truck lights on all surface ships to home in aircraft as they come toward the carriers."

"But even that won't tell those airmen which carrier is their own," Captain Burke said.

"I've thought about that, too," Mitscher said. "I also want searchlight beams from every carrier, beams in different colors: white from *Lexington*, blue from *Enterprise*, red from *Yorktown*, orange from *Monterey*, yellow from *Bunker Hill*, and—" he stopped and gestured. "You figure out the colors for the other carriers."

"Yes, sir."

"Be sure that each communications officer notifies his own air-group leader on the color of his searchlight beam. The air commanders in turn should notify all pilots in their groups. That's the only way to bring those planes home with a minimum of confusion."

Then, the faint drone of aircraft echoed from the dark sky to the west. Mitscher listened for several long seconds and he then turned to Burke. "O.K., get those goddamned lights on—fast. And notify all carrier communications officers to call their air commanders immediately."

"Yes, sir," Captain Arleigh Burke said again.

Chapter Fourteen

One squadron of American destroyers had already been released to speed westward to seek downed airmen. But now, Marc Mitscher asked that the entire complement of Willis Lee's surface ships also move west at top speed. He wanted as many vessels as possible to aid in the recovery of downed airmen. Further, the movement of these surface ships would put them into position to engage Ozawa's fleet if necessary. However, neither Admiral Spruance, the U.S. Fifth Fleet commander, nor Admiral Willis Lee, the TF 52 surface-ship commander, agreed to Mitscher's request.

"I don't want the battle line too far from the carriers," Spruance told Mitscher. "The entire force should be kept tactically concentrated tonight. You must simply move as fast as you can westward, so you'll be within striking distance of the enemy fleet by morning."

"Yes, sir," Mitscher answered, disappointed.

"However, I have asked Lee to release another destroyer squadron, so you'll have two Desron units at full ahead to speed recovery of downed airmen."

"That'll help," Mitscher said.

Mitscher's instructions to light up ships had reached all vessels of TF 58. Mitscher also sent aloft from the *Lexington* Lt. Cmdr. Evan Aurant in a night fighter Hellcat. Aurant, one of the few pilots of TF 58 with extensive night training, was a man who could "see in the dark like a cat," according to Capt. Gus. Widhelm. Aurant would loiter in the sky within full view of the TF 58 so he could shepherd home the mass of returning American aircraft.

By 2240 hours, all ships in TF 58 had lit up their vessels, including the glow lights on carrier decks, the truck lights, and the varicolored searchlights to identify themselves. Now, over a sprawling 20-mile square of the Philippine Sea, searchlights pointed west in a 30- to 40-degree arc through the black night.

At 2045 hours, as returning planes approached the American carriers, the U.S. destroyers threw up star shells from five-inch guns to further illuminate the carriers. Lt. Cmdr. Ron Mead of *Bunker Hill*, leading his pack of returning AG 8 bombers, was the first pilot to spot the array of lights in the distance. His eyes widened in astonishment. The sight resembled a huge carnival midway: colored lights on moving objects (the ships), the maze of blinking truck lights, the rows of glow lights on carrier decks, and the oscillating, varicolored searchlight beams.

Mead picked up his radio and called Ralph Shipley. "Do you see those lights down there? The lights?"

"Goddamn, Ron," Shipley said. "They're going all out to bring us home."

Then, Shipley got a call from *Bunker Hill*. "This is eight comm, eight comm; now hear this, Commander. Please watch for the yellow searchlight beam, the yellow beam. That's your *Bunker Hill* base. Yellow beam is your *Bunker Hill* base."

"I see it," Shipley said.

"Flagmen are ready on deck to recover," the *Bunker Hill* communications officer continued. "You can start coming in."

"Roger," Shipley said. "The bombers will come in first."

At 2053 hours, *Bunker Hill* commenced landing aircraft. The combat crews, the men who flew out to sink enemy ships or to destroy the enemy on land, were the glory boys of a carrier fleet. But, the men on the hangar and flight decks would be the heroes on this dark June 20th night. Their skill and stamina would save many airmen before this nightmarish evening ended.

Still, despite every effort, confusion reigned. Many pilots headed for the nearest carrier because of an obsession to land somewhere as soon as possible. Cmdr. Ron Mead alighted nicely aboard *Bunker Hill*, and four other AG

8 Dauntlesses followed him down smoothly. But then, a Dauntless pilot from *Hornet* broke the landing pattern ahead of the sixth *Bunker Hill* Dauntless. The flag officer frantically gestured a wave-off. However, the *Hornet* pilot simply alighted on the deck, and at considerable speed. The Dauntless slammed into the safety barrier and then, like a buzz saw, the aircraft's propeller cut into the deck. Miraculously, neither the pilot, the gunner, nor deck crew was hurt.

But then, an Avenger from U.S.S *Cabot* suddenly flopped down on *Bunker Hill*'s deck, despite the wave-off from the signalman. As the plane hit the deck, the Avenger veered to starboard and burst into flames. The ball of fire killed four deck hands, the crew in the *Hornet*'s Avenger, and the crew of *Cabot*'s Avenger. Luckily, deck hands quickly doused fires and crane men swiftly shoved the wrecked planes over the side, sending the wrecked aircraft, the charred deck hands, and the cindered airmen to watery graves.

The remaining *Bunker Hill* planes remained aloft, their pilots panicky, until crews cleared the deck. But, at 2144 hours, the signalmen again waved in planes. For another 40 minutes, *Bunker Hill* recovered aircraft. However, at 2236 hours, another intruder, this plane from U.S.S. *Wasp*, broke into the landing pattern and hit the barrier before deck crews had reset the barrier. The plane almost skidded off the deck. Crews quickly yanked pilot and gunner from the plane and then shoved the *Wasp* aircraft overboard before flagging in the rest of *Bunker Hill*'s aircraft. Finally, by 2305 hours, *Bunker Hill* had recovered all of its returning planes.

Five *Bunker Hill* Dauntlesses had failed to return home, another two Dauntlesses had luckily landed on a CVE jeep carrier, and a third had landed on *Enterprise* at 2245 hours with the gauge reading zero. Among the Hellcats, only seven landed safely on *Bunker Hill*'s deck. Two had been lost somewhere over target and two had dropped out of formation on the way home. Lt. Elbert McClusky made a water landing next to *Bunker Hill* because he had run out of fuel before he reached the carrier deck. A destroyer quickly plucked the *Bunker Hill* fighter pilot out of the sea.

Bunker Hill had also recovered five planes that belonged to other units, while two other intruders had cracked up on deck.

Meanwhile, U.S.S. *Monterey*'s communications officer radioed Lt. Cmdr. Roger Mehle. "We're the orange, Commander, the orange. Can you see us?"

"I see you," Mehle answered, squinting at the orange, vacillating searchlight.

"Deck crews are ready to recover. Please follow the orange light; be sure you await signals from flagmen."

As Lieutenant Commander Mehle droned eastward, he saw *Monterey*'s deck, now outlined in glow lights, loom larger and larger. He sighed in relief for his gas gauge showed less than ten gallons of gas. He picked up his radio and called his pilots. "This is 28 leader; 28 leader. Bombers will go in first; bombers first. They're worse on fuel than we are." Then, he spoke to Lt. Ron Gift. "O.K., Rip, take in your Avengers—and make it quick."

"We won't waste time," Gift promised.

Ron "Rip" Gift then glided toward *Monterey*, the deck easily visible from the glow lights on either side. He made an easy landing. As his plane hit the barrier and stopped, deck crews quickly yanked pilot and crew out of the plane, cleared the plane away and waited for the next plane. The second Avenger also came in safely before deck crews worked swiftly once more. In fact, deck crews flagged in and cleared planes at the rate of one a minute.

But not all of AG 28's bomber pilots made *Monterey*. Lt. Tom Dries saw his fuel gauge on empty and he feared he'd run out of gas in the holding pattern. So, he tried to come in prematurely. However, the flag officer waved him off. Dries cursed, arced his plane in the sky, and looked for another carrier on which to land. Then, Dries mistook the red truck lights of a destroyer as the red glow lights of a carrier. Dries came down quickly and he gaped in horror when the destroyer loomed large and clear. He veered away and then his engine sputtered to a stop—out of gas. Dries splashed into the sea and the destroyer quickly launched a boat to yank the Avenger crew out of the sea, even before Dries and his crewmen were wet.

The *Monterey* Corsair pilots fared better than Tom Dries. Lt. Cmdr. Roger Mehle and his fighter pilots came safely down at one-minute intervals, without interlopers from other carriers breaking into the landing pattern. By 2300 hours, all of *Monterey*'s planes had landed. The last AG 28 fighter pilot hit the barrier with a grand total of one quart of gasoline in his tank!

When Lieutenant Commander Mehle and Lieutenant Gift came into the *Monterey* ready room to write action reports, they appeared weary and spent. Yet, they protested vehemently when the operations officer insisted they could not claim five hits on the Japanese carrier without more corroboration. But, Dries, Bennett, and Edwards were missing, and only when one of these dunked Avenger pilots returned to *Monterey* to verify the hits, would the operations officer allow the hits on the record.

Cmdr. James Peters of *Yorktown*'s AG 1 felt a greater apprehension than did perhaps any other commander returning from the late-afternoon air strike. By his calculations, his AG 1 had flown 300–330 miles during the return flight from the target area. He himself had only 15 gallons of gas left in his tank. At 2050 hours, he called his carrier.

"*Yorktown?* Where are you? Must land soon; have no gas left. We're coming in. Please, *Yorktown*, where are you?"

"Follow the red searchlight to carrier deck; red searchlight. Do you see it?"

Peters scanned the east and his eyes brightened when he saw the sweeping red searchlight beam. "We see it."

"Deck crews are ready to recover. Come in."

Commander Peters called his pilots. "Keep your eyes on the red searchlight, ahead and off to port; ahead and off to port. That's home. Let's go."

Cmdr. James Peters landed first. As soon as he hit the barrier, deck crews yanked him from the cockpit, cleared away the plane, and waved in the other AG 1 aircraft at one-minute intervals. Within 30 minutes the *Yorktown* deck hands had brought in most of the returning planes, including the straggling Avengers of Lt. Warren Omark and Lt. Ben Tate, who had tried to guide the badly injured Lt. George Brown back to the carrier.

But, the landings were not without mishap. Lt. Mike Tomme had sighed in relief when he came to a stop on the flight deck. However, before Tomme got out of his plane, a second aircraft came in too quickly behind, hit the deck erratically, and bounced into the air. The plane landed squarely on top of the other Hellcat, smashing the canopy and killing Lt. Mike Tomme instantly.

And not all of *Yorktown*'s returning planes made her deck. Besides the earlier losses, five planes ran out of fuel before they got the O.K.

to land. These Avenger pilots simply splashed into the sea alongside the nearest ship that quickly sent out motor launches to pull pilots and crews from the water.

A further gloom descended over the sailors on *Yorktown* when they learned that Lt. George Brown, the VB 1 commander, had been lost at sea, and that two other Avenger crews and a pair of Hellcat pilots were missing.

Aboard *Lexington*, the communications officer called Cmdr. Ralph Weymouth at 2030 hours to bring in his aircraft.

"Do you have any damaged planes, Commander?"

"A few," Weymouth said, "but I think they can make it down. The worst had to ditch. They never got this far. I think we've got a string of airmen on life rafts for a couple hundred miles behind us. I just hope to hell that somebody picks them up."

"Two squadrons of destroyers are out," the communications officer said. "They're sweeping a thirty- to forty-mile arc with searchlights. That ought to catch most of those downed airmen."

"I hope so."

"O.K., Commander, we're the white searchlight. Bring down your aircraft and keep a sharp watch for the flag officer. We'll bring you in about a minute apart."

"Roger and out," Weymouth answered.

As Cmdr. Ralph Weymouth touched down on *Lexington*'s deck, crews quickly helped

Weymouth and his gunner out of the plane and then moved off the Dauntless to allow room for other planes. The first six Dauntlesses came in smoothly and deck hands handled them swiftly. However, the seventh Dauntless touched down too quickly, despite signals from the flag officer. The young, nervous pilot skidded alongside the deck, sideswiped plane number six and fouled up the deck. No one suffered injury, but the incident held up other planes because deck crews needed to clear away wreckage.

Despite the delay, most of the returning bombers touched down safely. However, the delay affected *Lexington*'s fighter pilots who waited to come in. By the time the signal officer waved in the Hellcats, only Cmdr. Bill Strean and a few other AG 16 fighter pilots still remained airborne. These few Hellcats came in nicely, with Cmdr. Bill Strean and Lt. Cmdr. Paul Buie leading the way. However, Lt. Alex Vraciu's gas tank was dry just as he circled to approach the deck of Lady Lex. He could not maneuver his plane toward the deck and he luckily missed the island structure of *Lexington* before he splashed into the water. Fifteen minutes later, a destroyer rescued the drenched Alex Vraciu.

Another *Lexington* pilot, Ens. Eric Wendorf, had been orbiting *Lexington* at 110 knots and he finally got the flag to come in. But, another plane cut him off and Wendorf veered to avoid. One of the landing wheels hit the water, the wing dipped, and the Hellcat cartwheeled on its back. Water poured into the upended plane and Wendorf struggled to free himself and the snagged parachute from the smashed canopy. He sank into 20 feet of water before he finally freed himself and came to the surface miraculously to survive. However, in Wendorf's case, no skimming destroyer came swiftly to his aid.

Aboard *Lexington*, every sailor feared they had lost most of the VF 16 pilots. However, as the night wore on, they learned that Alex Vraciu, the biggest hero of yesterday's turkey shoot, had been pulled safely from the sea. They also learned that eight other *Lexington* pilots had landed aboard other carriers.

Now, as Lt. Cmdr. Alvin Priel led his Dauntlesses toward carrier *Enterprise* he blinked his eyes in awe. Before him appeared a kaleidoscope of colors: glow lights on deck, blinking signal lights, truck lights on ships, and multicolored, sweeping searchlights. And in the air, contrails from arching planes seeking a place to land left white streaks across the black sky.

A dozen non-*Enterprise* planes had already landed on Big E. When Priel told communications he was coming in with AG 10 aircraft, the signalmen got orders to refuse any more wayward, non-*Enterprise* planes aboard Big E.

"Go find your own carrier," the *Enterprise* communications officer continually cried into his squawk box. "We've got our own aircraft to recover."

The communications officer of *Enterprise* may as well have shooed away pesky flies, however. As Lt. Cmdr. Alvin Priel came down toward the deck, he was astonished to see another plane, an Avenger from *Hornet*, land right in front of him. Both bombers skidded down the flight deck. The *Hornet* Avenger rolled the full length of the deck and barely stopped at the stern because deck crews had not yet reset the barrier. Luckily, the barrier was up before Priel crossed the deck.

Throughout a harrowing 15 or 20 minutes, other planes simply joined the *Enterprise* Avengers as they landed on the flight decks, some of them simply tightroping the port side to hit the barriers along with legitimate Big E planes that had been flagged in for landings. But, pilots were anxious, frantic, desperate. Most of them had drops of fuel left and they simply landed wherever they saw a flight deck.

Lt. Vannie Eason, the last AG 10 Avenger pilot still aloft, was just about to alight on the deck of *Enterprise* when a Hellcat came out of nowhere and landed right in front of him. Eason arced his plane away and then came back toward the carrier again. Now, the flight deck was clear and Eason sighed in relief. But, just as he approached Big E's ramp, the dive-bomber pilot ran out of gas. He quickly pulled up his wheels, made an S-turn to port, and landed in the water alongside the big carrier. He and his gunner scrambled out of the plane and a destroyer pulled them from the water in a few minutes.

Now came the *Enterprise* fighter pilots. The first half-dozen Hellcats came in safely, but Lt. Ed Lawton could not wait to come in because he was too low on gas. He veered away and luckily landed on CVE carrier *Princeton*. Lawton's plane was the last aircraft *Princeton* could handle.

"She's a small deck," Lawton grinned to the deck crew, "but I'm sure as hell glad to be here."

"Go below for some coffee, Lieutenant," the deck officer said.

Lt. Bob Shackford had tried twice to get his Hellcat on the deck of the *Enterprise*, but he continually veered off as uninvited planes from other carriers cut in front of him when signalmen gave him a wave in. Shackford finally headed away and found carrier *Lexington* who gave him permission to land. However, Shackford ran out of gas before he reached the deck and he landed in the water alongside Lady Lex. Again, a shuttling destroyer, one of many skittering about the sea, rescued Shackford.

But, when all planes were in, gloom prevailed aboard U.S.S. *Enterprise*. Cmdr. William "Killer" Kane had not returned. Kane had already been out three times, snagging a Zero and a Jill during the June 19th turkey shoot. He was a leader in the Eddie Rickenbacker tradition among carrier fighter pilots. He had been instrumental in leading VF 10 fighter planes against intercepting Zeros to save most of Alvin Priel's bombers from further punishment. Kane had also led his VF 10 pilots in strafing runs against battleship *Nagato* and cruiser *Mogami* to draw attention away from the AG 10 bombers that had given carrier *Ryuho* a working over.

TF 58 carriers spent about two hours in recovering planes. By 2330 hours, no more drones echoed from the skies overhead. Still, searchlights continued to probe the darkness, while destroyers continued to weave about the 20 square miles of sea with their own piercing searchlights.

By 0100 hours, a stack of reports had filtered into the flag room of U.S.S. *Lexington*. When Adm. Marc Mitscher and his aides made calculations, they found that six Hellcats, ten Dauntlesses, and four Avengers had been shot down over the target area by Japanese fighter planes or ack-ack fire. Seventeen Hellcat, 35 Dauntlesses, and 28 Avengers had been destroyed in deck crashes, had splashed in the water near the task force, or had dropped out of formation during the long flight home.

"What about personnel?" Mitscher asked.

"Not too good, either," Captain Arleigh Burke answered. "We've got one hundred pilots and one hundred nine crewmen missing, although destroyers have been plucking airmen out of the sea for a couple of hours. So, we can assume that will reduce the casualty list."

Admiral Mitscher nodded. "Slow to half-speed on our westward course. I don't care if we need to sail all the way to the Philippines; I want to find any man who may be floundering on the sea.''

"Yes, sir,'' Captain Burke answered.

Throughout the night of June 20–21, the TF 58 task force continued westward on a 260° course at a leisurely 15 knots. American destroyers sliced the van, their searchlights sweeping across the black sea in search of downed U.S. airmen. In the determination to save as many downed airmen as possible, the U.S. ships had simply defied the possibility of night air attacks or submarine attacks.

The effort proved fruitful because the sailors aboard the tin cans saw flashlights blinking everywhere, the winks resembling a sea full of fireflies. Destroyers ignored none of them and launch-boat crews continually pulled men from wallowing rubber rafts or men in Mae West life jackets. Before dawn, the American destroyers had pulled 51 pilots and 50 air crewmen out of the sea.

As the sun rose over the eastern horizon on June 21st, big, long-range Dumbo Catalinas and PBM navy flying boats joined the search for downed airmen. The big planes covered an area between 16° 20' north latitude, and 13° 50' south latitude.

At 0614, as the sun rose from the east, an aircraft carrier, one of the last in the TF 58 fleet moving westward, found Lt. Eric Wendorf on his raft. Men aboard the carrier had heard his shouts before getting him aboard.

The pilot was utterly spent. He had vomited repeatedly during the night from swallowing salt water spiked with oil from the plane. Sharks had glided around his raft for hours, but had not attacked him. Several times during the night, he had fired his pistol with tracer bullets, but without success.

Lt. Warren McClellan, meanwhile, had remained relatively comfortable during the night of June 20–21 on the warm sea. He had watched the Japanese carrier *Hiyo* belch fire and smoke from the series of explosions that had ripped huge chunks of the carrier from her side and had sent debris into the air like skyrocketing balls of metal. He had looked in awe as *Hiyo* finally went under. At 0700 hours, a big Dumbo spotted McClellan on a patch of empty sea where once had loitered the Japanese 1st Mobile Fleet. The big Catalina landed and took McClellan aboard.

The PBY had barely taken off when they sighted the rubber raft with George Platz and Ellis Babcock. Again, the big Dumbo landed, this time to pull the two Avenger crewmen aboard. All during the flight back to Saipan, McClellan, Platz, and Babcock chattered endlessly about the awesome sight of viewing a Japanese carrier in her death throes before sinking.

In the same area, another Dumbo and a navy PBM picked up a dozen more TF 58 airmen who had scrambled out of downed planes during the TF 58 air attack on Ozawa's carrier fleet.

At about 0930 hours, a crow's-nest lookout in front-running destroyer U.S.S. *Hickox* spotted another raft. The destroyer hurried to the rescue. To the amazement of the *Hickox* crew, they pulled Lt. Ken Musick out of the water, a man they had rescued from the sea when Musick went down in combat on June 15th. Following tradition, the sailors had painted on the stack of the destroyer the miniatures of Japanese planes shot down. When they had first rescued the *Bunker Hill* pilot, the *Hickox* sailors had painted a caricature of Musick on the stack. And now, with this second rescue, the crewmen quickly painted a second caricature of Musick next to the first.

"Jesus, Lieutenant," one of the sailors told Musick, "if we keep pulling you out of the sea, we ain't gonna have no more room on that stack."

Lt. Ken Musick only grinned, grateful to be alive.

At about noon, June 21st, destroyer *Hickox* got its second catch of the day—Cmdr. William "Killer" Kane. After they brought Kane aboard and discovered he was the AG 10 commander from *Enterprise*, they grinned eagerly. The *Hickox* sailors knew that the crewmen of Big E had promised to give up their ice-cream supply to anyone who found "Killer" Kane. The sailors aboard *Hickox* now contacted *Enterprise*: "We have "Killer" Kane. Send us ice cream and we send you Kane."

The men aboard *Enterprise* were jubilant. They had no ice cream, but they had recovered their popular air commander.

By the end of the day, searching surface ships and aircraft had rescued an additional 16 pilots and 26 air crewmen from the sea. At 1920 hours, TF 58 was at 16° north latitude by 135° east longitude, far west of the Japanese fleet's position on the late afternoon of June 20th, when TF 58 planes had attacked 1st Mobile Fleet. Now, Adm. Raymond Spruance decided they could never catch Ozawa's fleet, and he also believed they had probably rescued all of the TF 58 airmen they were likely to find. So, he ordered Mitscher to reverse course and sail back to Saipan. This time, Mitscher did not protest.

At about the same 1920 hours, June 21st, Adm. Jisaburo Ozawa had sailed within 300 miles of Okinawa, far to the northwest of Saipan. After the evening meal, Ozawa called Captain Toshikazu to his cabin. "Captain, you will take a letter for the Honorable Admiral Toyoda, commander of the combined fleet."

"Yes, Admiral."

Admiral Ozawa then dictated a letter of resignation. He expressed regret that he had lost the opportunity to lead Japan to a glorious victory. He ascribed his defeat to his own inadequacy as well as to the inadequacy of his airmen who had not had enough training. He then tendered his resignation as commander of the 1st Mobile Fleet. However, Admiral

Toyoda refused the resignation, blaming ill fortune for the Philippine Sea disaster, and not Ozawa.

Ozawa reached Nakagasuka Bay in Okinawa on the afternoon of June 22nd, but there were no cheers from the sailors aboard 1st Mobile Fleet nor from the sailors on shore. A dispiriting quiet prevailed everywhere because of the heavy losses in aircraft and ships during the Philippine Sea engagement between the Japanese and American carrier fleets. First Mobile carried into Okinawa only 35 serviceable planes, with most of the fleet's airmen lost. Further, battleship *Hurana*, cruiser *Mayo*, and four of Ozawa's remaining six carriers needed to return to Japan for repairs.

Japan no longer possessed a naval air service.

On the same June 22nd afternoon, Adm. Marc Mitscher refueled his huge carrier fleet at sea and then continued to Saipan waters to complete the job of supporting the U.S. Marine invaders of that island.

And truly, the crushing Japanese defeat at sea had spelled doom for the Japanese defenders of Saipan. On June 22nd, Gen. Holland Smith, the marine commander on Saipan, mustered his troops for a final push. His men had already suffered heavy casualties. But, without sea or air support, a Japanese defeat on Saipan appeared inevitable. Day after day, despite hard resistance, the American Marines pushed the Japanese deeper into a corner.

On July 6, 1944, the marines closed on Marapi Point, the last pocket of Japanese resistance. Both Gen. Yshitusuga Saito, the ground commander, and Adm. Chuichi Nagumo, the naval commander, knew the end had come. Both men, along with a number of staff officers, put pistols to their heads and shot themselves in a mass demonstration of hara-kiri.

Admiral Chuichi Nagumo, the man who had led the Japanese carrier-fleet attack on Pearl Harbor in a thrilling Nippon victory, the man who had always been a faithful servant of the emperor, now ended his life in a fitting manner. In truth, Nagumo and the Japanese carrier fleet had perished together.

Admiral Masatome Ugaki, commander of the Batjan force surface fleet, wrote a haiku to mark the sad occasion:

"The battle is ended,
    But the gloomy sky of the rainy season
Remains over us."

AMERICAN PARTICIPANTS AND UNITS

U.S. Fifth Fleet—Adm. Raymond Spruance
U.S. Task Force 58—Adm. Marc Mitscher
    Chief of staff—Capt. Arleigh Burke
    TF 58 Commander—Capt. William "Gus" Widhelm

Aircraft Carriers
U.S.S. *Lexington*—Capt. Ed Litch
    AG 16—Cmdr. Ralph Weymouth
    VF 16—Cmdr. Bill Strean

U.S.S. *Enterprise*—Capt. M. B. Gardner
    AG 10—Cmdr. William "Killer" Kane
    VB 10—Lt. Cmdr. Alvin Priel

U.S.S. *Yorktown*—Capt. R. E. Jennings
    AG 1—Cmdr. James Peters
    VB 1—Lt. George Brown

U.S.S. *Bunker Hill*—Capt. T. P. Peters
    AG 8—Cmdr. Ralph Shipley
    VB 8—Lt. Cmdr. Ron Mead

U.S.S. *Monterey*—Capt. S. H. Ingersoll
    AG 28—Lt. Cmdr. Roger Mehle
    VB 28—Lt. Ronald Gift

U.S.S. *Essex*—Capt. R. A. Ofstie
    AG 15—Cmdr. David McCampbell
    VF 15—Lt. Cmdr. Charles Brewer

U.S.S. *Hornet*—Capt. W. D. Sample
    AG 2—Cmdr. Jack Arnold
    VF 2—Lt. Everett Hargreaves

OTHER participating TF 58 U.S. aircraft carriers:
    U.S.S. *Belleau Wood*, U.S.S. *Bataan*, U.S.S. *Wasp*,
    U.S.S. *San Jacinto*, U.S.S. *Princeton*, U.S.S. *Langley*, U.S.S. *Cowpens*

TF 58.7—Battle line surface fleet—Adm. Willis Lee
TF 17—Submarine fleet—Adm. Charles Lockwood
    U.S.S. *Cavella*—Lt. Cmdr. H. J. Kossler
    U.S.S. *Albacore*—Lt. Cmdr. T. W. Blanchard
    U.S.S. *Flying Fish*—Lt. Cmdr. R. D. Risser
    U.S.S. *Seahorse*—Lt. Cmdr. S. D. Cutter
TF 52—U.S. Marine Expeditionary Force, Saipan—Gen.
H. M. Smith

JAPANESE PARTICIPANTS AND UNITS

Japanese Combined Fleet—Adm. Soemu Toyoda
1st Mobile Fleet—Adm. Jisaburo Ozawa
    Chief of staff—Adm. Matake Yoshimura
    Communications officer—Capt. Toshikazu Ohmae
    1st Mobile Air Fleet—Capt. Mitsuo Fuchida

Cardiv 1—Adm. Jisaburo Ozawa
    Carriers: *Taiho, Shokaku, Zuikaku*
    601st Air Group—Cmdr. Akira Tarui
Cardiv 2—Adm. Tajaji Joshima
    Carriers: *Junyo, Hiyo, Ryuho*
    652nd Air Group—Cmdr. Joyotara Iwami
Cardiv 3—Adm. Sueo Obayashi
    Carriers: *Chitose, Chiyoda, Zuiho*
    653rd Air Group—Cmdr. Masayuki Yamaguchi   *BACK*

Raid I—653rd Air Group   *69 SENT / 57 LOST / 12*
    Bombers—Cmdr. Masayuki Yamaguchi
    Fighters—Lt. Shoichi Sugita   *128 SENT   97 LOST*
Raid II—601st Air Group
    Bombers—Cmdr. Akira Tarui
    Fighters—Cmdr. Masatake Okimiya   *46 SENT / 7 LOST?*
Raid III—652nd Air Group
    Bombers—Cmdr. Joyotara Iwami
    Fighters—Lt. Takeo Tanimizu
Raid IV—601st Air Group   *94 SENT*
    Bombers—Capt. Mitsuo Fuchida
    Fighters—Lt. Toshohiko Ohno

Batjan force surface fleet—Adm. Masatome Ugaki
1st Air Fleet, Guam—Adm. Kakuji Kakuta
1st Submarine Fleet, Saipan—Adm. Takeo Takagi
31st Army, Saipan—Gen. Yshitsugu Saito
1st Naval Defense Force, Saipan—Adm. Chuichi Nagumo

GRR-185
P103

P 152

BIBLIOGRAPHY

BOOKS

Barbey, Daniel. *MacArthur's Amphibious Navy*, Annapolis: U.S. Naval Institute Press, 1969.

Belote, James H. and William, M. *Titans of the Seas*. New York: Harper and Row, 1975.

Blair, Clay. *Silent Victory*, Vol. II. Philadelphia: Lippincott, 1975.

Constable, Trevor, and Toliver, Raymond. *Fighter Aces of the U.S.A.* Fallbrook, Cal.: Aero Publishers, 1979.

Craven, W. F., and Cate, J. L. *The Pacific: Guadalcanal to Saipan*. Vol. IV, Chicago: Univ. of Chicago Press, 1950.

Dull, Paul S. *The Imperial Japanese Navy*. Annapolis: U.S. Naval Institute Press, 1978.

Fitzsimmons, Bernard. *Warplanes and Air Battles of World War II*. New York: Beekman House, 1973.

Hughes, Terry, and Costello, John. *The Battle of the Atlantic*. New York: Dial Press, 1977.

Ito, Masanori. *The End of the Japanese Navy*, translated by Roger Pineau. New York: Norton Publishers, 1962.

Jablonksi, Edward. *Air War*, Volume II. Garden City, N.Y.: Doubleday & Co., 1970.

Lockwood, Charles Admiral, and Adamson, Hans Christian. *Battles for the Philippine Sea*. New York: Thomas Cromwell & Co., 1967.

Morison, Samuel. *New Guinea and the Marianas*. Boston: Little, Brown & Co., 1952.

Potter, E. B. *The Great Sea War*. Englewood Cliffs, N.J.: Prentiss Hall, 1960.

Pratt, Fletcher. *Fleet Against Japan*. New York: Harper & Brothers, 1946.

Reynolds, Clark G. *The Fast Carriers: Forging of an Air Navy*. New York: McGraw-Hill, 1968.

Roscoe, Theodore. *U.S. Destroyer Operations in World War II*. Annapolis: U.S. Naval Institute Press, 1957.

Roscoe, Theodore. *U.S. Submarine Operations in World War II*. Annapolis: U.S. Naval Institute Press, 1953.

Shores, Christopher. *Fighting Aces*. Toronto, Canada: Hamlyn Publishers, 1975.

Smith, S. E. *The U.S. Navy in World War II*. New York: William Morrow & Co., 1956.

Steinberg, Rafael. *Island Fighting*. New York: Time-Life Books, Inc., 1978.

Toland, John. *The Rising Sun*. New York: Random House, 1970.

RECORD SOURCES

News Accounts:

The New York Times, July 6, 1944, "Dying Pilot Torpedoed Japanese Carrier"

The New York Times, May 28, 1945, "Hero Killed on Saipan"

The New York Times, June 20, 1944, "American Fleet Attacked by Japanese in Air"

The New York Times, June 22, 1944, "Japanese Report Fierce Sea Fight"

The New York Times, June 22, 1944, "Nimitz Bares Blow at Japanese Navy"

New York Sun, June 29, 1944, "Bronxville Flyer Finds Jap Fleet"

U.S. Marine Corps *Gazette*, October 1944, "Saipan Tank Battle"

Personal Accounts:

Fukaya, Hajima, "The Shokakus—Pearl Harbor to Leyte Gulf," *In Proceedings*. Annapolis: USNI, 1952.

Gray, James Seton, "Development of Night Naval Fighters in World War II," in *Proceedings*. Annapolis: USNI, 1952

Archive Records—Naval Historical Center, Washington, DC

Reports of carriers taking part in the Philippine Sea battle, including the "Mariana Islands Turkey Shoot."

Microfilm Records:

NRS 1977-17, Air Group Mission Reports, 6-1-44 to 6-30-44

   AG 16, U.S.S. *Lexington*
   AG 10, U.S.S. *Enterprise*
   AG 15, U.S.S. *Essex*

AR 248-77, Air Group Mission Reports, 6-1-44 to 6-30-44
  AG 1, U.S.S. *Yorktown*
  AG 8, U.S.S. *Bunker Hill*
  AG 28, U.S.S. *Monterey*
NRS 1974, Carrier Battle Reports, TF 58, 6-1-44 to 6-30-44
  U.S.S. *Lexington*, U.S.S. *Enterprise*, U.S.S. *Essex*, U.S.S. *Wasp*, U.S.S. *San Jacinto*
AF 249-77, Carrier Action Reports, TF 58, 6-1-44 to 6-30-44
  U.S.S. *Yorktown*, U.S.S. *Bataan*, U.S.S. *Hornet*, U.S.S. *Bunker Hill*, U.S.S. *Cabot*, U.S.S. *Monterey*

Japanese Records:
Japanese Monograph #90, A-Go Operations, May–June, 1944
Japanese Monograph #91, A-Go Operations Log, supplement, May–June, 1944
JD 1-B—Operations orders and records for Battle off the Mariana Islands, A-Go Operation, June, 1944
  Detailed Action Report, 1st Mobile Fleet, 13-22, June, 1944
  War Diary, Cardiv 5, 1-30 June, 1944
  War Diary, Batdiv 1, 1-30 June, 1944
  War Diary, Desron 10, 1-30 June, 1944
  Detailed Action Report, carrier *Chiyoda*, 15-22 June, 1944
  Detailed Action Report, carrier *Shokaku*, 15-22 June, 1944
  Detailed Action Report, Desdiv 61, 20 June 1944
Japanese Defense Agency War History Records (BKS), translated and stored in National Archives, Washington, DC
  BKS, Volume 12, pp 567-87
  BKS, Volume 12, pp 548-51
Imperial Japanese Navy, postwar interviews:
  Maj. Kiyoshi Yoshida, Volume No. 43, 25 October 1945 (Nagumo staff officer)
  Capt. Tatsui Nakamura, "Report on Japanese Defense Plans for Saipan"
  Capt. Masataka Nagaishi, Hachiman Group, 1st

Air Fleet, "Impressions and Battle Lessons"

Capt. Toshikazu Ohmae, "1st Mobile Fleet Order #77"

Commander Fukaya, 601st Air Group, "The Shokakus," USNI, Volume LXVIII

Photos and Maps

All photos and maps from the U.S. Naval Historical Center, Washington, DC, and from National Archives Still Picture Section, Washington, DC.